Logan struggled, but the tentacle drew him calmly down into the freezing water until he was floating opposite a giant eye. The kraken stared at him for a long moment, and then it began making odd noises. Logan was starting to feel lightheaded, and the noises wouldn't have meant anything to him anyway. But he got the feeling the kraken was trying to tell him something.

THE MENA

KRAKENS

HE

GERIE

and LIES

TUI T. SUTHERLAND
KARI SUTHERLAND

HARPER

An Imprint of HarperCollinsPublishers

The Menagerie #3: Krakens and Lies
Copyright © 2015 by Tui T. Sutherland and Kari Sutherland
Map and glossary art by Ali Solomon
All rights reserved. Printed in the United States of America.
No part of this book may be used or reproduced in any
manner whatsoever without written permission except in
the case of brief quotations embodied in critical articles and
reviews. For information address HarperCollins Children's
Books, a division of HarperCollins Publishers, 195 Broadway,
New York, NY 10007.
www.harpercollinschildrens.com

ISBN 978-0-06-078069-2

Typography by Torborg Davern
16 17 18 19 20 OPM 10 9 8 7 6 5 4 3 2 1
❖
First paperback edition, 2016

For Adalyn—

may your dreams be filled with griffins

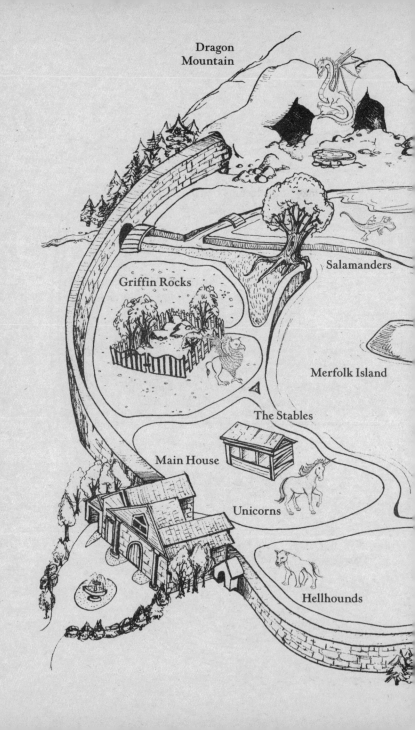

Dragon
Mountain

Salamanders

Griffin Rocks

Merfolk Island

The Stables

Main House

Unicorns

Hellhounds

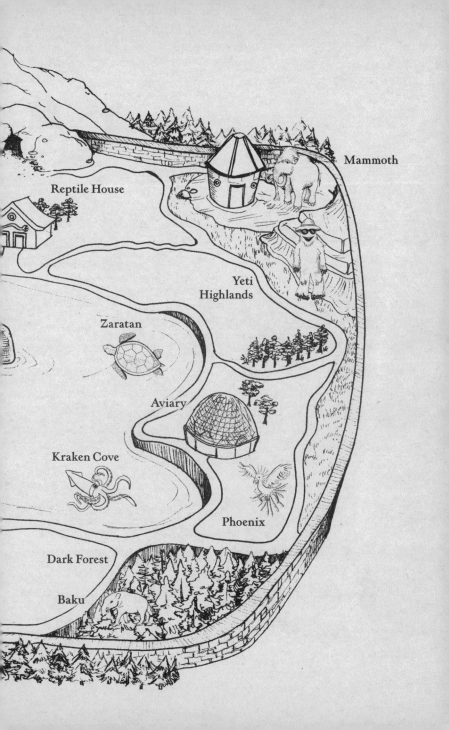

Mammoth

Reptile House

Yeti
Highlands

Zaratan

Aviary

Kraken Cove

Phoenix

Dark Forest

Baku

THE
MENAGERIE
KRAKENS
and
LIES

ONE

Logan Wilde stared down at the map in his hands. Mr. Sterling's oak-paneled study seemed to be spinning around him.

Dragon Lair.

Flight of the Griffins.

Unicorn Safari.

One week earlier, he had discovered that his little town of Xanadu, Wyoming, contained a secret home for mythical creatures called the Menagerie. Emphasis on *secret*. As in, nobody was supposed to know about it, and anyone who accidentally found out would get their memories wiped with kraken ink.

He'd only been allowed in because he could communicate with the baby griffins and because of his mom's ties to the Kahn family, who ran the Menagerie. But he understood how important it was to hide these endangered magical animals from the world.

The map in his hands represented the exact opposite of all that: a vision of the Menagerie as an amusement park where rich tourists could snap pictures of mermaids, ride a chained-up woolly mammoth, and probably buy yeti-fur blankets and baby pyrosalamanders of their own at the large GIFT SHOP marked prominently in the corner.

Logan's heart was hammering in his chest. The Sterlings didn't just know about the Menagerie. They knew all the details—the layout, the animals who lived there. But how? Ruby Kahn had given all the Sterlings kraken ink, which should have wiped their memories of the Menagerie. Why hadn't it worked?

He slipped his phone out of his pocket and snapped a photo of the map. The Kahns needed to see this right away.

It was awkward working with the fake fur and claws of his werewolf costume. Across the hall, he could hear the noise and thumping music of Jasmin Sterling's Halloween party. It was the first party he'd been invited to since moving to Xanadu—and now he needed to find a polite way to bolt out of there two hours early.

"What on earth are you looking at?" Jasmin said from

behind him, making him jump. He'd almost forgotten that she and his friend Blue Merevy were even in the room.

Logan fumbled his phone back into his jacket and tried to roll up the map, but she was already reaching around to take it from him.

"There can't possibly be anything interesting in my dad's boring papers about boring real estate and boring politics and—" Jasmin stopped, raising her eyebrows at the map. "Oh, *Dad*."

"What?" Blue asked, leaning over her shoulder to look. Jasmin glanced sideways at him with a smile and tilted it so he'd lean closer to her.

"Isn't my dad so cheesy?" she said. "Remember that Wild West theme park he tried to start a few years ago? The huge enormous failure?"

"Oh yeah," Blue said, looking at her instead of at the map. "We went with Zoe on opening day."

"Right," she said, laughing. "And we all got totally sick on the free root beer, and you fell off a horse that was *barely* moving, and then Zoe nearly locked herself in the old jail cell while I was pretending to be sheriff." She paused, and a wistful expression crossed her face that was almost an exact match for the look Zoe got whenever she talked about Jasmin.

She misses Zoe, too, Logan realized. Zoe had had to stop being friends with Jasmin six months ago, when the whole Sterling family was dosed with kraken ink after Jasmin's brother, Jonathan—Ruby's boyfriend at the time—tried to steal a jackalope.

He tried to shoot *PAY ATTENTION, TIME TO FREAK OUT* vibes at Blue, but the blond boy was . . . what *was* he doing? Giving Jasmin a rather goofy-looking grin, for one thing.

"Anyway, look," Jasmin said, shaking her hair back. "Dad's got another brilliantly terrible idea. A theme park full of imaginary creatures? Who does he think is going to drive out to the middle of seriously absolutely nowhere for some lame animatronic unicorns? I mean, really, right?" She giggled and waved one hand at her Halloween costume. "Maybe you and I can play a couple of the mermaids."

Logan saw the moment where Blue realized what he was looking at. Even without the terrifying labels, it would have been easy to recognize the Menagerie from the giant lake in the middle of it—the lake where Blue's father, King Cobalt, ruled over the merfolk.

The normally unflappable merboy jumped back as though the map had snarled at him. All the color drained out of his face.

"Blue?" Jasmin said, turning toward him. "Are you all right?"

"We have to go," Logan said quickly. "I was just telling Blue—that's why we're in here, sorry."

"No!" Jasmin cried, genuinely upset. "Blue, you can't leave

already. You just got here. We haven't danced or anything. And there's, um—there's red velvet cake! In the shape of a ghost! You *can't* leave before the cake."

Blue shook his head and ran one hand through his hair. "Sorry, Jasmin. It's, uh—"

"My cat," Logan jumped in, right as Blue said, "My mom."

Jasmin glanced between them suspiciously.

"His mom," Logan agreed.

"Got bitten by his cat," Blue blurted.

Logan shot him a look. *You are the worst liar.* Poor Purrsimmon, as if she would ever bite anybody.

"What?" Jasmin said. "Is she all right?"

"Yes," Logan said.

"No," said Blue, and Jasmin's eyes went wide.

"His *mom* is *fine*," Logan said firmly. "He means my *cat*, who is now *missing*, and we have to *find her*, so we need to leave *now*." *Before this lie gets any more absurd.* He pushed Blue toward the door.

"Are you taking your disturbing sixth grader with you?" Jasmin asked. "Because she just dared Cadence to bite off one of her own fingers, and then got all outraged when she wouldn't. I'm not sure she completely understands that Truth or Dare is a game. Also, she might be a psychopath."

"Keiko, yes," Blue said distractedly. "We should get Keiko."

"This is going to go over well," Logan muttered. He took

out his fake fangs as they left the study. At least he wouldn't have to wear his uncomfortable costume any longer.

They found Zoe's adopted sister, Keiko, perched on the kitchen counter, chatting to three seventh-grade girls, while Marco Jimenez stood beside her holding two plates of snacks. Keiko took a tiny meatball from one plate and a mini-quiche from the other without looking at him. Her blue fox ears twitched, but no one seemed to notice that they were real.

"Terrible idea," Keiko said to her fascinated audience. "Getting you together would be an utter waste of time. Violet, stop liking him at once. There are much more useful things you can be doing with your brain than thinking about idiots and how to get those idiots to pay attention to you."

"Aidan's not that bad," Marco protested faintly.

"And he's so cute . . ." Violet said.

"He is twelve, and a boy," Keiko said, as if this were boringly obvious. "He'd require an exhausting amount of training. You wouldn't have any time for soccer." She speared another meatball.

"What kind of training?" Marco asked. "I'm a fast learner. Just in case you were wondering."

Keiko gave him a skeptical look and then spotted Logan and Blue heading toward her. Her expression shifted into a glare.

"Absolutely not," she said, pointing her toothpick at them. "Take those pathetic faces elsewhere. I will rip off your eyelashes if you try to make me leave right now."

"It's an emergency, Keiko," Blue said.

"*You're* an emergency," she said.

"Seriously, we have to go right now," Logan said.

"Aw, really? Already?" Marco held up the plates. "Look, she's letting me hold her fancy miniature foods!"

Keiko studied Blue's eyes for a minute, then growled softly. "Help me down," she ordered Marco.

He hurriedly dropped the plates on the counter, scattering crumbs everywhere, and took Keiko's outstretched hand. She jumped lightly to the floor and patted him on the head. "Think about what I said," she said to the three girls. "See me in school on Monday if you have any questions."

Logan turned toward the exit and nearly ran into a woman wielding a gleaming knife.

"Aah!" he yelped, leaping back.

"It's all right, you're safe from me unless you're a cake," Mrs. Sterling said, smiling. Her gold-rimmed glasses caught the light so it was hard to see her eyes.

"Oh—sorry, Mrs. Sterling," Logan said awkwardly.

"I'll forgive you this time, young man," she said, tipping the knife slightly toward him. Her dark hair was swept back from her face and pinned into a bun. Her orange-and-black dress was made from some kind of shiny material and she had on what looked like ten pounds of jewelry, between the diamonds dangling from her ears, the bracelets sparkling on her narrow wrists, and the giant pearl nestled in a gold-and-silver pendant at her neck.

Logan's mom would never have worn any of that. She wore her wedding band on one hand, a black-and-silver ring on the other, and that was usually it, apart from her charm bracelet. Jewelry would have gotten in the way of wrestling chimeras or whatever she had to do in her secret Tracker job.

"Jasmin says you're leaving already?" Mrs. Sterling said to Blue. He nodded, and she made a little fake sad face with her mouth. "What a shame. I hope we get to see you again . . . soon."

As an exhibit in your theme park? Logan wondered. She must know Blue was one of the merfolk, if the Sterlings knew everything else. She probably knew about Keiko being a kitsune, too. He felt a sudden flare of anger. Blue and Keiko weren't specimens; they were his *friends*. Well, Keiko was more like the unpredictably grouchy younger sister of a friend, but still. He'd do anything to protect her, or Blue, or the Menagerie.

"Come on," Logan said, taking Blue's arm and dragging him away. He could feel Mrs. Sterling's eyes on his back as they left the kitchen, as if she were thinking, *I know where you're going. And it will be mine soon.*

TWO

In the main entrance hall, Logan and Blue found Jasmin sitting on the stairs with her chin on her hands and her elbows on her knees, staring sadly into space. Her mermaid tail was a green, glittery waterfall flopping over her feet, and her hair was a dark curtain around her thin shoulders.

Blue hesitated, glanced at Logan, and then went over to sit on the stair beside her. He gently put one hand on Jasmin's back.

"I'm sorry we can't stay," he said. "I'm sure it'll be an awesome party."

"Of course," she said, mustering a smile. "All my parties

are awesome. You're so missing out." She looked into his eyes for a minute, then turned away, wrapping her arms around her legs.

Blue tucked a strand of her hair behind her ear, leaned over, and quickly kissed her cheek. "See you Monday," he mumbled, jumping up and practically running for the door.

Keiko was already outside, so Logan was the only one who saw the radiantly hopeful expression spread across Jasmin's face. He waved good-bye to her and followed Blue out.

"Don't say anything," Blue warned him as they walked down the long driveway, past the eerie glowing jack-o'-lanterns. Logan hadn't noticed it on his way in, but now half the carvings made him think of mythical creatures. Was that one an octopus, or a kraken? That one could be an ordinary ghost . . . or the yeti the Sterlings were planning to imprison and exploit. And that one was definitely a dragon. Its orange eyes seemed to be glowering malevolently at him.

"I'm not saying anything," Logan said. "Jasmin seems . . . kind of okay once you get to know her."

"Yeah," Blue said, kicking the gravel. "She's not really like how she acts at school now. It was always great hanging out with her, before . . . everything with Jonathan. I don't get it, Logan. How do the Sterlings know about the Menagerie?"

"Agent Dantes said some people have stronger resistance to kraken ink, didn't she?" Logan pointed out. "Maybe Ruby didn't give them enough."

"Or maybe she didn't give it to them at all," Blue said grimly.

"Wow," Logan said. "And then lied and told everyone that she did? That would be *so* unfair to Zoe."

"Tell me about it," Blue said. "Zoe dosed Jasmin and stopped speaking to her, to protect the Menagerie. It was pretty much the worst thing she ever had to do. And if it was for nothing—if Ruby didn't even dose the other Sterlings—"

"Then we should feed her to a . . . a . . . what's the most dangerous mythical creature?" Logan asked.

"Yeah!" Blue said. "We should feed her to a pyrosalamander!"

The tiny fire-eating lizards weren't quite what Logan had had in mind. He'd been thinking something larger and toothier.

"You're the one doing my math homework for the next month," Keiko informed Blue as they caught up to her at the bottom of the driveway. "As for you—how's your Spanish?" she added to Logan.

"Keiko, when you hear why we had to leave, you'll understand," Blue said. "You're in danger, too."

She tossed her head. "In danger of being *lame*," she muttered. "Leaving a Jasmin Sterling party before nine. My followers are not going to believe this." She growled at a passing group of trick-or-treaters and a tiny pirate shrieked and hid behind his mom.

Soon they turned up the drive to Zoe's house, and Logan breathed a sigh of relief. The sprawling colonial-style house looked just the same as when they'd left it, although Zoe was no longer staring mournfully out the front window. An enormous wall stretched in either direction, abutting the sides of the building and hiding the Menagerie from view. Everything seemed quiet.

"Oh, look at that," Keiko said snidely. "Still standing. I was expecting *at least* a smoldering pile of rubble, given all the *extreme panic-stricken urgency* and everything."

"How do you guys keep people from asking what's inside those walls?" Logan asked Blue. "The Sterlings must drive by this place every day—but they can't be the only people who've ever been curious about all the land hidden back there."

"It's the thing," Blue said vaguely.

"The thing?" Logan asked.

Blue scrunched up his face. "We have a—well, you know."

Logan blinked at him. "No, I don't. How would I know? What are you talking about?"

Blue waved his hands. "The . . . thing."

"Blue! WHAT thing?"

"The whatchamacallit that makes you not think about it so that—hey, your wig is falling off." Blue didn't seem to notice that he'd shifted topics midsentence.

Logan reached up and pulled off his werewolf wig, rubbing his head. If he understood Blue's evasive weirdness right, it sounded like there was some kind of device that could block anyone from noticing it, and its power worked on the whole—

The front door flew open. A vampire in a long, slinky red dress stood framed in the doorway, flashing her fangs at them.

"HAPPY HALLO—oh, it's you," she said.

"Don't let any real vampires see you dressed like that," Blue said, frowning at her. "Those fangs are just insultingly wrong. And why are your arms all sparkly? Are you a vampire or a pixie?"

"I'm not dressed as a *real* vampire." Zoe's sister Ruby sniffed, rearranging her black wig. "I'm dressed as a *Twilight* vampire."

"Oh, much better," Blue said. "Nothing makes a real vampire more likely to bite you than bringing up those books. There's a safety tip for you," he said to Logan.

"Okay, thanks," Logan said, following him into the house as Ruby sashayed off up the stairs.

A furry head with two enormous, flapping ears poked around the corner.

"EEEEEHHHH-WEEEEIIIIHHHH-NUUUU!!!" The woolly mammoth trumpeted in excitement and bounded into the hall.

"Ew, no, get off!" Keiko shrieked as Captain Fuzzbutt tried to pat her with his trunk. "Don't you dare touch me, you overgrown hairy elephant!" She swatted him away and the mammoth turned happily to Logan, stretching out his trunk. Logan stepped forward and gave it the fist bump the mammoth was looking for.

Zoe appeared behind the Captain. "Why are you guys back so early? Is Jasmin all right?" She narrowed her eyes at Blue.

"*They* made me leave," Keiko said huffily. "Apparently it's the end of the world. Can't you tell? Now I have to go wash mammoth drool out of my hair, so—"

"Wait, Keiko," Blue said. "You should hear this, too. Zoe, where are your parents?"

"In the kitchen," she said, twisting her hands together anxiously. "What's wrong?"

Logan pulled out his phone as they went after Blue into the kitchen. Mrs. Kahn was reading from a cookbook while Zoe's dad shaped a mound of lumpy oatmeal dough into giant dog biscuits. Two of the hellhounds sat below them, slavering rivulets of drool all over their paws. The room smelled like pumpkin bread, and cello music played softly on the stereo in the corner. Logan could see Zoe's older brother, Matthew, doing homework at the large table in the next room.

They all looked so peaceful. Logan wished he didn't have to be the one to tell them that their troubles weren't over after all. It was only yesterday that the Menagerie had escaped being shut down by SNAPA, the SuperNatural Animal

Protection Agency. Logan and Zoe had found and returned Pelly, the abducted goose who laid golden eggs, and they'd rescued Scratch, one of their dragons, from being exterminated for Pelly's supposed murder. He'd hoped that maybe they'd all have a minute to relax—and perhaps even think about trying to find his mom.

But that wasn't happening tonight. He opened the photo of the map and held it out to Zoe.

"We found this in Mr. Sterling's study," he said.

Zoe stared at it for a long moment, and then passed it to her mom, blinking away tears. Captain Fuzzbutt crowded up beside her and wrapped his trunk around her arm. She turned to bury her face in his fur.

Mrs. Kahn took one look at the picture, gasped, and covered her mouth with one hand.

"The Sterlings know about the Menagerie," Zoe said in a choked voice.

"That's impossible," Mr. Kahn said, taking the phone from his wife. He zoomed in to the picture and studied it, running one hand through his hair so it stood up in horrified tufts. "A theme park," he said. "This must be why Mr. Sterling has been buying up so much nearby land. But how—why—"

Keiko snatched the phone and scowled at it. "Oh REALLY. 'Kitsune Pavilion'? I've got a better idea: how about a 'Sterling Pavilion' featuring the stuffed heads of all the Sterlings I'm going to hunt down and disembowel?"

"Let me see," Matthew said, leaning over the pass-through. Logan took the phone from Keiko and handed it to him. "Holy chupacabras." Zoe's brother whistled softly. "This is a major kraken ink situation. Right? Like, we might need SNAPA for cleanup. And a massive dose for the whole family, obviously. I hereby volunteer to hold down Jonathan."

"I don't understand." Mrs. Kahn's voice faltered. "Ruby—Ruby said—"

"RUBY!" Zoe's dad bellowed. "RUBY, GET DOWN HERE RIGHT NOW!"

"Ooooh," Keiko said, hopping up to sit on the counter. "*Now* this is going to get fun."

"I knew Jonathan was a weasel," Matthew said vehemently. "I knew Ruby was wrong; I *knew* he would tell his parents. He's always trying to impress his dad by doing stupid things like going out for sports when he hates them. I bet he was taking that jackalope to show Mr. Sterling. I bet they've been planning to expose the Menagerie for months."

"We're getting to the bottom of this," said Mr. Kahn. "RUBY!"

"WHAAAAAAAT," said Ruby, flouncing into the kitchen. She threw herself into a chair and started picking through the candy in the Halloween bowl. "You don't have to *shout* at me. Ew, who got all this candy corn? Tell me there's *something* chocolate in here."

"Ruby," Mrs. Kahn said in a dangerously quiet voice.

Zoe's sister looked up and finally noticed their expressions. "Uh-oh," she said. "Oh no. What's wrong? What's Zoe done now?"

"ME??!!" Zoe yelled.

"Ruby," said Mr. Kahn. "Did you lie to us about dosing Jonathan and his parents with kraken ink?"

"What? No!" Ruby cried—a little too quickly, Logan thought. Her eyes darted sideways and she stood up, flinging the dark hair of her wig back over her shoulders. "How could you even *ask* me that? You know what a huge *sacrifice* I made! I gave up what might be my only chance at true *love*! I may be emotionally scarred for *life*!"

"You definitely gave them all kraken ink?" Mrs. Kahn said. "All three of them?"

"Of course I did," Ruby said, putting her hands on her hips. "This is an outrage! I can't believe you don't BELIEVE me!"

Her parents stared at her for a long moment and she stared back with her chin lifted defiantly.

"Matthew," Mr. Kahn said. "Go get the qilin."

Ruby and Zoe both gasped. Matthew dropped Logan's phone on the counter and bolted out the sliding doors into the dark night.

Logan hadn't thought of that, but it was smart. The qilin—a kind of Chinese unicorn—could determine a person's guilt or innocence. This one, Kiri, had been a part of Scratch's trial and was set to be sent back to Camp Underpaw on Sunday.

Her horn would turn yellow for innocence or blue if the person was guilty.

"You would use a qilin on me?" Ruby demanded, waving her hands dramatically. "How *could* you? Where is the trust? Where is the faith? I am your *daughter*. I refuse to stand here and let you interrogate me like some common dragon!"

"This is very serious, Ruby," Mrs. Kahn said. "Beyond serious."

"I know!" Ruby said. "Doubting your own flesh and blood! Threatening her with backward unicorns! If I could tell my Facebook friends about this they would be so totally appalled!"

Mr. Kahn picked up Logan's phone and held it out to her. "Can you think of another explanation for this, then?"

Ruby scrunched up her face, studying the map. She prodded the screen, moving it around and zooming in and out.

"Is this some kind of joke?" she said finally.

"That," said Mr. Kahn, "is what your friends the Sterlings are planning on doing with our Menagerie."

"Look how much they know," Mrs. Kahn said. "They couldn't have remembered all that if you really gave them kraken ink."

Ruby reached up unconsciously and touched one of the shimmering red hearts dangling from her ears. "No," she murmured. "There's no way! Jonathan would never let this happen. He loves me!"

"Loves?" Zoe said accusingly. "Present tense?"

The glass doors slid open and Matthew came in, leading the delicate qilin. Captain Fuzzbutt waved his trunk cheerfully at her, and the qilin tiptoed lightly across the kitchen tiles. Her little hooves didn't even make a sound. Logan felt the quiet peace of her aura calming down the turmoil inside of him.

He held his breath. Was Ruby lying?

The qilin took one look at Ruby and her horn instantly turned blue.

Guilty.

THREE

Zoe stared at the qilin's glowing blue horn.

Ruby had *lied* about the kraken ink. She'd put the whole Menagerie in danger for a stupid, backstabbing *boy*. She'd broken all the rules they'd grown up with. Zoe couldn't even imagine it—if her parents told her to do something for the safety of the animals, she would have done it in a heartbeat.

In fact, she *had* done it. She'd given kraken ink to Jasmin. She'd given up her best friend.

Zoe reached for Captain Fuzzbutt and felt the mammoth's trunk wrap around her waist.

"Thank you, Kiri," said Zoe's dad.

The qilin gave a little bow with her head, then turned and trotted back out into the Menagerie.

"All right, fine," Ruby said. She slammed Logan's phone down on the counter and Zoe saw him wince. "I didn't give Jonathan the kraken ink, okay? What we have is true love forever!"

"But didn't you care about the danger to the Menagerie?" Mr. Kahn asked. "He tried to steal a jackalope—can you imagine what would have happened if he'd succeeded?"

Zoe had never heard him sound so bewildered. Or maybe a better word was *betrayed*—that was certainly how she felt. Mom and Dad had always trusted her and Ruby and Matthew. They'd let them do almost anything as long as everyone followed one rule: keep the Menagerie safe.

"I can't believe you lied to us," Mrs. Kahn said.

"*I* can," Keiko offered. "She's an enormous liar. I mean, that is *not* her actual hair color, for one thing."

"And for Jonathan, of all people!" Matthew said. "That double-crossing jerk!"

"He is not!" Ruby flared. She threw her hands up dramatically, waving her sleeves like wings. "You don't understand him! None of you do! He's a good person! He's wonderful and *heroic*!"

"He's a thief," Matthew said, "and he obviously lied to you, if you don't know about this theme park plan."

"I'm sure he knows nothing about that," Ruby said. "He

was stealing the jackalope for a noble reason! Which nobody even bothered to find out except me!"

Matthew crossed his arms. "Oh, right. And what noble reason is that?"

"He did it for Jasmin," Ruby declared, as if she were standing in the middle of a Broadway stage with one spotlight on her and dim blue mist all around. She pressed her heart with one hand and gave Zoe a pitying look. "He was trying to *save* her."

"Save her from what?" Zoe demanded. Something jumped and twisted inside her stomach. "*Save her from what*, Ruby?"

"I'm sorry, Zoe," Ruby said. "Jasmin is very sick."

"She is not!" Zoe yelled. Captain Fuzzbutt let go of her and backed away, trumpeting anxiously. Zoe clenched her fists, her heart pounding. "That's another lie!"

"It's true!" Ruby hollered back. "Jonathan told me!"

"Everyone calm down!" Mr. Kahn said. "Ruby, what are you talking about?"

Ruby paused again, like the most annoying Hamlet right before his big speech. "Jasmin . . . has a terrible secret disease," she said in a hushed voice.

"No. I would know if she did," Zoe said furiously. "She would never never keep that from me." *Would she? Has she been sick all these months? Did I abandon her when she needed me the most?*

"Jonathan told you he was taking the jackalope to save

his sister?" Mr. Kahn asked, giving Zoe a worried look. "From what? What does she have?"

"Oh, I don't know," Ruby said, waving her hands. "Something that sounded like sarcophagus? I can't remember. Anyway, whatever, it's terrible."

"Maybe he was completely lying," Matthew suggested. "That would fit with everything else he's done."

"Why didn't you tell us?" Zoe asked. "How could you not tell *me*, if you think it's true?"

Ruby wound a strand of the wig's hair around her finger and sighed. "Jonathan said the family didn't want anyone to know. Anyway, by the time he told me, it was too late. You'd already sent me over there with the kraken ink. And I *did* give it to his parents, *by the way*, whatever you think. But once I found out about Jonathan's true, heroic reasons, I couldn't do that to him, so we just . . . pretended I gave him the kraken ink."

"Wait," Mr. Kahn said, rubbing his forehead. "Are you telling me that you *told* Jonathan about what the kraken ink does?"

Ruby bit her lip. "Well, I—I mean, I had to explain why he needed to act as though we'd never dated."

"*Ruby.*" Mrs. Kahn shook her head sadly. "How are we going to get the Sterlings to forget about the Menagerie if they're already on alert for kraken ink?"

"Jonathan wouldn't tell them! He wouldn't do that to me! This is insane!" Ruby shouted.

"AAAOOOROOOOOOOOO!!!!!!!" Captain Fuzzbutt charged out from behind Zoe and started blundering around the living room. The vibrations from his feet shook books off the shelves and overturned a vase of yellow lilies on a side table.

"Fuzzbutt!" Zoe yelled. She ran to the doors that led out to the Menagerie and slid them open. "Help me get him outside!"

Logan, Blue, and Matthew ran to cut the mammoth off and herd him toward the doorway. Fuzzbutt rolled his eyes and trumpeted again, stamping his feet, then suddenly bolted out into the darkness.

"I'm going after him," Zoe said to her parents.

"Are you all right?" her dad asked.

"Yeah, I just—need some air." She ducked out the door and ran down the hill.

Captain Fuzzbutt was sitting by the unicorn stable, his shoulders slumped gloomily. The cool air smelled of pine trees, and a chilly wind swept right through Zoe's skin. She wished she'd brought a jacket, but she wasn't going back into that house or anywhere near Ruby right now.

"Don't worry," she said, hugging one of the mammoth's giant legs. "It's just a fight. Everyone will be fine."

She wished she believed that. She wished she knew *what* to believe. Was Jasmin really sick? Or was Jonathan a totally evil liar as well as a sneak and a thief?

Sneakers swished in the grass and she turned to find Blue and Logan behind her.

"You know what we have to do," she said.

"Catch a jackalope, milk a jackalope, and then find some way to slip the world's most disgusting-smelling substance into Jasmin's Coke at lunch on Monday?" Blue guessed. "No problem."

"WHAT?" Logan said.

"Exactly," said Zoe. "Except I can't wait until Monday. We find a way to get it to her tomorrow."

"She seems fine," Blue said. "It's much more likely that Jonathan was lying, right? Really, Zoe, I think she's okay."

"But if she's not—" Zoe said. "If there's even a *chance* Jasmin is awfully sick, and I—I just left her—I've been the worst friend, and she might . . ."

She covered her face with her hands. A warm arm went around her shoulders and she turned to let Logan hug her. It was comforting, but at the same time, she kept thinking that Jasmin hadn't had anyone to comfort *her* all these months.

"Let's go now," she said, pulling free. "The jackalopes might be sleepy and easier to catch in the middle of the night. Captain, you stay here."

The mammoth made a mournful noise and flopped down on his side. Zoe rubbed his head once more, knowing exactly how he felt.

"Um, so," Logan said as he followed her down to the path

around the lake. "I'm totally on board, of course. But *what* are we doing?"

"Jackalope milk is supposed to cure anything," Blue said. "But it's kind of unpredictable. SNAPA has been studying it for years, trying to figure out a way to reliably reproduce it and get it into the world as medicine, but for one thing, it doesn't always work, and for another, they'll have to invent an explanation for where it comes from. Also there's this rare side effect where one percent of people who take it grow antlers. So there's a lot more testing still to do."

"But Jasmin—" Zoe said.

"Oh, I agree," Blue said. "No need to convince me. We're doing this. I'm ready."

"Then go get a thermos or something," Zoe said. "Don't let my parents see you." He turned and ran back toward the house.

They crept up to the jackalope enclosure, a small fenced-in field near the pine grove between the Aviary and the yeti's ice sculpture garden. Everything was quiet. Zoe guessed the jackalopes were asleep in their hutch, which looked much like an ordinary rabbit hutch, except that the entrance and the roof were extra-tall to accommodate their antlers.

She crouched behind the hedge, waving Logan to the ground as well, and held up a finger to her mouth.

"Be vewy, vewy quiet. We're hunting jackalopes," Logan whispered.

"What?" Zoe said.

"Seriously?" Logan said. "From the . . . cartoon . . . do you even own a TV?"

"What's a TV?" Zoe asked.

He goggled at her for a minute, and then she couldn't keep a straight face anymore and collapsed into giggles.

"Would you quit teasing me?" he said, punching her shoulder. "I'm still figuring you all out."

"We're not aliens, goofus," Zoe pointed out. "And seriously, yes, we should be quiet. Jackalopes can mimic any voices they've heard, so the best way to approach them is without talking. That way, we know not to follow someone's shout when they try and throw us off track."

"Oh," Logan said, "good call."

"It's okay, Logan." Zoe smiled at him. "I know you haven't had time to memorize all the tips in Matthew's Tracker guide yet. We don't expect you to be an expert until, say, next week."

"Funny," Logan said, pointing at her. "I got it that time."

Blue came jogging up with an empty water bottle in his hand. "Hope this'll work," he whispered, crouching beside them.

Zoe peeked at the hutch again. "We can't just reach in and get them—the hutch is designed to make them feel secure, so they can hide in there as long as they want—which is what they usually do when they see us coming. So Logan and I will go around to the back opening and Blue, you take the front. Sneak up and then make a loud noise, and hopefully they'll bolt out the back. We need to grab the female one, so follow my lead, okay, Logan? And try not to get impaled by their antlers."

"Ha-ha?" Logan said. "Hilarious?"

"No, that's real," Zoe said. "They're not as sharp as deer antlers, but you still don't want to get stabbed in the neck with one."

"Someone should get you an ordinary pet one day," Logan said. "Something that doesn't impale or bite or breathe fire or plan to take over the world. Like a goldfish."

"Oh, you'd be surprised what some goldfish are planning," Blue said.

"I have Captain Fuzzbutt," Zoe said. "All he can do is break my foot if he steps on it. Otherwise, he's perfect. Okay, Blue, are you ready?"

Blue nodded.

"Remember, no talking. Or if you really have to tell us something, say the word 'banana' first so we know it's you and not the jackalopes."

"Banana? Really? That's the best code word you can come up with?" Blue said.

"Okay, fine, what do *you* want to use?"

"How about 'merfolk rule!'?" Blue suggested.

Zoe rolled her eyes. "Way too long."

"Gadzooks?" Logan suggested.

"Are you ninety-seven years old?" Zoe asked.

"Fish sticks!" said Blue.

Zoe sighed. "'Fish sticks' it is. Now get out of here."

Blue saluted her and they split up, circling around the hutch.

"This fence is mostly to keep the hellhounds out," Zoe explained to Logan. "The regulations say we need to provide a separate enclosed space for the jackalopes. Plus they like to rub up against the wooden barriers; it helps when they're molting."

Zoe tucked her hair behind her ears. Was this a terrible idea? How much trouble would she be in when her parents found out? Less trouble than Ruby, surely. And they had to understand it'd be worth it for Jasmin . . . if she was really sick.

Zoe eased forward to a break in the hedge and threaded her way through two of the wooden planks of the fence. Logan copied her and she was glad to note that he moved quietly. *Those natural Tracker skills again.*

The long grass tickled her ankles and she wished she were wearing socks. As she and Logan approached the hutch, she turned, caught his eye, and motioned that she'd go in from the left. He nodded and started curving to the right.

We should have brought the night-vision goggles. Zoe mentally kicked herself. Matthew would have remembered them.

He had a whole checklist pinned to his bulletin board for what Tracker equipment to pack depending on which creature you were hunting.

But even without goggles, Zoe was close enough now to make out the details of the hutch. It was raised half a foot off the ground. The water bowl sat in one corner, next to a pile of alfalfa sprouts. A plain cardboard box took up most of the hutch's space. It was stuffed with shredded paper and she could see two pairs of antlers sticking out the top.

The sound of gentle whuffling breaths told her the pair was sleeping. *Maybe this will be easier than I thought.*

Just then, Logan stumbled. His feet scuffed the ground as he righted himself, and then he froze in place. Zoe eyed the hutch, not daring to move.

One. Two. Maybe they're still sleeping. Three. Four.
WHOOSH.

The two jackalopes leaped from the box and sprinted out of the hutch in opposite directions.

Zoe let out a little cry of dismay and bolted toward Clover. She could only tell it was the female jackalope from the slightly smaller size of the antlers. Logan followed Zoe and tried to head Clover off.

"Over here!" Zoe heard her own voice call from behind her. It was surreal. Did she really sound that high-pitched?

"Fish sticks! Blue, she's heading for the fence!" Zoe called out.

"Fish sticks, on my way!" he answered.

"Wait, Blue, you're going the wrong way!" a jackalope squeaked in Zoe's voice.

Clover turned sharply and darted under a patch of scrub, emerging on the other side at full steam. Logan vaulted after her as Zoe ran around the bush.

"I've got one!" Blue's voice shouted triumphantly from her left. Zoe nearly turned toward him, before she realized there was no code word. She swerved back and spotted Clover bounding over a rise.

"Fish sticks, Zoe, Logan, where are you?" Blue's voice came again, this time from in front of her.

"Fish sticks, right here! Keep coming, we've almost got her," Logan shouted back.

"Fish sticks, what are you doing? That's not the one we want!" Blue said.

Logan slowed and sent a questioning look over his shoulder at Zoe. Zoe squinted at the jackalope she and Logan were chasing. *No,* she thought, *that's definitely Clover. They must have figured out our code.*

"Banana, they've caught on. Logan, keep going!" she cried.

Logan picked up his pace as Clover pelted toward the border of the field. Mooncrusher's yurt was visible up ahead. Zoe hoped they wouldn't wake the yeti. For a nocturnally named guy, Mooncrusher was an early-to-bed kind of yeti, and would not appreciate three twelve-year-olds and a jackalope crashing through his ice sculptures at this hour.

Blue suddenly appeared out of the darkness, racing toward them. Clover's back legs slid sideways as she veered away from him, but Logan took a chance and dove forward, pinning the jackalope's back half down and tucking his head between his arms to avoid her antlers.

Clover squeaked in alarm and twisted her head frantically to see what had her.

"Fish sticks, let her go! You're hurting her!" Zoe's voice cried out in alarm.

"Banana, no! It's okay," Zoe panted as she dropped to the ground next to Logan and Clover. "I've got her." She reached out and gently scooped Clover up, flipping the jackalope over onto her back so her antlers dangled down on either side of Zoe's left arm. Clover's hind legs pushed against Zoe's chest—that was going to bruise. "Shh, Clover, it's okay," Zoe crooned.

"You're going to be in big trouble for this, young lady," the jackalope said sternly in Zoe's father's voice. Zoe winced. It really sounded exactly like him.

Blue joined them, resting his hands on his knees as he caught his breath.

"Whew, I'm glad that's done," Logan said.

"Well, next is the hard part," Blue said. "Now we've got to milk her."

"I BEG your pardon," said the jackalope, sounding like

Melissa Merevy, Blue's mom, this time. "Under whose authority? Where are your SNAPA badges? I demand to see your requisition forms!" Even coming from an upside-down rabbit with antlers, Melissa's voice was intimidating.

"Clover, it's really important," Zoe said, stroking her fur softly. "Please don't be mad."

"Have you ever done this before?" Logan asked.

"Nope," Blue said. "Can't say that we have. SNAPA sends in special vets to do it occasionally, but it's not exactly standard procedure around here."

"I've read how to do it, though," Zoe said. "We just need to calm her down first."

"Calm me down, indeed," Clover grumbled in, hilariously, Pelly's voice. "After barging through my home and waking me up and practically traumatizing my antlers right off, what makes you think I'll—oooh, right there, that's been itching all day."

The jackalope nestled into Zoe's arms as Zoe scratched under her chin. Clover's mate, Parsnip, peeked out of the bushes nearby, but once he seemed satisfied that Clover was not being harmed, he slipped away.

After five minutes or so, Clover's heart rate finally started to ease off turbo-speed, her legs relaxed, and her eyelids drooped. Zoe nodded toward Blue's jacket. "Get the bottle ready."

He produced the empty water bottle as Zoe flattened

Clover's fur. She told Logan how to hold it, and then she began massaging Clover's belly. Gradually, some milk began to drip into the bottle. Zoe nearly cried in relief. She hadn't been sure this would even work. Logan looked up and met her eyes, a grin spreading across his face. Zoe felt herself beaming back at him.

"How cool is this?" he asked. "Although, wow, with the smell. That is . . . going to haunt me for a while."

"This is very undignified," the jackalope pointed out in Zoe's voice.

"Sorry, Clover," Zoe said. "It's for a good cause."

Clover flopped her head sideways and rolled her eyes up toward Blue. "You don't look busy, young man," she said, switching back to Melissa's voice. "You could at least be scratching my ears."

"Okay," Blue said, crouching at Clover's head. "But could you use a different voice, please? I could have gone through life without ever hearing my mom ask me to scratch her ears."

"And you should comb your hair, too," the jackalope said, obstinately staying in Melissa's voice. She closed her eyes and poked Blue's hand with her little nose. "Also shower. You smell like you've been bathing with squid."

Zoe giggled. She'd heard Melissa say almost those exact words to Blue before.

"Okay, that's just eerie," Blue said.

Gradually, the pace of the milk picked up until the bottle was halfway full.

"That's probably good enough," Zoe said.

"Are you sure? I don't want to have to do this again," Logan said.

"Hmm. Good point."

SPLOOOOSH!!

Streams of milk shot up from several different points on Clover's belly all at once. Zoe felt one hit her chin, while Logan got some in his eye and even more in his mouth.

"YERGH," he sputtered. "Ugh. Holy *cow*. That tastes even *worse* than it smells."

"AHEM! There is no need to be *rude*," Clover said sniffily, back in Pelly's voice. "Considering I am doing you an enormous favor in the first place." She waggled her upside-down antlers at Logan, not very menacingly. "A little *gratitude* would be in order, I *do* think."

Blue started cracking up. Zoe looked at the milk dribbling down Logan's face and giggled. Logan grinned back as he wiped his face with his sleeve.

"Seriously, though," he said. "I have no idea how we're going to get Jasmin to drink that."

Zoe's joy fizzled out. She had no clue, either . . . but for Jasmin's sake, she knew they had to try.

FOUR

Logan's cell phone rang while Zoe was hiding the jackalope milk between two blocks of ice near Mooncrusher's yurt.

"It's my dad," Logan said to Blue. They were leaning against the wall of the Aviary, waiting for her.

"Something wrong?" Blue asked. "You usually look a lot happier than that when he calls."

"We had a fight on the way over here," Logan said. "Which never happens."

"A fight about what?"

"About being friends with Zoe, basically. Hang on." He answered the phone. "Hey, Dad."

"How's the party going?" Dad was trying to sound upbeat and enthusiastic, maybe to make up for how they'd left things.

"Great," Logan said. "Fine. Normal."

"Super. Well, I can come get you at Jasmin's anytime you're ready."

Logan thought about sticking around the Menagerie for a while, but most of the animals—including the griffin cubs, his favorites—were asleep. And he didn't particularly want to hover around the edges of the massive Ruby fight that was probably still going on. Safer to come back tomorrow, when things had calmed down.

"I'm ready now," he said. "But can you pick me up at Blue's?"

There was a short silence.

"Yes," Logan said. "I mean Zoe's."

"I'm on my way," Dad said, in his let's-not-argue-about-this voice. "Love you."

"You, too." Logan hung up and shoved the phone back in his pocket. "It's weird, Blue. I think my dad must know about the Menagerie—why else would we be here in Xanadu? He must know my mom knew you guys, and that she was on her way here with something. But then why wouldn't he come talk to the Kahns about her, and why is he acting so crazy about me being friends with Zoe?"

"Maybe he's worried that the Kahns will wipe his memory," Blue said with a shrug.

Logan scratched his head. He hadn't thought of that. "You're right—if he knows about kraken ink, he'd be smart to be careful. I wish there was a way to figure out how much he knows."

"Maybe it's time to talk to him about all this," Blue suggested.

"I was kind of hoping he'd talk to *me* first," Logan said. "But yeah, maybe."

Logan only knew that his mother was a mythical creature Tracker because Zoe had told him. Abigail Hardy had brought in Captain Fuzzbutt—rescuing him from a cloning facility in Siberia—and the unicorns and several other inhabitants of the Menagerie.

But then she had disappeared six months ago, on her way to the Menagerie with a Chinese dragon, and no one had seen her since.

Could the Sterlings have had anything to do with her disappearance?

Logan shook his head. He didn't know where to go with those thoughts.

Zoe emerged from the darkness and they all headed around the Aviary and back to the house. Logan could hear tiny splashes coming from the lake. He wondered if it was the kraken, who was supposed to be hibernating but had popped out at least twice in the last week.

"I've been thinking," Zoe blurted suddenly. "What if the

Sterlings are the ones sabotaging the Menagerie?"

"I had the same thought," Logan agreed.

"Sabotaging?" Blue echoed, startled.

"Logan and I think someone's been trying to get us shut down," she said. "First by letting the griffin cubs escape— *someone* cut that hole in the river grate so they could get out. And then we think that same someone stole the golden goose and framed Scratch for her murder. I thought they wanted us to get in trouble with SNAPA. But maybe it's the Sterlings, and they're hoping we'll lose control of the Menagerie so they can swoop in, expose us, and take it over."

"How could they have done any of that?" Blue asked. He pointed back at the dragon caves in the cliff. One of them glowed with a small, eerie red light—the fire of whichever dragon was on duty tonight, Logan guessed. "I mean, you know I don't trust the dragons, but surely at *some* point they would have sounded the intruder alert if the Sterlings kept coming into the Menagerie."

"Not the night Pelly was stolen," Zoe reminded him. "There was no alarm. Scratch was out eating sheep, remember?"

"But he could only do that because someone had already tampered with his chain and the electric fence," Blue argued back. "The Sterlings couldn't have done that."

Zoe fell silent.

"So if the Sterlings are the saboteurs," Logan said slowly,

"then either they found a way around the dragons' intruder alarm, or . . ."

"Or someone inside the Menagerie is working with them," Zoe finished.

"It's not me," Matthew said, popping out from behind the Doghouse. Zoe shrieked and jumped back, nearly knocking Logan over.

"Sorry, sorry," Matthew said. He held up his hands with a grin. "I just wanted to put that out there, since you always think it's me. I swear I am not working with the Sterlings."

The ground shook as Captain Fuzzbutt came barreling up the hill, trumpeting anxiously. He threw his trunk around Zoe and lifted her off the ground.

"I'm all right! It's okay, Captain, put me down," she said.

Grudgingly he set her on her feet and patted her all over with his trunk.

"What did Mom and Dad do to Ruby?" Zoe asked Matthew, rubbing the mammoth's forehead.

"They were still discussing it when they kicked me out," he said, shaking his head. "I heard them say something about sticking her in a SNAPA OOPSS course during all her school breaks for the next three years."

"No *way*," Zoe said in a voice that was equal parts awe, delight, and horror.

"What's an oops course?" Logan asked.

"Official Overview of Protective Security Standards," Zoe said.

"Essentially the most boring thing associated with mythical creatures *ever*," said Matthew. "It's, like, remedial 'don't tell anyone about the animals' classes. Shut Your Yap 101. You're stuck in an underground facility for months on end, reading long boring articles about the rules and what happens when people break the rules. Ruby would haaaaaaaate it."

"Perfect," Zoe said firmly. "I hope they really do it."

"I voted for sending her to the Tanzania menagerie to work with the Giant Mythical Insect research team," Matthew said. "I think feeding enormous talking cockroaches and cleaning out monster spider dens would serve her right."

"That's a good one, too," Blue said. "I guess SNAPA will have to decide."

"As long as it's awful," Zoe said, shaking her head. "I still can't believe what she did."

"I'm going to head out front," Logan said. "My dad will be here soon, and I'm guessing nobody wants him ringing the doorbell right now."

"All right," Zoe said. To his surprise, she came over and gave him a hug. "Thank you for your help. And for finding that map. I don't know what's going to happen, but I know it would have been a lot worse if you hadn't found it."

"I'll be back in the morning," Logan said. "If that's okay?"

"You better be," Blue said, punching his shoulder.

Nobody was in the kitchen as they went through, but they could hear the murmur of voices from upstairs. The Halloween candy bowl sat abandoned on the table. But as Logan went past it, he could have sworn he saw a Three Musketeers bar suddenly . . . disappear from the bowl. He stopped and blinked at it.

I'm just tired and imagining things, he told himself.

He slipped out the front door and found his dad's car parked in the driveway, its front windows rolled down.

But his dad was nowhere to be seen.

"Dad?" Logan said, glancing around at the dark woods that surrounded the Kahn property. "Dad?" he called, a bit louder.

Is this what happened to Mom? Did she just vanish like this?

A bolt of fear shot down Logan's spine. He reached into the car and grabbed a flashlight from the glove compartment. The light did hardly anything to illuminate the spaces between the pine trees, but he stepped closer to the wall, sweeping it around.

"DAD!" he shouted.

Twigs cracked in the woods off to his right. Logan whirled around and caught his dad right in the beam of the flashlight.

Jackson Wilde threw up his hands to shade his face. "Whoa, buddy. Spare an old man's eyes."

Logan lowered the light and frowned at the darkness

behind his dad. "What were you doing out there?"

"I thought I saw something moving," his dad said. "Some kind of animal, maybe a coyote. You know we've had something eating the sheep around here. I figured I should investigate. Wildlife department and all." He tapped his shirt, although he wasn't wearing his badge.

"Without a flashlight?" Logan said skeptically. "Or a weapon? You may be taller than a sheep, but you could be just as edible."

Logan's dad laughed and slung an arm around Logan's shoulder, a little awkwardly given how tall Mr. Wilde was. "I'd like to meet the coyote who'd dare to try and eat me."

How about a dragon? Or a kelpie? Logan thought. He glanced back at the woods as they climbed in the car. Had his dad really seen something? Or was he trying to snoop around the Kahns' house?

"Those are some tall walls," his dad said. "What do they keep in there? Cattle? I don't recall seeing a license for them in our files. . . ."

"I'm sure they have one," Logan said, evading the question. He knew SNAPA would have given them some kind of cover story and paperwork to guarantee no one from any other government agency came poking around.

It was a quiet drive back to their house. Logan's dad asked a few halfhearted questions about the party, but Logan could tell he was thinking about something else.

Whatever it was, he seemed to make a decision as they opened the front door.

"Logan—" he said.

"I'm really tired, Dad." Logan didn't want to have another argument about Zoe and her family tonight. He wanted to go back to his room, wash off the werewolf makeup, curl up with his cat, Purrsimmon, and think about who might be helping the Sterlings sabotage the Menagerie.

"Okay, just . . . I want to give you something," his dad said.

"A puppy?" Logan joked. That was his line, the joke they always ran through whenever his dad gave him anything.

His dad reached into his jacket pocket and pulled out a necklace. Logan raised his eyebrows at it as it dangled from his dad's huge hands.

"Really?" he said. "Jewelry? Is it our anniversary?"

"I think it's important that you have this," said his dad.

Hanging from the black cord of the necklace was a small glass square, and inside the square was something that glinted green and gold. Logan took it in his hands and peered closer at it. It wasn't a jewel. It was a beetle.

"Yikes," Logan said. "Which one is the insect anniversary?"

"It's cool, isn't it?" his dad said.

It *was* really cool looking. The beetle's hard folded wings shimmered like sunlit green stained glass with layers of dark blue and gold underneath. Six little black legs stuck out from its sides and tiny black antennae-like jaws protruded from its head.

And then, as Logan was staring at it, he saw one of the legs move.

"AAAAAH!" he yelped, nearly dropping the necklace. His dad reached out and grabbed it from him. "Dad! It's alive! It's alive in there!"

"I know," his dad said. "Like I said, cool, right?"

"But HOW IS IT ALIVE, Dad?" And then, of course, Logan realized how.

It was magic. His dad was giving him a mythical creature.

"I don't know," his dad said with a shrug. "Your mom gave it to me a long time ago, when we first got engaged. She said— she said it would protect me."

"By scaring the daylights out of anyone who tries to mug you?" Logan asked. *Or with magical creature powers? Do you know what you're holding? Does anyone know you have this? Surely not; SNAPA couldn't possibly let mythical creatures like this float around being worn as accessories. So if Mom had broken the rules by giving him this, she could have broken them some more by telling him everything about her job.*

"The thing is, I think it's worked so far," his dad said, twisting the cord between his fingers. "And now—I really want you to have it."

"Why?" Logan asked. "This is Xanadu, Dad. We're not

in Chicago anymore. What could I possibly need protecting from out here?"

He waited. This would be a good time for his dad to say something like, "I don't know, maybe grumpy unicorns?"

But instead he said, "Please take it, Logan. If you're—I just want to know you're safe."

If I'm going to be hanging out with the Kahns, Logan guessed. *Inside the Menagerie. He does know.*

He took the beetle necklace and slipped it over his head. The glass square with the beetle inside rested over his heart like a warm hand. It glowed like there was a sunbeam trapped inside it, casting a soft light over his brown skin.

"Weird," Logan said. "I do feel safer."

A look of relief spread across his dad's face, and Logan suddenly felt guilty. He remembered the surge of fear he'd had when he thought for a moment his dad might be gone, too. Of course his dad was worried about him. Neither of them knew what had happened to Mom.

But if his father met the Kahns, he'd see there was nothing to worry about.

Maybe it was time for the truth.

"Dad—" Logan said as his dad turned toward the kitchen. "Yeah?"

Logan's phone buzzed, and then buzzed again, and then a third time in rapid succession.

"Hold on." He pulled out his phone and saw that it was a text from Blue. Three texts from Blue, all in a row.

LOGAN.
911!
DO NOT TELL YOUR DAD ANYTHING.

What? Logan blinked at the screen.
The phone buzzed again.

We think he's the one sabotaging the Menagerie.

FIVE

"Explain this," Logan said, holding up his phone as Zoe answered the door Saturday morning.

"It's an advanced technological device," Zoe said, yawning. "People use it to communicate over long distances and to take pictures. But its primary use is for watching videos of sloths being tickled. So I hear."

"Ha-ha," Logan said. "My dad? Sabotaging the Menagerie? Are you crazy?"

"Come in," Zoe said. "You're up really early."

"I haven't exactly slept," he said, following her into the kitchen.

"Me neither." She got out two mugs with rainbow

unicorns on them. "I went out and did half my chores at five a.m. because I couldn't lie in bed anymore. Tea or cocoa?"

"Cocoa if you have mini-marshmallows," he said.

"Of course we do," she said. "What are we, savages? Also the baku is kind of obsessed with them."

"The what?" Logan said. "Wait, no. Don't distract me. Tell me on what planet you think my dad would ever be working with the Sterlings to steal golden geese and frame Scratch."

"I don't know if he has anything to do with the Sterlings," Zoe said. "But come look at this." She stuck the two mugs of milk in the microwave and led the way into the living room. They passed Captain Fuzzbutt snoring softly, flopped out on one of the giant orange pillows. At the far end was the door to Melissa's office. Zoe tapped on the door lightly and listened.

"I think she went out early," she whispered to Logan, "but just in case."

There was no answer. After a moment, Zoe pushed the door open and headed straight for the bank of video screens in the corner. Logan had been here once before, when they were checking the video feeds for the night the griffin cubs had escaped.

"Remember the security updates SNAPA wanted us to install last week?" Zoe said. "The ones Matthew swears crashed the system, but Melissa thinks someone else came in and hacked us? Well, SNAPA finally got us new versions of the software, so Matthew installed it all again yesterday.

And last night we didn't want to go upstairs while my parents were still fighting with Ruby, so Blue and I came in here with Matthew to check on everything."

She leaned over and typed something quickly. One of the screens blipped and started zipping backward.

"Part of the upgrade is that SNAPA insisted we put a new camera in the Dark Forest," Zoe said. "We used to have one there, but the mapinguari and the baku never do *anything* interesting, so when it broke, we just left it that way. But now it's up and working again, which means we've got footage from this last week."

She hit a button and the video stopped, then started playing at a regular speed. The screen showed a thick tangle of vines and leaves woven around a small grass hut. It was night, so the video had that blurry night-vision grayness. Something furry and huge shuffled out of the hut, its eyes glowing. It scratched its back on a nearby tree and shuffled back in.

"What was that?" Logan whispered.

"Not the important part," she said. "Look back there." She pointed at the top left corner of the screen, beyond the creature's hut. When Logan squinted, he realized there was a wall there, through the vines—the outer wall of the Menagerie.

A head suddenly appeared over the wall.

Followed by an arm, and a leg, and a whole body, as someone pulled himself over the wall. Whoever it was scrambled down, using the vines like climbing ropes, and hopped to the ground.

He looked around furtively, touched his chest, and then edged away from the hut, into the trees, and off the screen.

Zoe looked up at Logan. "Still think we're crazy?"

Logan sat down in the nearest chair, his head spinning. "But maybe—I mean, we couldn't clearly see his face—" He stopped and rubbed his eyes. There still wasn't any doubt. Xanadu wasn't exactly teeming with six-foot-two bald African-American men, and Logan recognized that nose.

That was his dad on the video, sneaking into the Menagerie.

"When was this?" he asked. "Last night?"

"Last night?" Zoe said. "No, what? Should we be checking last night's feed, too? This was from Monday night."

"Monday." Logan tried to remember the crazy week that had just passed. "That was the morning you came over and he realized we were hanging out. Maybe he was just checking up on me. Maybe he wanted to see what you guys were like."

"By climbing over our wall and sneaking past our enormous mythical sloth in the middle of the night?" Zoe said. "Maybe they do things differently in Chicago, but here most parents would, just hypothetically, call up the other kid's parents and say hello." She touched Logan's hand to stop him from protesting. "There's more. After we saw this, we went back through the tapes. We found him climbing over in the same spot at least two other times before."

"That doesn't mean he's sabotaging the Menagerie!" Logan said, standing up so fast the rolling chair banged into Melissa's desk. "Why would he do that?"

"We were hoping you'd have a guess," Zoe said.

Logan felt queasy. "He must have a good reason. I mean, this is my *dad*. Even when I'm mad at him, he's kind of awesome, Zoe."

"I'm sure that's true," Zoe said. "But we have to figure out what he's doing, right? Could he have broken Scratch's anklet? Or cut that hole in the river grate?"

"I guess maybe—but wait, why didn't the intruder alarm go off when he came in?" Logan asked.

"I have no idea," Zoe said with a sigh. "Maybe we should ask the dragons. I'll put it on my list for the day, along with figuring out how to get the jackalope milk to Jasmin. Mooncrusher was complaining already this morning about a weird smell coming from his yurt. I was able to sneak over, grab the bottle, and hide it in our fridge, but someone is *definitely* going to notice it there soon."

"Do you have a plan?" Blue asked from the doorway. He looked rumpled, as if he'd just woken up, in a blue-green shirt that matched his eyes and gray cargo shorts. "Hey, Logan."

"Hey," Logan said. He leaned against the desk and rubbed his eyes again. *Dad, what are you up to? Why would you want to take down the Menagerie?*

Zoe gave Blue a speculative look. "I might have a plan."

"I have a bad feeling about this," Blue said. He crossed his arms and shook his blond hair out of his eyes. "You're all 'don't toy with Jasmin's feelings' and then you're like, 'well, except when we need you to.'"

"But we have to, don't we?" Zoe said. She cleared the video screens and stood up. "She's not going to drink anything *I* give her. I figure you can go over there, apologize for leaving early last night, and, like, make her coffee or something to make up for it."

"That is weird, Zoe," Blue said, stepping aside as she went out the door. "Guys don't show up at girls' houses to make them apologetic coffee in their own kitchens. And definitely not apologetic coffee that smells like moose breath."

Logan followed them back through the living room, trying to concentrate on the conversation, when what he really wanted to do was run home and freak out at his dad. What would Dad say if Logan asked him about this?

One of the hellhounds was sitting on the grass right outside the glass doors, panting and slobbering, with an enormous grin all over his shaggy black face. He saw them coming and wagged his tail. Zoe stepped around Captain Fuzzbutt and slid open the door.

"Morning, Sheldon," she said, scratching his head. The hellhound poked his nose into her neck, tipped his head at Logan for a considering moment, and then went to sniff around the sleeping mammoth. Captain Fuzzbutt made a grumbling noise and whacked the rhino-sized dog with his trunk.

Sheldon yipped amiably and wandered into the kitchen, where he promptly sprawled out and took over most of the floor.

Logan felt the weight of the beetle necklace under his shirt. Would it protect him from hellhounds? How could a little beetle do that? Not that Sheldon was much of a threat. He'd meant to ask Zoe about the necklace first thing, but he also kind of wanted to keep it to himself. If his mom had broken SNAPA rules by giving it to his dad, he didn't want to get her in trouble—or have to give it back.

"Have your parents figured out how to give the Sterlings kraken ink?" he asked. "Maybe you could slip the jackalope milk in the same way."

Zoe shook her head. She took the two mugs out of the microwave and climbed on the counter to reach the cocoa and marshmallows. "From what we can tell, the Sterlings are being really careful. They'll only drink bottled water from, like, the Alps, or something. They even brush their teeth with it."

"How on earth did you figure that out?" Logan asked.

"My parents can be very resourceful when the Menagerie is in danger," she said. "What it means is that we won't be able to fix this by slipping kraken ink into the town water supply, which is what SNAPA usually does."

The bag of marshmallows suddenly tipped over as Zoe was climbing down, even though she wasn't touching it. A shower of mini-marshmallows cascaded to the floor and Sheldon sat up with a hopeful expression.

"I got it," Logan said, coming around the table to help pick them up.

A small creature was sitting on the floor, gobbling up marshmallows as fast as it could. Logan caught a glimpse of honey-colored fur and enormous dark eyes when it looked up at him, and then it vaulted onto the table, up to the top of the doorframe, and out of the room before he could even blink.

"What was that?" Logan asked.

"What was what?" Zoe said, picking up the bag.

"That thing eating the marshmallows," Logan said.

She gave him a quizzical look. "Thing eating the marshmallows?"

"Didn't you see it?" Logan said. "Was it the baku?"

"No, the baku is nocturnal and moves very slowly," Zoe said. "We'd know if it was in the kitchen. You must be seeing things."

"Yes, I did," Logan said. "One actual thing, eating marshmallows. Seriously, it was right there!"

"Anyway," Zoe said. "My parents have gone to meet with the SNAPA agents this morning to tell them everything. Actually, they're making Ruby tell them, which I kind of wish

I could be there for. They decided we'll need SNAPA's help, and for once, I kind of agree. Stopping the Sterlings is a bigger problem than we can solve, but SNAPA cleans up potential disasters like this all the time. I think. I hope."

"Wait," Logan said, struck by an awful thought that chased the mystery creature right out of his head. "Zoe, what if . . . what if the Sterlings know something about my mom? What if SNAPA gives them kraken ink and they forget everything?"

Zoe set down the cocoa and stared at him with wide brown eyes. "Oh my gosh, Logan."

"Hang on," Blue said. "There's no reason to think there's any connection between what happened to Abigail and that map in Mr. Sterling's office."

"But there could be," Logan said. "Right?"

"What if the Sterlings *have* her?" Zoe said. "Maybe they tried to grab the Chinese dragon and ended up getting Abigail as well."

"Jasmin's parents aren't kidnappers," Blue said, but Logan thought he didn't sound so sure. "They wouldn't . . ."

"They might at least know what happened to her, or where she is," Logan said. "And if they do—"

"Logan's right," Zoe said. "If they have Abigail and the Chinese dragon, and we dose them, they might forget where they're keeping them. We might never find them." She pulled out her phone. "We can't risk it. I'll text my parents right away."

Logan looked down at his hands, clenching them into fists and then opening them again. His stomach felt like a yawning pit full of angry dragons.

Was it possible? Did the Sterlings have his mother trapped somewhere?

"I feel like I'm in a Hardy Boys book," Blue said.

"Well, I've been in Narnia all week," Logan said. "It's not that big of a jump from there."

The doorbell rang.

Zoe and Blue blinked at each other. Neither of them moved.

"What?" Logan said. "Why do you guys look so spooked? It's just the doorbell. Most people find those *less* scary than man-eating hellhounds." On the floor, Sheldon thumped his tail twice as if to say, *Yup, that's me, I'm terrifying!*

"The doorbell never rings," Zoe said. "Nobody ever comes over. Who is that?"

"Can't be SNAPA," Blue said. "Leftover trick-or-treaters?"

"Maybe we shouldn't answer it," said Zoe.

"Oh, come on," Logan said. "It's probably a delivery or someone selling Girl Scout cookies. *I'll* go get it, if you want."

"Wait, Logan," Zoe said, hurrying after him.

Logan pulled open the front door.

And found himself face-to-face with Jasmin Sterling.

SIX

Zoe froze in her tracks. Jasmin was *here*. At her *house*. This never happened even when they *were* friends. As far as Jasmin knew, Zoe owned at least seven cats, which Jasmin had to stay far away from because of her crazy allergies.

"Hi, Logan!" Jasmin said brightly. She had her dark hair swept up into a cute messy ponytail and she was wearing a soft sage-green shirt that flared at the wrists, plus jeans with sneakers. She was carrying something dark blue draped over one arm. No tall boots, no fancy jacket, no expensive jewelry. She looked like she always had when she was Zoe's best friend.

She didn't look sick, either. Zoe felt tears pricking at the back of her eyes. More than anything in the world, in the *whole world*, she wanted to run over and throw her arms around Jasmin and hug her and never let go.

Jasmin's gaze shifted past Logan and she saw Zoe standing in the hallway. "Oh," she said. "Um. Hey."

"Hi," Zoe said, swallowing the lump in her throat.

"ROWF ROWF ROWF!" Sheldon suddenly boomed from the kitchen, loud enough to shake the pictures on the walls. *Delayed reaction, doofus,* Zoe thought.

Jasmin looked startled. "What the heck was that?"

"That's . . . our dog," Zoe said. They were lucky you couldn't see into the kitchen from the front hall. She just had to pray that Blue would keep Sheldon in there. He might *sound* kind of like a dog, but he *looked* like something that ought to be guarding a fire-breathing demon's mansion.

"Loud, right?" Logan said, rubbing one ear.

"Crazy loud," Jasmin said. She scrunched her nose at Zoe in the way that used to signal something they would both find hilarious.

"How are you?" Zoe asked. What she meant was, *are you sick, are you okay, I miss you, I'm sorry,* and *do you need my kidneys because you can have them if you do.*

Jasmin looked at her like she almost understood all that.

"Just looking for Blue," she said. She sounded casual, but Zoe could tell she was nervous from the way she hooked her hands in her pockets and tipped her toes toward each other. Nervous about coming to see Blue, Zoe guessed, but also nervous about talking directly to Zoe for the first time in months.

"Is he here?" Jasmin asked. "Is it too early? I'm sorry if it's too early—my parents got the cleaning crew in first thing this morning to deal with the party mess, even though it's, like, barely anything, but someone put slime and fake bugs on the walls, and you know how my parents are about their glorious *walls* and their beloved *couches*, so, anyway, there was vacuuming, it was loud, I couldn't sleep."

Zoe laughed. She did remember how Jasmin's mom was about her furniture—the girls weren't even allowed to have popcorn if they watched movies in the den, and Jasmin had once lost her bike for a month because she scuffed a wall by throwing her crayons at Jonathan.

Jasmin smiled at her, then ducked her head and looked down at her shoes.

"I'll go get him," Zoe said. "We were just, um—" *This is it,* she realized. *This is our chance! If we can get her to drink something, we can slip her the jackalope milk!* She glanced at Logan, who was giving her a wide-eyed look like he'd had the same thought.

"Making smoothies," she blurted. "We were making smoothies. Be right back."

She bolted into the kitchen and found Blue sitting on top

of Sheldon, pinning him to the floor. The hellhound wagged his tail furiously at Zoe, his glowing red eyes shining with delight, and wriggled toward the door even with Blue on top of him.

"Why is she here?" Blue whispered. "Sheldon, stay! Chill out!"

"Go be nice to her," Zoe whispered back. "Give me two minutes and then offer her a smoothie. *Do not let her say no.*"

"Oh, man," Blue said. He stood up and Zoe grabbed Sheldon's collar, leaning all her weight into holding him back. Blue brushed fur off his clothes and then ran his hands through his hair. "How do I look?" he asked.

Zoe stared at him as if he'd grown an extra fish tail. "You look the same as you always look. Don't be weird!"

"All right, all right," he said, sauntering out into the hall. Sheldon tried to lunge after him and Zoe yanked him back.

"Logan!" she called. "A little help in here?"

"Hey, Jasmin," she heard Blue say. "Great party last night."

"Like you would know," Jasmin joked. "You were there for what, three nanoseconds? You completely missed Cadence and Violet accidentally pushing Aidan into the pool. It was so funny."

Logan ducked into the kitchen and saw Zoe struggling with Sheldon. He glanced around, grabbed the giant cookie jar next to the toaster, and pulled out one of the monstrous dog biscuits Zoe's parents had made the night before.

Sheldon immediately sat down and gave Logan his full slavering attention.

"So, anyway," Jasmin said, "I found this jacket after the party and I wondered if it might be yours, so I figured I'd bring it over and check."

Zoe shook her head sympathetically. She was sure Jasmin remembered exactly what Blue was wearing at any given moment, and whatever jacket she'd found was clearly not his. What it was, in fact, was a convenient excuse to come over and see Blue. *Smart, Jasmin.* And brave; Jasmin had been flirting with Blue for years, but she'd never risked looking ridiculous before.

"Oh, thanks," Blue said, "but it's not mine."

"Okay," Jasmin said, and Zoe could hear her courage failing. "Sorry, I'll just—go."

"No, wait," Blue said quickly. "Uh—I want to hear more about Aidan falling into the pool."

"Really?" Jasmin said.

"Yeah, totally." Zoe peeked around the corner and saw Blue lean sideways against the doorframe, closer to Jasmin. He grinned down at her. "Was he wearing his cowboy hat?"

Jasmin giggled. "He *was*." She launched into the whole story.

Zoe turned back to Logan, thinking. The look on Blue's face . . . he wasn't that good an actor. *Blue and Jasmin? Could it actually happen?* In some ways, that would be awkward for

Zoe, but in all the ways that it would make Jasmin happy, it would be worth it. Given the Ruby-Jonathan debacle, everyone could take their ban on dating and shove it up a harpy's nose.

"Come on," Logan whispered, waving the dog biscuit just out of Sheldon's reach. He backed toward the glass doors in the living room, with the hellhound trotting after him and Zoe close behind. Carefully Logan eased one of the doors open and threw the dog biscuit out into the dew-covered grass.

Sheldon bolted after it, but at the same time, three more giant black shapes came tearing out of the Doghouse, snarling hungrily.

"Oops," Logan said.

Zoe ran into the kitchen, grabbed three more dog biscuits, ran back into the living room, and flung them at the squabbling hellhounds. Logan slammed the door shut.

"Did you hear that? Zoe's dog sounds kind of like twelve dogs," Jasmin said, out in the front hall. "Or, like, seven bears."

"Yeah, he's a character," Blue said.

Zoe beckoned to Logan and darted back into the kitchen. "Smoothies," she whispered, frantically hunting through the cupboards. "Find me stuff that can go in a smoothie. Come on, we have to have a blender in here somewhere."

She started yanking pots and pans and mystery kitchen appliances out, leaving them scattered across the kitchen floor. She knew they owned a blender. Matthew had once made himself a smoothie every day for a month after one of the visiting Trackers told him—jokingly, Zoe suspected—that kale and raw eggs would make him strong enough to wrestle a wampus cat.

"You have one banana," Logan reported. "And three half-dead strawberries."

"Here it is," Zoe gasped, dragging the blender out from behind a bread machine wrapped in duct tape. She set it on the counter and dove back into the cabinet, looking for the top.

Logan grabbed the blender and rinsed it out in the sink, then dropped in the banana and the strawberries and a handful of ice. "You also have hardly any milk left," he said. "Apart from jackalope milk, but it can't be all jackalope milk or she won't even try it."

"Use this," Zoe said, crawling out with the blender top and picking up her cup of cocoa. She dumped it in, milk and cocoa and marshmallows together. "What else? Honey? No, wait, I left the honey in the unicorn stables yesterday."

Logan took the jackalope milk out of the fridge. Even with the top on the bottle, Zoe could still smell it from across the kitchen.

"How much should we put in?" he asked.

Zoe clutched her hair. "I have no idea!" she whispered frantically. A drop? The whole bottle? What would work?

They couldn't get this wrong. What would happen if someone drank too much jackalope milk?

"Want to come in and, uh . . . have a smoothie?" she heard
Blue say.

"Oh—I shouldn't," Jasmin said. "Zoe's cats, remember? I'd
turn into Little Miss Sneeze, which is not my most glamorous
look, by the way."

"Cats," Blue said. "Right. No, well, actually, the cats,
uh . . . the cats are all gone."

"Gone?" Jasmin echoed, startled. "All seven of them?
What happened?"

"Um . . ."

"Please don't tell me her new dog ate them," Jasmin said.
"Because he sounds like he could."

"No, no. Nothing terrible. They, uh, went to live on a
farm in the country. That's all."

"Hmm," Jasmin said skeptically. "That sounds like code
for 'the dog ate them,' Blue. But okay. If you guys don't have
cats anymore, then sure, I can stay for a bit."

"Wait," Zoe said, darting into the hall and blocking their
way. "I have to—we just—um, let me clean up the dog hair.
Just in case. Give us one second." She bolted around them and
up the stairs.

"Where is she going?" Jasmin asked.

"To get the . . . vacuum," Blue said unconvincingly.

"You keep your vacuum upstairs?" Jasmin said. "Should

we remind her I'm not allergic to dogs?"

Zoe ran down the upstairs hall and pounded on Matthew's door.

No response.

She knew he would kill her, but she burst in anyway.

No Matthew. The room was empty, and a total mess, as usual. *Where is he?* Zoe scanned the room and spotted one of the walkie-talkies on the floor, under his jacket. She threw herself at it and pressed the call button.

"Matthew? Can you hear me? It's an emergency."

There was a long, frustrating silence, and then the radio crackled.

"What's up? I'm on my way to feed the salamanders."

Zoe took a deep breath. "Matthew. I have a really important question I need you to answer right now without giving me a massive big-brother hard time. Okay?"

Crackle. "That sounds . . . ominous," he said.

"Suppose you were going to give someone jackalope milk," she said, pressing her fingers to her forehead. "How much would you need to give them for it to work?"

Another long, long pause.

"ARE YOU KIDDING ME?" Matthew yelled into the walkie-talkie. "ZOE, ARE YOU SERIOUSLY OUT OF YOUR MIND? With everything that's going on with the Sterlings right now?"

"She's *here*, Matthew," Zoe said, starting to cry. "And if

she's sick—can't you understand? I have to do this and I have to do it now."

"For the love of krakens," Matthew said. "Zoe, she's not really sick. Jonathan was totally lying."

"We don't *know* that," Zoe said. "She might be awfully sick, and I could save her. I *have* to."

There was another pause, and then Matthew sighed. "One tablespoon. That's it. Any more than that and she might end up living forever and never getting zits or something."

"Thank you!" Zoe cried. "Thank you, Matthew!"

"You are *never* hearing the end of this," he said. "Both my sisters are cracked in the head."

Zoe ran back down the stairs, around Jasmin and Blue, and into the kitchen.

"Where's the vacuum?" Jasmin asked.

"Couldn't find it!" Zoe called. "One more minute!" She dropped the walkie-talkie on the kitchen counter and took the bottle from Logan.

"One tablespoon," she said, pulling out the measuring spoons. She poured an exact tablespoon out and dumped it in the smoothie. Logan re-capped the bottle and shoved it into the back of the fridge.

"Okay, you can come in," Zoe called. She pressed the button on the blender and everything inside began to spin around with a deafening whirring sound as Blue led Jasmin into the kitchen.

And then, through the pass-through window, Zoe saw a huge furry head slowly rise up, flapping its ears.

The blender had woken Captain Fuzzbutt.

If she thought a hellhound would be difficult to explain, a baby woolly mammoth was probably going to blow up Jasmin's brain completely.

She shot Logan a desperate look and he followed her gaze to the living room, where the Captain was yawning hugely and swinging his trunk in an exploratory circle.

Logan sidled quickly out of the kitchen, giving Jasmin a manic smile. Jasmin still had her back to the living room, but if she turned around, she would have an excellent view of Logan trying to shove a mammoth out of sight. Zoe watched in petrified horror as he threw his weight against the Captain's side and Fuzzbutt grunted with amusement, poking Logan cheerfully with his trunk.

"So," Blue said. "Smoothie? Zoe?"

"Right," she said, snapping back to attention. "Here." She shoved the blender toward them and grabbed a glass out of the cabinet.

"I can't believe I've never been in here before," Jasmin said, setting the jacket on a chair and twisting her fingers together as she glanced around. "My allergies seem fine so far. What did you do with your fire alarm dog?"

"Ha-ha!" Zoe said. "I mean, he's around. Probably in the living room. Don't go in there!"

Jasmin started to turn toward the living room. Logan frantically grabbed Fuzzbutt's tail and tried to tug him out of sight. The mammoth snorted and swatted him away.

"Hey," Blue said, reaching out and touching Jasmin's hand. She pivoted back toward him with a dazzling smile. He held out the drink, which was a hideous reddish-brownish-greenish color. "You can have this one."

"Oh, thanks," she said, and then, as she lifted the glass to her mouth, she stopped. Her nose crinkled and she lowered the glass again, eyeing the thick concoction inside doubtfully. "Um. Sorry . . . what's in this? It smells a little . . . unusual."

"Wheatgrass," Blue said promptly.

"Greek yogurt," Zoe said at the same time.

"Uh-huh," Jasmin said, raising her eyebrows. Zoe realized she was staring at Jasmin like a crazy person. She ducked below the island and started putting away the pots, trying to look casual. Her heart was thumping. *Please drink it. Please drink it.*

"You know, I don't really love Greek yogurt," Jasmin said to Blue. "Maybe I'll skip it."

"Oh, try it," Blue said charmingly. "This is my favorite. I make them all the time."

"Yeah?" Zoe heard Jasmin sniff the drink again. "You know what, then you should have it."

"I want *you* to have it," Blue said, a little too intensely.

"I'm okay, really," Jasmin said, setting it on the counter. "I mean, that's really sweet, but—well, my doctor said maybe I should eat less, uh . . . wheatgrass."

Doctor?!

It *was* true!

Zoe leaped to her feet. "Jasmin, you have to drink it!" she cried.

Jasmin jumped back, startled. In the living room, Captain Fuzzbutt wheeled around to face Zoe, alarmed by her tone of voice. Logan frantically started throwing blankets over the mammoth's back, as if hoping that perhaps Jasmin would be like, "Ah, yes, just your average elephant-sized pile of blankets there, nothing remarkable."

"It's only a smoothie, Zoe," Jasmin said, glancing at Blue.

"Zoe, calm down," Blue said. He had on his maddening "the universe will work itself out" face.

"It's *not* just a smoothie!" Zoe said passionately. "It could save your *life!*"

"What?" Jasmin took a step toward the door. "You know, maybe I should—"

"Blue, hold her down!" Zoe shouted. She charged around the island and grabbed the smoothie. Holy mother of dragons, it did smell completely disgusting.

Jasmin shrieked and bolted toward the front door. Blue lunged and seized her around the waist. She yelped and kicked the air.

"It's okay!" he yelled. "Zoe's just being crazy! Don't panic!"

"I'm not being crazy!" Zoe cried. "Jonathan told Ruby that you have some awful terrible disease! This will cure you! I promise!" She advanced on Jasmin with the smoothie.

"Do NOT MAKE ME DRINK THAT," Jasmin shouted. "Zoe Kahn! I will seriously bite you! Blue, put me down! GET THAT HORRIFYING SLUDGE AWAY FROM ME! I don't know what you're talking about! I am NOT SICK! There's nothing wrong with me! I SWEAR BY THE SECRET BOOKS OF WONDERLAND, ZOE!"

Zoe stopped, shaking. When she and Jasmin were eight years old, they'd been in love with *Alice's Adventures in Wonderland* and *Through the Looking-Glass*. They'd written their own "secret untold stories" of Wonderland together and hidden them under Jasmin's bed. No one else knew about those.

"You're . . . not sick?" she said.

"I am *definitely not sick*," Jasmin said. Blue lowered her to the ground but kept his arms wrapped around her. "I have no idea why Jonathan would say that, but he's the worst and you know it. I'm super-healthy. I'm beyond healthy. I'm Wonder Woman, okay?"

Zoe folded both her hands around the glass. "Are you sure?"

Jasmin gave her a quintessentially Jasmin exasperated look. "I would *know* if I had a terrible wasting disease, wouldn't I?"

"Maybe your parents haven't told you for some reason,"

Zoe said. "Maybe you should drink this just in case." She took another step forward.

Jasmin broke out of Blue's arms and ran.

But since Blue was between her and the front door, she darted past Zoe instead. She tore through the kitchen into the living room . . . and crashed straight into the side of a woolly mammoth.

SEVEN

Captain Fuzzbutt trumpeted and stamped his feet in a panic, flinging all the blankets off at once.

Jasmin was knocked back onto the floor. She looked up at the mammoth and screamed, which sent the Captain into an even bigger tizzy. He flapped his ears and shuffled backward, nearly trampling Logan's foot.

"It's all right," Logan yelped, dodging out of the way. "Captain, shhhhh. Jasmin, he's harmless."

"Oh my God," Jasmin said. She scrambled to her feet and stared at the mammoth. "Oh my *God*."

Fuzzbutt trumpeted again, eyeing Jasmin warily.

"She's a friend," Logan said, although a week ago that was

just about the last thing he'd thought he'd ever say about Jasmin Sterling. He stroked the Captain's trunk between his eyes.

"It's true," Zoe said, coming into the room with Blue. She set the smoothie down on the table and came over to lean against the mammoth's side. "I love her, Captain. She's safe." Logan felt the Captain's breathing start to slow down. He held out his trunk and Zoe took the end of it in her hand.

"First of all," Jasmin said, "no one who loves me would ever make me drink whatever *that* is. And second of all: Zoe! THERE IS A MAMMOTH IN YOUR HOUSE."

"I was *trying* to save your *life*," Zoe argued. "And his name is Captain Fuzzbutt."

Jasmin stared at Zoe for a long minute. And then she started laughing.

"Zoe!" she said, wiping away tears of laughter. "Okay, now I know he's yours. Remember that toy elephant I gave you for your sixth birthday?"

"Colonel Flopnose!" Zoe said. "Of course I do. She's on my shelf between *When You Reach Me* and *Walk Two Moons*."

Jasmin looked at Zoe, and then her eyes started to fill with real tears. "Zoe," she said.

A heartbeat later, Zoe was across the room with her arms around Jasmin. The two girls leaned into each other, crying. Blue edged around them and flopped down on one of the beanbags. Logan shifted uncomfortably and focused on patting the Captain's side.

"I miss you," Jasmin sobbed.

"I've missed you *so much*," Zoe said. "I'm sorry, Jasmin. I'm so so sorry."

"I still don't know what I did," Jasmin said, pulling back and wiping her eyes with the backs of her hands. "Was it because of Jonathan and Ruby breaking up? We always knew *that* would happen."

"No, it's—it was all—this," Zoe said, waving one hand at the mammoth and the rolling grassy hills of the Menagerie outside the glass doors. "It's complicated."

One of the unicorns chose that moment to gallop past as though its tail was on fire.

Jasmin blinked several times, then rubbed her eyes hard. "Did I—was that—?"

"What do we do now?" Blue asked Zoe. He leaned back with his arms behind his head. Logan tried to match his coolness by leaning casually on Captain Fuzzbutt, but the mammoth shifted sideways and he nearly fell over.

"Don't kick me out," Jasmin said. She whirled and grabbed Zoe's hands. "Don't stop talking to me again. Please, Zoe."

"Maybe she can help," Logan said. "With your . . . other problem." Would Jasmin be willing to help them stop her parents? Was it too risky to involve her? He didn't know her as well as Zoe did. For one thing, he would never have expected to see her cry, and he still felt a little nervous that she might write snide things about them on Twitter later.

But if Zoe decided to trust her, he would, too.

"Yes, maybe I can help!" Jasmin said. "Besides, if Mr. Random over there can be friends with your mammoth, why can't I?"

That sounded more like the Jasmin Logan was used to.

A high-pitched squeal went off in the kitchen, followed by static and then a crackling noise, and then Matthew calling, "ZOE! ZOE! PICK UP!"

Zoe hurried into the kitchen and grabbed the walkie-talkie. "Matthew?"

"There's been an accident at the Reptile House!" Matthew shouted.

"I knew it!" Blue yelled, surging to his feet. "The pyrosalamanders have escaped! This was their sinister master plan all along! Evacuate the town! Evacuate the state!"

"BLUE, SHUSH!" Zoe hollered at him. "Matthew, what happened?"

"It's Basil." The walkie-talkie hissed and crackled again. "Something blew a hole in his cage and now he's gone! He's somewhere in the Menagerie!"

Logan saw Zoe turn the color of chalk. He remembered the ancient-looking giant lizard from the Reptile House— the one Zoe had to put to sleep before they could go in to feed the salamanders. He also remembered her saying something about how it was the most dangerous animal in the Menagerie.

"The what?" Jasmin said.

Blue took the walkie-talkie from Zoe's hand. "What about the pyrosalamanders? Are the pyrosalamanders contained?"

"Yes, Blue, they're all in their cages, half-asleep as always," Matthew said in an irritated voice. "Can you please try to wrap your mind around the fact that there is a *basilisk on the loose* somewhere?"

"Oh, thank Neptune," Blue said. He saw the look on Zoe's face and added, "I mean, that's bad, too."

"Basilisk?" Jasmin said. "He didn't just say *basilisk*, did he?"

"We have to find him," Zoe said, sounding completely panicked. She took the walkie-talkie back. "Do you have any idea where he is?"

"The hole is in the west wall, so he could have gone toward the dragons or the lake," Matthew said. "Or . . ."

"Into the river that leads out of the Menagerie," Zoe said. She started pacing up and down the living room.

"Wait," Jasmin said. "Dragons?"

"Oh no," Zoe said, biting her nails. "Oh no oh no oh no. Blue, did the merpeople ever fix the hole in the grate?"

Blue shrugged. "I have no idea."

"Knowing mermaids, I think we can assume they didn't," Zoe said.

"MERMAIDS?" Jasmin said.

"Should I call Mom and Dad?" Captain Fuzzbutt made

an "oooooorgh" noise and sidled into her path so Zoe had to stop pacing and hug him. "Matthew, what do we do? Oh! The emergency kit!" She ran over to the big table and slid out a hidden drawer.

"Is it that terrible?" Logan asked. "Can't you use your rooster ringtones to just knock him out and drag him back?"

"You have to be at fairly close range for the rooster crow to work, especially because our basilisk is four hundred and practically deaf," Zoe said, pulling things out of the drawer and spreading them across the table. "If any of us get close enough to use our cell phones, we'll be close enough for Basil to make eye contact or hiss at us, and then we're dead."

"I am *so confused*," Jasmin said.

"We take care of mythical creatures here," Blue said to her. "It's top secret; no one can know."

"Well, yeah, that makes sense," Jasmin said. "Like, my dad would totally freak out if he knew there were dragons next door." She stopped with a gasp and stared at Blue. "That map—the one in Dad's study!"

"Let's deal with that crisis after we neutralize the killer lizard," Zoe said. "Matthew! Are you still alive?"

"I'm inside the Reptile House," Matthew's voice came back. "I'm trying to figure out whether a brave Tracker would charge out there and search for it, or whether a smart Tracker would stay put in here."

"I vote stay put," Zoe said into the walkie-talkie.

"Says the twelve-year-old who's about to hunt it down armed with what, earplugs and a sleep mask?" Matthew said. "I know you, Zoe. Don't do something dumb."

Zoe regarded the sleep mask in her hand thoughtfully.

"Basilisks are totally deadly," Blue said to Jasmin.

"I know about basilisks," she said, putting her hands on her hips. "I read fantasy, Blue."

"You stay here, put a blanket over your head, and wear these," Zoe said, handing Jasmin a pair of earplugs.

Logan had a funny wave of emotions all at once: pride, that Zoe wasn't telling *him* to stay put, which meant she thought he could be useful, but also terror, because *deadly killer lizard.*

"Absolutely not," Jasmin said. "I know what to do with a basilisk. And if there are mermaids in danger, I am so there. I am so *there* for saving mermaids!" She pulled a compact out of her back pocket. "Besides, I have this. Check me out. Do any of *you* have mirrors in your pockets? If so, you clearly never use them. I'm just kidding." She burst into giggles.

"Jasmin, this is serious!" Zoe cried. "Do you know what I would do if anything happened to you?"

"Something appropriately dramatic and grief-stricken, I hope," Jasmin said. "Now, do you have a rooster?"

"Of course we do not have a rooster," Zoe said, and then stopped as if struck by lightning.

"What do you mean, *of course* you don't have a rooster?"

Jasmin said. "You have a mammoth and a unicorn and apparently a horde of menacing salamanders. A rooster does not seem that unlikely, in context."

Zoe turned to Logan and he saw a gleam in her eye. "Marco," she said.

"Yes!" Logan agreed. He couldn't believe he hadn't thought of their wererooster friend himself.

"Oh, poor Marco," said Blue. "Not again."

"Is there literally a single more useful thing he could do in his entire life?" Zoe asked, pulling out her phone and heading into the kitchen. "He'll be the hero, he'll love it. And we're not even in school, so his mom can't yell at him."

"*Marco* knows about this place?" Jasmin said. "Okay, now I'm seriously offended. *Marco?*"

"There's . . . a little more to him than you might expect," Blue said.

"Like he owns a rooster, you mean? Yeah, I wouldn't have guessed that."

Logan and Blue glanced at each other. Logan wasn't sure whether it would be okay with Marco for them to reveal his secret.

"Sure, okay, he owns a rooster," Blue said, in his "I'm lying, but obviously, so now we both know it and let's move on" voice.

Jasmin pulled out her ponytail, shook her hair loose, and then pulled it back up again like she was preparing for battle.

"Well, I'm ready," she said. "Point me at this basilisk."

"We have to figure out where he is first," Logan said. "Right, Blue?"

"Let's check the video monitors," Zoe said, barreling through the room toward Melissa's office. "Marco's on his way. Blue, where is your mom?"

"She had a meeting at the bank this morning," Blue said. "I think we're the only ones here."

"Except your dad!" Zoe said, alarmed. She stopped at the door to Melissa's office. "They're right there! The basilisk could be at the lake already! We have to warn them!"

"I'm on it," Blue said. He hurried out of the room and they heard his footsteps thumping up the stairs. Logan pointed questioningly after him.

"They have a communication device linked up in Blue's room," Zoe explained.

"Does the basilisk's power work on the creatures?" Logan asked as he and Jasmin went after Zoe into the office. He scanned the bank of screens and shivered. "Are the griffins safe?"

"It only works on people-creatures, not animals," Zoe said. "Although it can make the talking ones kind of sick and sleepy for a while by looking at them."

"Oh, wow," Jasmin breathed, leaning over Zoe's shoulder to study the screens. "No way. That is really a dragon."

In the top left screen, Clawdius was sitting outside his

cave, frowning down at the Menagerie. Smoke spiraled up from his nostrils and he looked decidedly concerned. After a moment, he took a step backward, and then another, and then he backed all the way into his cave and vanished in the dark.

"I bet he knows Basil is loose," Zoe said. "Thanks for the warning, Clawdius! Sheesh."

"Dragons," Jasmin said, shaking her head. "So unreliable."

"That's what Blue always says!" Zoe said. "Oh, you're joking."

Logan was searching each screen for anything that looked like a person-sized iguana. There wasn't a lot of movement in the Menagerie at the moment. The griffins were all inside their cave—maybe their parents could sense the danger, too. Inside the Aviary, the birds were fluttering around, but the basilisk probably wouldn't get in there. There was no sign of Mooncrusher by the ice garden, and nothing moved in the Dark Forest.

No sign of the basilisk anywhere.

"Wait," he said, leaning forward. "Zoe, look. Is that— is one of the islands in the lake—it looks like it's *swimming*. That's not the kraken, is it?" He suddenly remembered his first day in the Menagerie, when he'd thought he'd seen one of the two islands move. He'd forgotten about that until now.

"No, it's just the zaratan," she said distractedly.

"Oh," Logan said.

Jasmin caught his eye and grinned. "Just the zaratan," she said. "Obviously."

"I should have guessed," he said, smiling back.

"Me too," she said. "I just had him over to tea, after all."

"Are you guys being sarcastic?" Zoe asked, glancing over her shoulder at them.

"Not at all," Jasmin said innocently. "Everyone knows what a zaratan is. I think we learned about them in between polynomials and semicolons."

"Okay, smart aleck," Zoe said. "It's a giant turtle, like, *really* giant, and it can live for about a thousand years. They're really good at acting like islands and staying inconspicuous." She zoomed in on the shot of what looked like a mossy green island slowly perambulating across the lake. "Wait. Do you guys see what I see?"

Something long and gray was draped across the zaratan's shell.

"There he is," Zoe yelped. "He's on top of the zaratan. Oh, man. The mermaids really are in danger. I hope Blue reached his dad." She started biting her nails again. "Basilisks are good swimmers. He could slide off the zaratan and swim out through the river any minute. If he gets out into Xanadu—"

"Stop that," Jasmin said, swatting Zoe's hand away from her mouth. "How do we get to it? Is there a boat?"

"There is," Zoe said. "But we should wait for Marco. But do we have time to wait for Marco? What if Basil escapes before he gets here? But we can't go out there by ourselves; it's way too dangerous. What would Abigail do?"

It took Logan a moment to realize that (a) Zoe was talking about his mom and (b) she wasn't asking him, she was talking to herself. She closed her eyes and rubbed her temples furiously.

"Who's that?" Jasmin asked, pointing at one of the screens. "Is she a mermaid?"

With a sickening drop in his stomach, Logan saw Keiko sauntering out of the Dark Forest and along the path around the lake. She was wearing her white kimono. Her fox tail was out and swishing along proudly behind her.

"Wait," Jasmin said. "Zoe, isn't that . . ."

"Keiko!" Zoe yelped. "I am the worst sister ever! I completely forgot about her!" She leaped up. "We have to go get her. With her fox hearing, she might even be able to hear Basil from where she is now."

To her credit, Jasmin did not ask a million fox-related questions. She just raced after Zoe as Zoe hurtled into the living room and started grabbing earplugs for all of them.

"Jasmin, won't you please stay here?" Zoe asked.

"No way," Jasmin said. "Can you remember the last time you were able to stop me from doing something?"

"Fine," Zoe said. "Logan, what about you? You don't have to do anything this dangerous. I promise it's not in the Menagerie contract." She shot him a smile that didn't at all hide how worried she was.

"You know perfectly well I'm coming with you," he said, and felt that rush of warmth again at her grateful expression.

"Blue!" Zoe shouted up the stairs. "Basil is on the zaratan and might be near the mermaids and Keiko is down by the lake and we're going to rescue her so come with Marco as soon as he gets here, okay?"

"Okay," Blue called back, as if Zoe had said "pork chops for dinner tonight."

Zoe stuck the earplugs in her ears and slid open the glass doors. Outside it was chilly and a little windy. Logan could see ripples scudding across the lake, which reflected the overcast gray sky. It felt like the weather was saying, "Yes, now it is November, suck it up."

Just like it had looked on the video screens, the Menagerie was eerily silent. No yelps of playful glee from the griffin enclosure; no splashing and catcalling from mermaids sunning themselves in the lake; no raucous squawking from the Aviary. A strange, skin-prickling aura of doom hung in the air.

Logan fitted the earplugs into his own ears and wondered if they would really work. They looked like they'd been lifted from some airplane overnight flight kit.

Jasmin stared around her with wide eyes as they hurried down the hill, going straight through the grass instead of following the path the golf cart usually took. She mimed *This place is huge!* at Zoe, and Zoe shrugged as if to say, *Eh, it's okay, but no secret passages like your house has.*

As they reached the lakeshore, Logan glanced out at the water and, with a shiver of horror, realized that the zaratan had vanished. Maybe it had figured out what was on top of it and submerged itself.

But that meant the basilisk was nowhere to be seen.

He reached to grab Zoe's sleeve, but just then she spotted Keiko coming toward them.

"Keiko!" she called, waving her arms frantically. "We have to get back to the house! Right now!" Logan was alarmed to realize he could hear her fairly clearly, although muffled somewhat by the earplugs.

Her adopted sister stopped on the path several feet away and frowned. "Is that Jasmin Sterling?" she shouted. She sounded like she was speaking through a voice distorter, but she was still audible. Logan hoped that a basilisk's hiss was much quieter than a truculent sixth grader.

"Keiko, the basilisk has escaped!" Zoe cried. "We have to get out of here!"

Keiko's eyebrows shot up, and then, very suddenly, she was gone. A beautiful glossy red fox sat in her place; she eyed them archly and then went scampering up the hill toward the house.

"Whoa. So, *that* was amazing," Jasmin said, her voice reaching Logan as though she were miles away and under-water. "Is she a kitsune or a werefox?"

"You do read too much fantasy," Zoe said with delight.

"And also I love you. Now we run back to safety."

Jasmin nodded, grabbed Zoe's hand, and set off running. As Logan turned to follow them, he suddenly felt something coil around his ankle. Alarmed, he looked down and had a moment to realize that the *something* was a long dark-purple tentacle reaching out of the lake. And then he was yanked suddenly off his feet and dragged toward the water.

Logan's hands scrabbled in the pebbly sand, trying to grab onto something, but all he felt were grains of sand slipping through his fingers. A moment later, the kraken had dragged him all the way into the freezing water.

The lake closed over his head and Logan had a horrible memory of something like this happening one week earlier, when the kelpie had taken him underwater to drown him. But that time the kraken had mysteriously saved him. Why was it trying to kill him now?

He struggled, but the tentacle drew him calmly down until Logan was floating opposite a giant eye. The kraken stared at him for a long moment, and then it began making odd noises. Logan was starting to feel lightheaded, and the noises wouldn't have meant anything to him anyway. But he got the feeling the kraken was trying to tell him something.

Bubble. Squerk. Wheek. Fwelk. Bubble.

Maybe it was trying to warn him the basilisk was loose. Maybe it was just saying hi.

Logan waved his hands at his face, trying to convey, *I'm sorry, but can we chat sometime when I'm not drowning?*

The kraken let out a long stream of bubbles like a sigh, and then it released Logan's ankle.

Logan kicked and kicked his way back to the surface, bursting out into the air with a gasp. He could see Zoe and Jasmin running up the hill; they hadn't noticed yet that he wasn't behind them. Only a minute had passed. He paddled toward the shore, glancing around. Still no sign of the zaratan . . . or the basilisk.

He looked down at his clothes, wringing them out as he staggered onto the beach. He'd have to borrow something dry from Blue again. He twisted around to look back at the Reptile House across the lake. No sign of Matthew.

His foot hit some kind of enormous log and he tripped, falling forward to land on his face.

"Ow," he groaned, rolling over and feeling his forehead to see if he was bleeding.

The enormous log lifted its scaly, greenish-gray head . . . and slowly turned it toward him.

Logan slammed his eyes shut.

The basilisk.

It was RIGHT. THERE.

Don't look at it. Don't let it look you in the eye. Oh, please let the earplugs work. Maybe it'll go away without hissing. Don't open your eyes. Is this how I die? Mom isn't going to be pleased. I don't even have a mirror or anything. If I survive, and when I find her, I will tell her this is why I need to go to Tracker training camp.

He tried to inch backward, away from it. Maybe he could scuttle away before it made any noise.

But then a weighty claw slowly settled on Logan's knee and he froze. An eternity later, another claw came down on his stomach.

The basilisk was crawling on top of him.

Maybe it's just climbing over me, Logan prayed. *On its way to somewhere else. Don't look. Don't look.*

The basilisk dragged itself up, one millimeter at a time. Logan could sense its head coming closer and closer to his face. The smell was overwhelming, worse than the jackalope milk, like a thousand crocodiles had just eaten a thousand rotting antelopes and were now breathing all over him.

Something flicked his nose lightly.

Don't look. Do not look. The basilisk's eyes had to be directly over Logan's eyes now. It was staring down at him, waiting for him to give in, open them up, and die.

Something tickled his nose again, faintly rough and slightly damp.

The basilisk's tongue, Logan guessed.

From far away, he thought he heard screaming.

And then he felt the basilisk lean forward so its tongue was touching his ear. It poked his ear for a minute, and then with a sudden flick, dislodged the earplug.

Logan tried to clamp his hands over his ears, but his arms were pinned by the basilisk's weight and it was too late, anyway.

"HIIIISSSSSSSSSSSSSSSSSSSSSSSSSSSSSSSSSSSSSSS
SSSSSSSSSSSSSSSSS."

EIGHT

Am I dead? Logan wondered. *I assume I'm dead now. Is this what being dead feels like?* It didn't feel all that different. His clothes were still sticking wetly to his skin and the wind was still freezing him all over. And the basilisk still felt as heavy as a boulder on top of him.

"*Hisssssss,*" the basilisk said irritably. "*HIIIISSSSSSSS-SSSSS.*"

Wait, there was something new. A burning heat suddenly seared through Logan's upper chest, like a small supernova going off right above his ribs. Was that from the basilisk?

The basilisk's front claws clamped over Logan's shoulders. He squeezed his eyes shut even tighter.

"Cock-a-doodle-doo!" a rooster crowed. "Cock-a-doodle-doo! COCK-A-DOODLE-DOOOOOOOOOOO!" It was the most aggressively furious crow Logan had ever heard; it sounded less like "hey, morning's here" and more like "DIE, BASILISK!"

Just as he had that thought, the basilisk slumped forward. Its head landed on Logan's shoulder and its claws went limp. The giant lizard flopped down over him like a scaly blanket.

Logan risked squinting his eyes open and saw the basilisk's fast-asleep face only inches from his own. Drool was already sliding out of the corners of its mouth.

He tried to wriggle backward and shove it off, but it was too heavy to move.

Another eye appeared, very close to his own—this one black and beady, and topped by a fine cheery crest of red feathers. It peered at him, then stalked around to scrutinize the basilisk.

"Bkk-KAWK," it said with great satisfaction.

"Thank you, Marco," Logan gasped.

"Logan! LOGAN!" Zoe slid to her knees beside him. She started shoving at the basilisk and he saw that she was close to tears. "Logan!"

"I'm alive," he said, reaching out and grabbing her hand. "It's okay. I'm alive."

She let out a breath that was half sob. The basilisk was

too heavy for her to move, either. "Marco, turn back into a human and help me with this."

"Bkk-KAWK bkk-kawk," the rooster said, ruffling its feathers in outraged dignity.

"All right, fine," Zoe said. "Go get dressed and then come help me with this."

The rooster fluffed his tail and stalked away, muttering roostery things that Logan guessed were about ingratitude.

Jasmin and Blue came pounding up.

"Dude, Logan," Blue said, shoving his hand through his hair. "No *way*. No one survives meeting the basilisk that close up."

"I got you," Jasmin said to Zoe, kneeling beside her. Together the two girls heaved the basilisk up and off of Logan. It flopped over onto the sand, belly up, and made a small "zzzzzz" noise.

Logan sat up and a wave of nausea hit him. He scrambled away from the others and threw up onto the sand, shaking all over.

"That was completely terrifying," Jasmin said. "Are you all right?" She handed him a little packet with a wet wipe inside, produced from one of her pockets. He ripped it open and wiped his face. The smell of the basilisk was still haunting his nostrils. He had a feeling it would be there for a while. Like possibly for the next century.

"I'm okay," he said. "Thanks."

"How is that *possible*?" Zoe cried. "Did you, like, *talk* the basilisk out of killing you? Are you just so inherently awesome that it restrained itself? I know you're basically a mythical creature superhero, BUT SERIOUSLY, WHAT JUST HAPPENED?!"

"I have no idea," Logan said, leaning forward with his hands on his knees. "It hissed in my ear. I thought I was dead." He fished the other earplug out and stuck it in his pocket.

"Hang on," Zoe said. She darted toward him and reached down his shirt. He started back with a yelp, but not before she'd pulled out the beetle necklace. It thumped against his chest, winking bright blue-green-gold in the gray light.

Zoe and Blue stared at him with their mouths open.

"Why are we shocked?" Jasmin asked. "I agree it's definitely not fashionable. I'm not sure wearing insects has ever been in style. But this seems like a bit of an overreaction. I mean, you're hardly Heidi Klum yourself, Zoe."

"I don't know who that is," Zoe said. "Logan. Why are you wearing a scarab?"

"And where did you get it?" Blue asked.

Logan fingered the glass box, looking down at the beetle. "My dad gave it to me last night. He said my mom gave it to him."

Zoe let out her breath with a whoosh. "Oh," she said. "*Oh.* That's how he's been getting around the Menagerie without being attacked by anything. Wow. Your mom must really love him. Giving away a scarab—that's, like, *definitely* against protocol."

"There's only about fifty of them in the world," Blue said. He stepped closer and studied the beetle. "Most of them are in SNAPA custody—Trackers check them out when they're going on particularly dangerous missions. I bet Abigail told them she lost this one so she could give it to your dad."

"*That's* why the basilisk didn't kill you," Zoe said.

"A scarab is protection against other mythical creatures?" Jasmin asked, catching on. She lifted the necklace and watched how the beetle's wings flashed in the light. "I've never heard that before. Okay, the fashion police will allow a life-or-death exception, just this once." She smiled at Logan.

"Is this also how my dad was able to get in?" Logan asked Zoe. "Could the scarab trick the intruder alarm?"

She shook her head. "It shouldn't. I still don't understand that." She looked down at the sleeping basilisk and sighed. "Let's get Basil back to his cage and then maybe we can talk to the dragons."

"Yes!" Jasmin said excitedly. "I mean, yeah, okay, that sounds fine, if you want to."

"They *should* be yelling about you," Zoe said to Jasmin. "They must have been distracted by the basilisk escaping."

"I'm telling you," Blue said. "Worst alarm system ever."

"Yes, all right, maybe you're right," Zoe said.

Marco came galloping toward them, followed more sedately by Keiko.

"Did you see that?" he crowed. "I saved the day! I slew the basilisk!" He turned to Keiko with a grin. "Me! I'm like a dragon slayer! I just took it down, pow pow!" He punched the air like a ninja.

"Yes," Keiko said. "What a fortuitous genetic accident that you are capable of growing feathers and making horrible noises. It's so impressive."

"Exactly," Marco said. "Impressive! That's me!"

"Thank you again, Marco," Logan said sincerely. "Really, I will literally never be able to thank you enough."

"Me too," Zoe said. "We should tell Matthew it's safe to come out." She unhooked the walkie-talkie at her belt.

"And my dad," Blue said. He stepped toward the water and whistled, a high and swooping noise like a whale flying overhead.

"Um," Jasmin said. "Do I want to know what's about to—"

She cut herself off with a yelp as a dark, bearded head broke through the surface of the water, rising up as King Cobalt stormed out of the lake carrying a trident.

He had decidedly *not* stopped to put pants on.

"AAAAAACK!" Jasmin, Marco, Zoe, and Logan all yelled, covering their eyes.

"Dad!" Blue cried. "The rule! About clothes!"

"THERE WAS A BASILISK IN MY KINGDOM,"

King Cobalt thundered. "THE INEPTITUDE OF THESE PATHETIC ZOOKEEPERS HAS ENDANGERED MY SUBJECTS. WE SHALL NOT STAND FOR THIS!"

Through his fingers, Logan saw Blue run over to a sturdy plastic trunk sitting on the side of the beach and pull out a pair of large yellow shorts decorated with vibrant pink flowers. "Dad, *please* put these on," he said.

King Cobalt snatched the shorts and a moment later, Blue said, "It's okay, guys, he's decent now."

Logan lowered his hands. The mermaid king was somewhat less intimidating in floral shorts, but he still looked very, very angry.

"A basilisk!" he roared. "The SNAPA agents were right! They said it wasn't safe housing a creature like that so close to my kingdom!"

"They did?" Zoe said skeptically. "They didn't tell *us* that, as far as I know."

"Dad, it's fine, we took care of it," Blue said. He shifted on his feet and glanced at Jasmin, who seemed entirely speechless for once.

"No," said the king. "It is *not* fine. We will not keep working for such an incompetent pack of useless humans. We demand to be sent to the Hawaii menagerie!"

"The Hawaii menagerie is full," Zoe protested. "You know that. Besides, Melissa and Blue live here."

"The prince will, naturally, come with me," King Cobalt

said, putting one arm around Blue's shoulders. Blue wriggled free and shook his hair out of his eyes, staring at his feet.

"That's not up to you," Zoe said fiercely. "And no one is going to the Hawaii menagerie. If you insist on leaving here, you'll be reassigned to Manitoba, if you're lucky. I don't know where any of you got the idea that Hawaii was even an option."

"We *know* someone can make Hawaii happen," Blue's dad said, pointing at Zoe. "Or Samoa would be an acceptable alternative as well. And until our demands are met, we are officially on strike. Do you hear me? ON STRIKE. You can groom the kelpie and feed the kraken YOURSELF." He struck the ground with his trident, making a *thud* sound and a small hole in the sand, and then turned and strode back into the water.

"Oh, Dad," Blue said halfheartedly.

King Cobalt stuck his head out of the lake, flung the wet shorts back at Zoe, and then dove again, splashing them all with his massive blue tail as he went.

There was a dripping-wet moment of silence.

"Wow," Jasmin said.

"Sooo," Blue said. "That was my dad."

"Are you a mermaid prince?" Jasmin asked him.

"I'm not a *mermaid*," Blue said. "I'm a mer*man*. But . . . yes."

"Zoe, I know this has probably been a rough morning for

you," Jasmin said to her. "But I want you to know I am having the best day ever."

"Hey, Logan," Marco said. "Are you okay?"

"I think your new employee is about to die of hypothermia," Keiko observed. "Which probably won't do much to discredit Cobalt's claims of incompetence."

Logan didn't feel okay. He felt extremely cold and sick to his stomach, and his teeth were chattering too hard for him to talk. He wrapped his hands around his upper arms.

"Oh, Logan, I'm sorry!" Zoe cried. She took off her jacket and threw it around his shoulders. "Why on earth were you in the lake? Never mind, tell me later. Let's get him back to the house."

Logan felt Marco put his jacket around Logan's shoulders as well, and then Blue added a blanket he must have gotten from the storage chest. In a daze, he let them turn him around and steer him up toward the house.

"Is that going to be a problem?" he asked through his shivers. "The mermaids? On strike?"

"You let us worry about the mermaids," Zoe said, rubbing his arm. "You need to worry about your dad."

And the kraken, Logan thought. *Was the kraken trying to kill me, or was it actually trying to tell me something? What could a kraken want with me?*

"Like, what does your dad know about this scarab," Zoe

went on, "and why is he sneaking into the Menagerie, and did he use the scarab to get close enough to the dragons to break Scratch's chains, but mostly *why* would he do that?"

"Maybe we could catch him in action," Blue said. He nudged Logan's shoulder. "What do you think? Sleepover tonight?"

Logan managed a shaky nod. There had to be a good reason for what his dad was doing. If they could catch him sneaking in, perhaps they could get one of their questions answered.

Dad . . . what are you up to?

NINE

Jasmin lay on her back on Zoe's bed, gazing up at the blank wall beside her. On the floor, Captain Fuzzbutt was flopped on another giant pillow and Zoe was leaning against his side. Logan was in the shower, with permission to use up all the hot water, and Blue and Marco were downstairs scrounging up lunch. Matthew and Mooncrusher had taken charge of getting the basilisk safely locked away again, which was the least they could do, Zoe thought, after Logan and Marco had risked their lives to knock it out.

Zoe still couldn't believe Jasmin was actually *in her room*.

She also didn't know quite what she was going to do about it.

Did she have to give her more kraken ink? She knew that was what Matthew would vote for. But would it erase Jasmin's memory of their reconciliation? What would it leave behind?

And how could they go back to being friends if Zoe had to lie to her all over again—only worse, now that she knew how thrilled Jasmin was about the mythical creatures?

But the Sterlings were perhaps the biggest threat the Menagerie had ever faced. Could she really let Jasmin go home to *that* house, knowing what she knew?

"Do you actually live here?" Jasmin asked, poking the empty wall with her toe. "Why haven't you put up any posters or anything?"

Zoe shrugged. "I don't have time to shop for that stuff. Besides, no one ever sees this room except me and Keiko."

"Who has made *her* half of the room very Keikoesque in less than a year," Jasmin pointed out.

It was true. Zoe knew Keiko had brought the two scrolls painted with fox-girls from home, but she wasn't sure exactly when Keiko had acquired the origami mobiles or cherry blossom landscape photographs.

"I have books," Zoe said, waving at the floor-to-ceiling bookshelves on her side. "And I have Captain Fuzzbutt."

"True," Jasmin said. She rolled onto her stomach and reached over to scratch the mammoth's ears. "I'm glad I'm not allergic to him."

"You know," Zoe said hopefully, "the jackalope milk could probably cure your allergies."

"Zoe, I'm really not sick, I promise. I have no idea why Jonathan told your sister that."

Because he's a stinking liar, Zoe thought. *Imagine pretending your little sister is sick just to hide the fact that you're a total thief. What a jerk.* She was tempted to tell Jasmin the whole story, but then the option of giving her kraken ink would definitely be off the table.

"So tell me about this Logan guy," Jasmin said. "You totally like him, right?"

"I've only known him for, like, a week," Zoe pointed out, feeling her face get warm.

"He doesn't really like Keiko, does he?" Jasmin said. "I don't get that vibe from him. I'm pretty sure he likes you."

"He's only known *me* for, like, a week," Zoe protested. "And we've both had bigger things to think about. His mom is missing. One of our dragons was accused of murder. Someone is trying to destroy the Menagerie." She hesitated. "Jasmin—"

"Let me guess," Jasmin said, cutting her off. "One of your many problems is that my parents somehow know about your top secret unicorn sanctuary, and they're planning something terrible that has to do with that map Logan found in Dad's study."

Zoe winced. "In a nutshell," she said.

"That sounds like my parents," Jasmin said with a sigh. "You say 'endangered pandas' and they say 'oooh, we can make money on that.' Plus I bet my mom is all up in arms about the experiments we should be doing to see if your animals have any magical healing properties."

"There's a branch of SNAPA for that," Zoe said. "Strictly overseen to make sure the animals are always treated humanely, and that they have chosen to give their consent."

"Oh," Jasmin said, imitating her mother's voice, "what a waste of time, asking a dragon its opinion about anything. Let's just chop off its claws and see if they're useful."

Zoe shuddered and wrapped her arms around her knees.

"Sorry, Zo," Jasmin said. She slid off the bed and put one arm around Zoe. "I was just kidding. I bet it feels awful. Listen, I promise we can stop them, okay? I don't know what we can do, but if I can help, I'm in. I don't want my dad selling tickets to ride this guy any more than you do." Jasmin thumped the Captain's side and he waved his trunk amiably at her.

"Really?" Zoe said. "You would do that? Help us to stop your own parents?"

"You know my parents," Jasmin said. "I like them some of the time, but they're all work work work and anytime I disagree with them, they just talk right over me like I'm not there. My dad's so wrapped up in his campaign he hasn't come to any of my dance recitals this year. If I were old enough to vote, I wouldn't even vote for him on Tuesday."

She stopped suddenly and her eyes got huge. "Oh no," she whispered.

"What?" Zoe whispered back.

"You might have a problem," Jasmin said. She stood up, tightened her ponytail, and cracked her knuckles nervously.

"Don't torture me," Zoe said.

"Okay." Jasmin started pacing in the narrow space around Fuzzbutt and the beds. "Well, my mom and dad have been talking in cryptic circles about something for months. When will everything be ready, what's the best strategy, this has to be done carefully, all that boring stuff I never listen to, right? So, last week I was doing my homework in the den and I heard Mom say to Dad something like 'We're all set for Election Day.' And he said, 'Cameras from every network, right?' And she said, 'Of course. All trained on you. You bring it out, and the entire country will have to believe you. There'll be no covering this up.' And he said, 'Win or lose? They'll still come for the speech?' and she said, 'Yes, but you're going to win. And even if you don't . . . we win anyway.' And then they got all mushy about how great they each are, so I put in my headphones and turned up the sound."

Zoe stared up at her.

"This is what they were talking about!" Jasmin said, throwing her hands out. "The Menagerie! Zoe, they're going to expose it on Election Day. Do you know when that is?

You live under a rock, so maybe not. It's *this Tuesday*. Do you know what today is? *Saturday*. You have *three days* to do something, or it's hello, mermaids, you're on camera, say hi to the world."

Zoe made a strangled sound and dropped her head into her hands. "I have to tell my parents," she said. Maybe they really *had* to give kraken ink to the Sterlings, whether or not they knew something about Logan's mom.

"What do you think they have?" Jasmin asked.

"What?" Zoe said.

"Mom mentioned bringing something out at the election-night party—at the Buffalo Bill Diner, I assume, where the cameras will be. Is there any chance they have one of your creatures? Or any way they might get one?"

Zoe felt her stomach drop even further. *The Chinese dragon*, she thought. If they did have Abigail, that meant they must have the Chinese dragon, too.

So they *couldn't* give them kraken ink, or else what would happen to Abigail and the dragon?

But if they didn't have Abigail . . . what if they were using Logan's dad to steal something else?

Zoe's phone vibrated—a text from her dad.

On our way home with Pelly. Who is in quite the wonderful mood. Batten down the hatches.

"Oh dear," Zoe said with a sigh. She did not particularly want to deal with the world's most passive-aggressive golden goose right now. But on the other hand, maybe that meant SNAPA had released Miss Sameera to them as well. Zoe was dying to sit the school librarian down and ask her a million questions—like who she followed to find Pelly. Whoever it was had to be the saboteur, surely. And if they caught him, they'd be able to use him to stop the Sterlings. Zoe was still hoping it wouldn't turn out to be Logan's dad.

"My parents are on their way," Zoe said, scrambling to her feet. "You should go before they get here."

"Or else with the awkward questions," Jasmin said, nodding.

Or else with the kraken ink, Zoe thought. "Last chance for a delicious jackalope milk smoothie?"

"Ha-ha, NO," Jasmin said. "I'm watching you, Zoe Kahn." She hesitated, and then threw her arms around Zoe. "Are we really friends again? This isn't a dream?"

"It's real," Zoe said, hugging her back. No matter what happened with the Sterlings, Zoe wasn't going to let anyone tell her she couldn't be friends with Jasmin again. "I'll tell you the whole awful story sometime."

"Sometime soon," Jasmin said. They headed out of Zoe's room and downstairs. Captain Fuzzbutt heaved himself up and tromped after them, making the entire house shake.

Blue looked up and smiled as they came into the kitchen. "Grilled cheese?" he said. "I'm putting seaweed in mine." Marco was leaning on the island, wolfing down a sandwich already.

"Sorry, I have to get home," Jasmin said.

"Oh." Blue poked the plate of sandwiches with his spatula. "Right. Okay."

She picked up the jacket she'd left on the chair and glanced around at everyone. "I wish I could stay. I didn't even get to meet any dragons."

"Next time," Zoe promised.

Jasmin looked at Blue again. He gave her an awkward smile and went back to spreading butter on a slice of bread. "Okay. Bye."

Zoe walked her to the door and gave her another hug. "Remember, don't say anything to anybody," Zoe said. "Especially your parents. Don't let them know you were here, or that you talked to me or Blue, or—"

"ZOmygoodness," Jasmin said. That was a phrase she'd made up long ago for whenever Zoe was worrying too much. Zoe hadn't heard it in months, and it made her giggle even through her anxiety. Which was, of course, the point. "I'll call you soon, okay?"

"Definitely," Zoe said. She watched Jasmin walk away down the long drive and felt the weirdest combination of soaring happiness and bone-crushing dread.

She might have her best friend back. Maybe. She wasn't entirely ready to believe it yet.

But the Sterlings were out there, planning whatever they were planning, and if Jasmin was right, they needed to be stopped before Tuesday.

She went back into the kitchen and found Logan staring mournfully at the sandwiches and wearing what looked like about four long-sleeved shirts on top of each other. The top one was pumpkin orange, which was a nice color on him.

Thanks a lot, Jasmin in my brain.

"I don't think I can eat," Logan said. "The basilisk smell is stuck in my nose and it's too awful."

"You should try, though," Zoe said. "Did you ask your dad if you can sleep over?"

"My phone is still drying out," Logan said, pointing at the windowsill where his phone sat in a beam of pale sunshine.

"Your brother just radioed," Blue informed Zoe. "Basil is contained. And Matthew and Mooncrusher found what looks like the remains of a fire extinguisher scattered from the Reptile House to about fifteen yards out. I guess it exploded."

"Like on *MythBusters*," Logan said.

"What?" Zoe asked.

"On *MythBusters*, they took the safety valve off a CO_2 fire extinguisher and it blew up," Logan explained.

"Wasn't it in a fire, though?" Marco said.

"You're right," Logan said, seeming surprised Marco watched the show, too.

"And anyway, how could any of our fire extinguishers not have their safety valves?" Zoe said. "We literally replaced them all just last week on SNAPA's insistence. Unless—"

"Unless what?" Marco said.

"Unless it was the saboteur,'" Logan finished for her. "We think someone's been messing with the Menagerie."

A rumbling sound echoed through the walls, and with her nerves as frayed as they were, it took Zoe a heart-stopping minute to realize it was just the garage door opening.

"That was quick," she said. They'd gotten Jasmin out just in time. "Remember, let's not mention Jasmin was here just yet. And, heads up, Pelly is back."

The boys stayed in the kitchen while Zoe went out to the garage, where Zoe's mom and dad were climbing out of the van. Ruby emerged after them and flounced into the house with a sullen look on her face. A squawky muttering was coming from the back of the van. Out in the driveway, Zoe saw the two SNAPA agents getting out of their car.

"Hi, Zoe," Delia Dantes said tiredly as she came into the garage. Zoe wondered if any of her other SNAPA work was as crazy or messed up as this week at the Menagerie had been. The agent looked like she hadn't slept in days, with dark rings under her pretty gray eyes. There was a small coffee stain on her white blouse and wrinkles in her tan linen pants.

Agent Runcible, by contrast, looked as perfectly pressed and impeccable as ever. And possibly even more unfriendly than usual, although that might be because Melissa Merevy had blackmailed him into letting the Menagerie stay open by threatening to reveal how many new-werewolf rules he'd broken lately. Otherwise he'd been planning to shut them down over any number of things, big (a missing golden goose, a dragon wandering around town eating sheep) or small (expired kennel cough vaccines for the hellhounds, not enough algae in the zaratan's diet, etc.). But now he couldn't.

So we're safe from one thing, at least, Zoe thought.

"Where's Miss Sameera?" she asked.

"We took her home," Delia answered.

"Oh," Zoe said. "We sort of promised she could see the unicorns. And I wanted to ask her some questions."

"You'd better not," Agent Runcible said sternly. "We gave her enough kraken ink to make the kraken itself forget it's not just a squid. This time it had better work, since it clearly didn't in Missouri." He stalked past her, oblivious to her mouth dropping open.

"Wait," Zoe cried. "You gave her kraken ink already? But what about all our questions?"

"We questioned her, don't worry," Delia said.

"But what if you asked her the wrong things?" Zoe said. "What if she knew something else that *we* need to know?"

"Zoe," her dad said warningly, taking a clipboard from Runcible and signing the papers on it. "I'm sure the SNAPA agents know what they're doing."

I'm sure they DON'T, Zoe wanted to shout. How could they wipe Miss Sameera's brain without even asking if the Kahns needed to talk to her first?

"Did you ask her who she followed?" Zoe demanded. "To find Pelly? Do you know who it was?"

"Someone she didn't know," Delia said. "A young man in a hooded sweatshirt. She didn't get a good look at his face."

"That's it?" Zoe said. *Could that be Jonathan?* "But where—"

"Zoe, save it for later, all right?" her mother said.

We don't HAVE until later, Zoe felt like screaming. But something in her mom's tone made her stop asking questions. Maybe her parents had already gone through this. Maybe they knew something and would tell her after the agents left.

Mr. Kahn handed the papers back to Runcible and opened the rear door of the van. The enormous goose who laid the golden eggs slowly turned to glare at him. Zoe saw that the interior of the van had been packed with at least forty pillows to cushion Pelly's ride.

"OOOOOOH good," Pelly said in her quacky drawl. "We're here. How wonderful." She stood up and paced to the edge of the van, regarding each of them balefully. "Just where I was hoping to be. Oh yes, this is much better than a private garden with an adoring caretaker devoted to my needs above all others. I simply cannot wait to get back to that crowded birdcage and all my featherbrained companions. I do *hope* it's as noisy as it was when I left."

"When you were kidnapped, you mean," Zoe's mother pointed out.

Pelly eyed her with enormous disdain. "If anyone could possibly take the trouble to help me down, that would be so delightful. But really, don't strain yourselves."

Mr. Kahn stepped forward and lifted Pelly down to the ground with an audible "Oof!" The goose was as tall as Zoe and quite a bit wider, especially after a week of being pampered and fed anything she wanted by Miss Sameera. Pelly waddled over to the door that led into the Menagerie, holding her beak in the air.

"The paperwork's in order," Runcible said, stowing the clipboard in his briefcase. "We'll just come along to check the goose's nest one more time."

Zoe's parents only nodded, but Zoe could see the little sigh that her mother was repressing. Wasn't SNAPA done with them yet?

Pelly paraded slowly through the grass toward the Aviary, turning her head left and right as though she were surveying her kingdom (and finding it quite disappointing). Shortly before they all reached the dome, she stopped and stared piercingly at the Kahns.

"Well, I must admit I'm mystified," she said sniffily. "Where is it?"

Zoe's mom and dad looked at each other. "Where is what?" her mom asked.

Pelly examined one of her wings as if she were really rather bored and not *that* interested in the answer. "My memorial, of course," she said. "I mean, you all thought I was dead, so I'm sure you must have erected some kind of beautiful monument in my memory. A marble likeness of me, perhaps? Life-sized or twice my size, which did you choose? I would never say so myself, of course, but there are those who have observed that I would look simply *gorgeous* in marble. If it's not too heavy, perhaps we could move it next to my nest so I can admire it from time to time. I mean, if it's not too much trouble. Gazing at it might help just a *tiny bit* to get me through the trauma of my terrible ordeal."

Zoe rolled her eyes. Her dad coughed.

"Um," he said. "You know. Funny story. We actually hadn't quite—gotten around to your memorial yet. Of course we *would* have," he added quickly as Pelly turned her full glare on him. "But we were all so, uh—"

"Devastated," Zoe's mom chimed in. "So very, very devastated. We hadn't gone through all the stages of grieving. You understand. We couldn't commission a, um—beautiful marble statue—until we'd really accepted that you were gone."

"Mmm-hmm," said the goose, clearly not mollified. "And

how was my touching funeral? Who did the eulogy? I certainly hope someone sang 'Amazing Grace.' Not that dragon who thinks she can sing, though; far be it from me to judge anyone's musical talent, but she quite obviously has none. Which poems did you read? I'm sure you all remembered my fondness for Robert Frost. Oh, I hope that phoenix wasn't invited. He wouldn't care if I was dead or alive and that color red would be entirely unsuitable for such a somber event. Did you videotape it?"

Has anyone ever videotaped a funeral? Zoe wondered.

"We . . . hadn't gotten around to that, either," Zoe's dad admitted.

Pelly swelled up indignantly, ruffling all the feathers on her chest. "WELL," she said. "INDEED. I SEE."

"Sorry," Zoe's mom offered.

"NO, NO," Pelly said ostentatiously. "Why should anyone bother to grieve MY death? I am ONLY a MERE GOOSE. There are a whole ELEVEN OTHER golden geese in the world; that makes me downright *expendable*, I suppose. Some would say my enchanting personality is irreplaceable, of course, but what do they know. Besides, I'm sure you would have found some other way to support this outrageously expensive operation IN NO TIME AT ALL."

They were going to be hearing about this for weeks, Zoe realized. Possibly years.

Pelly huffed her way inside as Mr. Kahn opened the doors

to the Aviary. She flung out her wings in the warm, damp air inside and honked loudly. One of the halcyons landed on a branch overhead and gave the Kahns a disappointed look, like, *Did you have to bring her back?*

"Oh, don't bother with a welcoming committee!" Pelly cried at the birds twittering all around the dome. "I wouldn't want you to trouble yourselves just because I've been to the brink of death and violently kidnapped and then brutally dragged back here. No reason to come see if I'm all right, no, no, please carry on flapping as if nothing has happened."

When this failed to provoke any response from the other birds, Pelly fluffed her feathers again and stalked through the curtains of vines, toward her nest in the center of the Aviary dome.

"Uh-oh," Zoe said suddenly. "Dad, has anyone checked Pelly's nest in the last couple of days?"

"We cleaned it up after SNAPA got all their evidence," her dad said. "Don't worry, all the blood and feathers should be long gone."

"But have you checked on whether anyone's been using it?" Zoe whispered. "It's the nicest creature home in the whole Menagerie. What if the alicanto decided to move in, thinking she was gone?"

"Or worse—" her dad said, but he was cut off by a shriek of fury.

"GET OUT OF MY NEST!" Pelly howled. "THIS IS

THE LAST STRAW! I AM GOING TO PLUCK YOU BALD, YOU GAUDY TRESPASSER!"

They burst through the vines to find Pelly chasing Nero, the only phoenix in the world, around and around her nest. He flapped his stunning red-gold wings furiously, yelping with alarm. He was still wearing the small dark-blue hooded sweatshirt that had materialized after Logan tried to put out the bird's resurrection flames with his own jacket.

"Why?" Nero yelled. "Why is she back? Why didn't anyone warn me? Why doesn't anyone *care about me at all*? Oh, I am so beleaguered! So neglected! So unloved!"

Pelly lunged at him, snapping her beak, and nearly caught one of the phoenix's long flowing tail feathers.

Nero's voice rose to a wail. "Help! She's going to murder me! Birdslaughter! Murder in the goose degree! Phoenixcide!"

"He's right!" Pelly yelled. "I am!"

"Now *stop this*," Mr. Kahn said. He stepped forward and scooped up Nero; at the same time, Zoe's mom jumped (very bravely, Zoe thought) in Pelly's path and blocked her way. Nero whimpered as pitifully as he could and buried his head in Mr. Kahn's shirt.

"Everyone calm down," Zoe's mom said.

"Calm!" Pelly squawked. She spread her wings at her nest, hopping from one foot to the other. Zoe had never seen her so animated. "That *fire starter* has been in *my nest*! He's SLEPT in it! He's breathed all over it! He's REARRANGED THE

PILLOWS! It's RUINED!" She started kicking and biting at the enormous nest, pulling out bits of straw and silk and fluff.

"Hmm," Agent Runcible said disapprovingly. His fingers twitched toward his case, as if he was dying to report this new evidence of Menagerie incompetence.

"Pelly, it is not the end of the world," said Zoe's dad. "Really. I'm sure Nero will stay as far away from your nest as you like, now that you're back."

"Oh yes," Nero said, poking his head out to frown at Pelly. "I'll just rearrange my flight patterns completely for a mentally unstable *farmyard bird*."

"Nero!" Zoe's mom yelled as Pelly let out a crazy-eyed honk. "Don't make things worse!"

"Right," her dad said. "Don't add fuel to the fire. Heh, get it?" He caught the look from Zoe's mom and shook his head. "Not the time, okay."

"I could just DIE," the phoenix muttered, flopping sideways in Dad's arms. "And no one would even CARE. No one would even NOTICE."

"Do not set yourself on fire while I'm holding you, please," said Zoe's dad. "Let's find you a safe spot for the time being, until everyone's feathers are less ruffled."

"That is enough terrible puns out of you," Zoe's mom said.

Agent Runcible cleared his throat. "Perhaps up by the roc," he said. "Rocs are traditionally fairly calm about unusual circumstances."

"Good idea, thanks," said Zoe's dad. He left the clearing with Nero, and a minute later they heard him climbing the spiral staircase toward the roc's platform.

"Well," said Runcible, "I think we're done here. Now we must focus on the potential exposure problem."

Zoe thought guiltily of how she'd let Jasmin go home knowing the truth. But if she hadn't let Jasmin in on everything, they wouldn't know about the Sterlings' Election Day plans.

Pelly eyed them all beadily. "Oh, sure," she said. "By all means, go. I'll just stay here and contemplate the wreckage of my home."

"Great," said Zoe's mom, evidently deciding not to play Pelly's game anymore today. "We'll check in on you again once you're a little more settled." She put an arm around Zoe's shoulder and steered her toward the exit with the SNAPA agents close behind them.

"That's just fine," they could hear Pelly grumbling behind them. "Everything SMELLS LIKE PHOENIX. I'm going to have nasty phoenix dreams all night."

Zoe pushed through the outer Aviary door, trying to think positive. Pelly was back, and alive, most importantly. Scratch was safe. Maybe SNAPA would be able to solve their Sterling problem. Maybe in a few days, everything would be back to normal.

They emerged into the cold gray afternoon.

"MERFOLK OF THE WORLD, UNITE!" somebody screamed.

"SAFETY FOR ALL FINS!" shouted someone else.

"WE DEMAND OUR RIGHTS!"

"AND HAWAII!"

"HAWAII! HAWAII! HAWAII!"

Agent Runcible's eyebrows shot up. Just offshore, in the lake, a crowd of mermaids and mermen was bobbing up and down waving enormous waterproof signs.

How did they manage THAT so fast? Zoe wondered. She'd already forgotten about Cobalt's threats from that morning.

"What on earth?" Zoe's mother said, coming to a startled halt. "Cobalt! What's going on?"

"THE MERFOLK ARE ON STRIKE!" the king bellowed across the water. "UNTIL OUR DEMANDS ARE MET!"

"Oh my," Delia said in a low, bewildered voice.

"What?" said her mom. "Why—"

"Um," Zoe said. "Right. A few things happened while you were gone."

"I see," said Agent Runcible. His eyes glittered coldly at Zoe and her mother. "It appears that we are not *quite* finished with you yet."

TEN

"They kraken inked Miss Sameera already?" Logan said in dismay.

"I know," Zoe said. "I'm so mad." She rubbed her arms, her eyes fixed on the lake below them, where Mr. and Mrs. Kahn were arguing with King Cobalt. Agent Dantes was listening with her arms folded, and Agent Runcible was on his phone, which didn't seem like a good sign.

Logan hadn't realized how many merfolk lived in the lake. From here he could see at least thirty, all of them shouting and splashing their signs around. It was enough noise that the zaratan was clearly displeased; the mossy green mound of its shell had moved to the farthest north corner of the lake. At one point Logan even saw the giant turtle's head poke out to stare at the mermaids.

"Maybe it won't work," Logan said. "They gave her kraken ink when she exposed the Menagerie in Parkville, too, right? And she still remembered it."

"True," said Zoe. "But that's not really a best-case scenario. Because then what do we do with her, if we can't wipe her memories?"

Blue and Marco came out of the sliding doors behind them. Marco offered Logan the sandwich he was holding. Logan shook his head with a shudder, so Marco shrugged and started eating it himself.

"Man," Blue said, shoving his hands in his pockets. "I can't stand it when my dad gets mad like this. Good thing my mom's not—"

Melissa Merevy came storming out through the garage door and strode down the hill toward the argument at the lake.

"Awesome," said Blue. He hunched his shoulders. "I think I'll go read in my room for a bit."

"Oh, no you don't," Zoe said. She grabbed his wrist before he could escape. "You need to help us with this problem, Blue."

"There's not really anything I can do," Blue protested. "I should just stay out of it."

"You can help me figure out which merfolk chores are the most urgent," Zoe said, pulling out her notepad. "And how we're going to do them. The lake is the one habitat I don't know how to cover."

Blue wrinkled his nose, looking deeply uncomfortable. "I'm not sure Dad would like that."

"Well, *nobody* is going to like a grumpy zaratan or a hungry kelpie," Zoe said. "Just tell me what the mermaids usually do, please."

"Normal stuff," Blue said, edging toward the house. "Feed the kelpie, feed the zaratan, check on the kraken."

"Which is still not hibernating, by the way," Logan said. "It pulled me into the lake earlier, right before I ran into the basilisk. I—I think it was trying to tell me something."

Zoe rubbed her forehead. "What is up with her? She's always asleep by November." She gave him a rueful smile. "Too bad you don't magically speak kraken, too. BLUE, GET BACK HERE."

Blue had darted inside; he poked his head back out, leaning on the glass door. "And keeping the lake clean and checking the river grates and harvesting kraken ink and then regular castle duties. That's all. Can I go?"

He really doesn't like watching his parents fight, Logan guessed. Cobalt and Melissa were now screaming at each other loud enough to drown out the protesting merfolk. Fighting with each other was just about the only thing Logan had ever seen them do. His own parents never fought, or at least, they'd never done it in front of him.

"There are CONTRACTS!" Melissa was yelling. "There are LAWS!"

"I am the king!" Cobalt bellowed. "I MAKE the laws! I'm making a law RIGHT NOW! Oh look, it says that my subjects and I should live in Hawaii! SO IT IS DECREED!"

"You signed a contract with SNAMHP!" Melissa shouted. "And with this Menagerie! And with ME!"

"Contracts are for landwalkers!"

"Blue, come back," Zoe said. "When do all these things usually happen? Like, how soon will the animals be hungry?"

"I don't really pay attention," Blue said. "I'm not allowed to help, remember? Royalty and stuff?"

"Don't even try that with me," Zoe said.

He sighed. "Noon for the zaratan," he said. "And then when he's finished, the kelpie, and after her, the kraken, if it's awake. You'll need the shaker for the zaratan and the sticks for all three of them. The food is usually prepared in the castle kitchens early in the morning, so it's probably ready for today, at least."

"That means they're hungry now! It's after noon!" Zoe said. "Blue—"

"No, no, no," he said, shaking his head vigorously. "I cannot help you. Dad will kill me. I refuse to pick sides. Uh-oh, here she comes." He fled into the house without even closing the door behind him.

Logan turned and saw Melissa Merevy coming up the

hill. It looked like the merfolk had gotten angry and splashed her; her dark-blue wool coat, pearl-gray skirt, and gray tights all had wet patches on them, and her usually perfect blond bun was a tiny bit disheveled.

"Hi, Melissa," Zoe said. "Any chance they're going to feed the lake creatures today?"

"It certainly doesn't seem like it," Melissa said grimly. "I have never seen him behave so childishly, not even when we were married. Someone has filled his head with nonsense." She stalked past and into the house.

Logan glanced at Zoe, wondering if she was thinking what he was thinking. Had the saboteur somehow been talking to the mermaids? Did they get their ideas about the Hawaii menagerie from someone who was trying to cause trouble?

That couldn't be my dad, he thought again. *He wouldn't do anything like that.*

"I guess we're suiting up," Zoe said to Logan. "You can swim, right?"

"Um," he said. "If I have to." His two experiences with the Menagerie lake had not exactly made it his favorite place in the Menagerie. Mythical creatures were still exciting, yes, but he was definitely less excited about the kinds that tried to kill him. What if the kelpie or the kraken grabbed him again? But he didn't want to look scared in front of Zoe, and he did want to help. If this was part of being involved with the Menagerie, he'd do it, whatever it was.

"In November in Wyoming?" Marco said. "Sounds AWE-SOME. I will stand right here and cheer very loudly. That is my plan. Unless—do you think Keiko would be impressed if I went in with you? Would she think I'm EVEN MORE amazing?"

"I highly doubt she'd notice," Logan admitted.

"Then I will be useful from here," said Marco. "With my coat on. Hey, I can hold towels for you! I am excellent at holding towels."

Logan trailed Zoe into the garage, where they found Matthew going through a large trunk of what looked like snorkel gear.

"Uh-oh," Logan said.

"This one might fit you," Matthew said, holding up a wet suit and eyeing it critically.

"I think Ruby should have to help with this," Zoe said. "As part of her punishment." She dragged out a wet suit and flippers with her name on them.

"Maybe tomorrow, if the strike is still going on then," Matthew said. "Right now we don't have time for a snotty temper tantrum."

Logan took the wet suit and went to change. It was as uncomfortable and weird looking as he'd feared, but he managed to struggle into it by thinking about his mom, and how she had traveled the world and done a million braver and crazier things than this. One day he might be a Tracker like her.

A Tracker who didn't care how cold the lake was going to be, or how close he'd have to get to a murderous water horse, or how much Marco was going to laugh at him.

On the plus side, Zoe and Matthew looked extremely silly as well. Zoe had a snorkel mask perched on her head, and she handed one to him as he stepped out of the warm living room into the chilly afternoon. Matthew was carrying a big metal box shaped kind of like a saxophone case, but lime green.

"We have to go to the merfolk castle first," Zoe said. "To get the food. That'll probably be the hardest part, because certain fishbrains aren't going to be too pleased about it."

"A real underwater castle?" Logan said with a grin. He had actually been wondering how and where all those mermaids lived and what Blue did when he was underwater with his dad. He had not expected to ever find out, though. "Okay, now I'm excited."

"That's the attitude we're looking for," Matthew said, grinning back.

"We'll try sneaking around them, but it's unlikely to work," Zoe said. She led the way to the golf cart, where Marco was already sitting with a pile of towels, trying hard not to laugh at the sight of them. Matthew climbed into the driver's seat and they zipped down the path and turned left to go around the lake.

"BOOOOOOOOOO!!!!!" several of the mermaids shouted at them.

"Scabs!" one of them shouted. "FINLESS SCABS!"

By the time they pulled up to the shore not far from the griffin enclosure and the river, most of the merfolk had swarmed over to that side of the lake and started vigorously beating their tails. Waves splashed across the sand, immediately soaking Zoe and Logan when they sat down to put their flippers on.

"Ignore them," Zoe said to Logan. "They know if they touch us they'll end up manning the Antarctic outpost. All they can do is splash and yell." She turned to Matthew, who was snapping open the shiny green case. Nestled inside were four odd-looking devices.

"Have you ever seen any James Bond movies?" Matthew asked Logan. Logan shook his head. "Well, this is kind of like a gadget he had called a rebreather, which made it possible for him to breathe underwater—sort of like portable gills. Easier than scuba equipment; you just put your mouth over this bit and breathe normally." He passed one to Logan, who inspected it curiously.

"What's this sparkly part?" he asked, pointing at a small disk on either side of the mouthpiece. They were shaped like guitar picks and glimmered like rainbows trapped in silver.

"Those are hippocamp scales," Matthew said. "Half-horse, half-fish, if you haven't gotten that far in the guide. They filter the oxygen in the water so you can breathe it."

Something moved out on the lake, and Logan turned to

look. Beyond the mermaids, on the one actual island, something was clambering up the rocks where the merfolk often sunned themselves. As the water poured off its mane, Logan recognized the kelpie.

The dark gray horse gazed menacingly at all of them—Logan, Zoe, Matthew, and the merfolk. Logan couldn't believe he'd once found it beautiful, although he knew that was its magic. But now he could see the sinister depths in its black eyes, and the way it ground its teeth together made him remember all too clearly that it had once planned to eat him—and gotten very close to succeeding.

"Are you all right?" Zoe asked him, following his gaze to the kelpie. "You don't have to do this."

"Totally fine," he said. "Mermaid castle, here we come." He stuck the hippocamp rebreather in his mouth and started toward the water, his flippered feet sticking out so far he had to lift them extra high to avoid tripping.

The water along the shoreline continued to surge in waves as the merfolk swarmed close by. Logan waded in, trying to look confident. His mom had joked around with these same people, he reminded himself. Blue's dad ruled them. Still, it was unnerving being glared at by an angry crowd.

Matthew and Zoe fell into step next to him. As they approached, the merfolk grudgingly retreated. Matthew gave them a cocky salute before diving under. Zoe raised her eyebrows at Logan.

He nodded back, adjusting his mask. Rebreather or not, he couldn't help taking in a big breath before plunging his head under the water.

Brrrrrr!!! The lake had decidedly *not* warmed up in the last few hours and his face immediately started stinging from the cold. He glanced down, suddenly grateful for the goofy-looking wet suit. Before he got too far away from the shore, he cautiously drew in an experimental breath. A clean burst of oxygen met his lungs. It was very cool.

"BBLLLOOOORRRRRBBBB!!!!!!"

Logan blinked to clear his eyes as a volley of bubbles surrounded him. A disgruntled-looking mermaid with pale hair was shaking her fist at him and screaming what he could only assume were merfolk obscenities.

"GRRROOOOOOUPER MELLLOOOON!!!"

Logan raised his shoulders in an apologetic shrug, trying to convey *I can't understand mer-language* as well as *I know you don't want me down here doing your job, but if you're not going to do it, someone has to, because we wouldn't want the kelpie wandering off to find her own food, now, would we?* He kicked off the sandy bottom to follow Matthew and Zoe, who had several mermaids circling them as well. The pale-haired mermaid kept up, shouting furiously.

"MMMANNOOOOO WARRT!"

Logan tried to ignore her, pointedly peering beyond her shoulder, but all he could see was darkness. Anything could be hiding out there in the murky water. Including a very hungry kelpie and a misbehaving kraken. Not to mention a zaratan Logan knew nothing about. He sped up a little so he wouldn't lose Matthew and Zoe.

The weak November sun did not reach down very far, barely lighting the swathe of water above him. But as they swam farther, Logan realized that there was a faint glow coming from up ahead.

The merfolk who had been hassling them suddenly broke off, but instead of returning to the picket line, they zoomed toward the blue light and then . . . disappeared.

Logan swam closer and discovered that the floor of the lake dropped off dramatically. Suddenly he was swimming above what looked like a giant coral reef.

Greenish-blue light shone up from the edges of paths that wound between house-sized spiral shapes. The doorways were round, like on hobbit homes in *The Lord of the Rings*, but there were no actual doors, just open tunnels with curving pearlescent walls. Some of the circular windows had lovely, dangling planters of purple and red sea anemones or curtains of dark green seaweed.

The lights grew brighter and the spiral shapes larger as they swam toward a massive bluish-white castle-like shape sticking out of the reef. Five wicked-looking spires towered around a central dome with several entrance holes. The rows of lights ran up the castle in parallel lines just a few feet apart, so it looked like the whole thing had strings of Christmas lights along it.

Matthew and Zoe curved around to the right. As Logan followed, he reached down to trail a hand along the lights. Ripples of more light blossomed from the contact, spreading in either direction, and as Logan lifted his hand back, he saw his fingers seemed to be coated in light, although he couldn't feel anything.

Whoa!

Zoe must have sensed Logan slowing down because she turned and gave him a thumbs-up, like, *I know, so cool, right?*

Just then, a dark shape rocketed out of the murk behind her. Logan caught a glimpse of gleaming teeth and glowering eyes.

The kelpie had found them.

ELEVEN

Logan waved frantically at Zoe as he kicked toward them. But he would never get there in time. The kelpie bared her teeth and lowered her head toward Zoe's shoulder.

Zoe spun around, pulled out her rebreather, and clocked the kelpie on the nose with it. The kelpie let out a neighing scream and backed up, glaring malevolently. She stamped one of her hooves as if to say *Where's my food?*

Zoe pointed toward the nearest castle entrance, where Matthew hovered in the doorway.

The kelpie shook out her mane, snapping her teeth at the same time. *Well, either hurry up or let me eat you,* her dark eyes implied.

Zoe put her rebreather back in and wagged a sharp finger at the water horse. Logan imagined her saying *Stay here and stop bothering us unless you want nothing but kelp burgers for the next year.*

The kelpie snorted, but kept its distance as Logan tugged Zoe toward Matthew.

They swam into the castle along a spiraling hallway. The walls were completely smooth and shimmered like an opal or the inside of an oyster. Every ten feet there was an enormous mollusk shell overflowing with plants and sea life—pops of red, yellow, purple, and orange anemones nestled among bright green fronds swaying in the current. Logan spotted tiny blue seahorses bobbing between the strands of sea grass. Then he rounded a bend and swept into a cavernous space alongside Zoe and Matthew.

Racks of seaweed hung to their right, next to plants growing in shell pots along the wall. Several circular stone pits took up the left side of the room with spears of fish balanced over them. Logan could see blasts of bubbling, boiling water shooting up from the pits to cook the fish. A barrel-chested merman was tending them, fiddling with some levers that directed the streams of hot water from below. He looked up in surprise.

"Sooooowwwerrppp?" he asked.

The water felt pleasantly warm as they got closer to the pits. Matthew pulled out what looked like a whiteboard and wrote on it with a charcoal pencil.

We're here for the kelpie's and zaratan's meals. He eyed the merman for a moment, then added, **Please**, and held it up.

The merman's eyebrows drew together and he crossed his arms. If this was the guy they needed to go through, things did not look good.

As Matthew launched into a negotiation with the merman, Logan followed Zoe to the far wall. She unhooked a long white cylinder with a strap and handed it to Logan. It was heavier than it looked and made a clunking sound as it pulled him down to the floor.

"Nnneeeeeeevvvaaaaahh!" A young mermaid, maybe eight years old, with curly brown hair in pigtails came zooming out of nowhere and tried to wrestle the cylinder away from Logan.

He held on tightly as the momentum from the girl spun them. Something rattled inside as they played tug-of-war with it. Out of the corner of his eye, Logan spotted an older mermaid with the same hair stop near them. Suddenly the cylinder slipped out of the mergirl's hands and she went flying, end over end.

"Mmmaaaaaaaammmmaaaaaa!!!" she wailed and fled to the mermaid's side. Her mother hugged her, looking unperturbed, even as Logan crinkled his face in apology.

"Bbbaaadraallaam ppeeettum!" The merman who'd been arguing with Matthew came over and huffed at the mermaid.

Even without speaking their language, Logan could tell he was basically saying: "Can you believe these landwalkers, invading our castle?" The merman gestured toward the cylinder and the long slender sticks Zoe was unhooking from the wall. "Fffeeenna rratha mmeeer."

Instead of getting riled up like the other merfolk, the curly-haired mermaid shrugged with a smug expression. She cocked her head at Zoe and waved a hand toward several large lidded pails lined up along the walls. *Be my guest.*

"Gggoooolaa?" the merman asked her, incredulous.

The mermaid made a face at him that looked like, *If they want to get bitten by a zaratan, I'm not going to stop them.*

The merman paused, considering. A smirk spread across his face. He picked up two of the pails and shoved them into Matthew's arms.

That was too easy, Logan thought. As he and Zoe claimed the remaining pails, he studied the superior and highly amused looks on the merfolk's faces. *They don't think we can do this. Or they're counting on us running into some very entertaining trouble.*

Sure enough, the three merfolk followed them out of the castle, burbling gleefully to each other. Outside, a crowd of merfolk was waiting for them, some of them armed with tridents.

The curly-haired mermaid from the kitchen called out something, which made an amused murmur run through the crowd.

Matthew pointed the whiteboard at Zoe and Logan. **Just ignore them**, he wrote.

Easier said than done, as the entire mob trailed after them into the murky dimness outside the mermaid village.

"EEEEEEEEEEEEEEEEIIIIIIGGGGHHHH!"

They had only swum a few feet when a very agitated kelpie thundered up and started nosing the pails, shouldering into Logan and Matthew. Matthew shoved her head away and she snapped at his flippers. Zoe tried to poke her off with one of the sticks, but the kelpie grabbed it in her teeth and yanked hard, tugging Zoe into an off-balance somersault.

The merfolk began nudging each other and guffawing.

Matthew kicked to the surface, and Logan followed. Zoe's head popped up a second after his. Matthew was already taking out his rebreather.

"This is impossible," he muttered. "Silverina is being so annoying."

Right on cue, something pulled him downward and he sputtered as he kicked back up.

"The kelpie's name is Silverina?" Logan asked.

"Ruby named her," Zoe explained. "To be fair, she was nine at the time. But you'll notice Mom and Dad never let her name anybody else."

"Seriously," Matthew said. "We'd have ended up with a dragon named Sparklepuff. KELPIE, GET OFF OR I WILL STAB YOU."

"Can't we just feed . . . Silverina first?" Logan asked.

Matthew shook his head. "The zaratan would get offended. We should stick to the routine as best we can. Logan, you're going to need to signal the zaratan to come to us with the shaker." He nodded toward the cylinder slung over Logan's shoulder.

"No problem."

"Oof!" Zoe cried as she was knocked sideways by the kelpie's head.

Matthew reached over and bopped the kelpie on the nose. "Zoe, you and Logan feed the zaratan. I'll try to keep Silverina in line. Ready?"

"Ready," Logan said.

"Stupid mermaids," Zoe grumbled. "Stupid Blue and his stupid royal status."

They all put in their rebreathers and descended. Matthew pointed ahead to a flat, clear stretch along the bottom of the lake. It was shallower here, so some light filtered down. A ring of merfolk had set up around the patch and seemed to be munching on calamari and toasting each other with conch shells. It reminded Logan of the sidelines of a Bulls game. Or, he guessed, what Roman spectators at an arena would have looked like.

Waiting for someone to get eaten by lions—or in this case, by a cranky water horse.

Logan set his pails down on the sand and pulled the shaker over his head. *Shhkkkashhkkkashhkkka*, rattled whatever was inside it.

A gray head suddenly snaked around his legs and snatched one of his pails. The lid came off as the kelpie dragged it away and tiny squid-like creatures floated out.

Zoe abandoned her own pails and swam over to wrestle the bucket away and slam the lid back on, but the kelpie was rapidly gobbling most of what had escaped.

"Aaaahh!" Zoe yelped as the kelpie's teeth narrowly missed her fingers.

Matthew grabbed one of the sticks and smacked the kelpie on the nose with it. She danced away, arching her neck to snap at another squid.

Tremendously helpful laughter and applause erupted from the watching merfolk.

Darkness spread over the sand below them. Logan looked up to see an enormous shape roughly the size of their school's gymnasium blocking the light.

The zaratan pivoted and began to dive toward them.

Zoe quickly grabbed one of the sticks and reached into a pail. She speared several large fish onto the end. Logan followed suit as the zaratan's head came level with them. A round, black eye studied him curiously.

Logan's hand shook a little as he held out his stick in front of the zaratan's beak, which was as wide as a cafeteria table was long. The zaratan cocked its head and then its mouth opened and shut so quickly Logan would have missed it if he hadn't felt the force of it swiping the fish off the stick.

Yikes! That thing is fast. Logan hastily re-threaded his stick as Zoe offered hers to the zaratan. They emptied two of their pails as Matthew poured out the rest of the squid for the kelpie. Logan's last pail held seaweed.

Logan and Zoe tried to spear the seaweed onto their sticks, but it was too fragile and kept breaking.

The zaratan's beak nosed forward impatiently. Logan slapped his stick together with Zoe's like chopsticks and together they lifted a ribbon of seaweed out of a pail and held it out to the zaratan, who grabbed it and began munching. Logan could have sworn a smile spread across its face.

"Boooo!" the merfolk cried. Logan glanced over his shoulder and saw them slumping in disappointment.

Guess they were hoping we'd lose a few fingers. Well, too bad. He and Zoe could do this. He gave Zoe a thumbs-up as they worked together to scoop out more of the seaweed for the zaratan.

Matthew was having a harder time with the kelpie.

"AAARRRGGGH!" Logan thought he heard Matthew shout, although it was distorted by the rebreather.

Logan glanced over to see Silverina making off with one of their last pails, which was intended for the kraken. Matthew chased after her and managed to get it back, but not before the kelpie gulped down half of the food and then danced off with a swish of her tail.

They'd have to hope the kraken wasn't too hungry.

Once the seaweed pail was empty, the zaratan pivoted to swim away, its wake knocking them over. The merfolk threw their conch shells down on the sand and dispersed, grumbling.

Logan, Zoe, and Matthew collected their gear and the pail and a half that was left for the kraken. Matthew tugged out his notepad and wrote: "Two down, one to go."

It took a monumental effort to launch off the lake bottom; the sand sucked at Logan's flippers and the pails thumped against his thighs. The buckets were lighter, but swimming felt harder and harder as they crossed the lake and exhaustion seeped into Logan's muscles.

Just how big was this lake? And why did the kraken live in the most remote corner of it?

Then again, if he had to share a lake with those mermaids, he'd choose to live as far away from them as possible, too.

The lake bed beneath him became rockier, with boulders and crags sticking up. Then the northeast shore came into view. Logan spotted an irregular opening with a hinged gate in the cliff side. But the kraken was nowhere in sight.

Zoe and Matthew poked their heads into the hole and conferred using the whiteboard while Logan took the opportunity to rest on a flat rock.

He felt the water stirring behind him and turned. The kraken's bulbous head was hovering next to him. She blinked slowly and ran one of her tentacles over his head. Then her whole body shuddered, almost in excitement, like a puppy not believing the good fortune of finding a roast beef sandwich on the floor.

"Ummm . . ." Logan mumbled into his mask. "Guys?"

Zoe and Matthew turned just as the kraken wrapped one of her tentacles around Logan's waist and jetted off. Logan saw them hurrying after him, but they seemed very small and very far away very quickly. Water whooshed around him and he clutched the rebreather to his face to make sure he didn't lose it. He wondered whether to panic. How often did people get kidnapped by the kraken around here? Was there a protocol for hostage negotiation with a giant sea creature?

The kraken slowed and finally set Logan down in a curved half bowl along the shoreline, pitted with nooks and tunnels. Logan gazed around in wonder.

He could see what looked like a giant rock slide sloping down from the land above and a series of different-sized holes were carved into another stone slab. A number of balls were tied to weights along the floor, floating at different heights, and one stretch of smooth black rock seemed to have a shelf with small limestone sticks next to it, like an underwater chalkboard. Someone—or something—had drawn some wavy lines on it that reminded Logan of Chinese characters.

This couldn't be for the kelpie or the zaratan. Maybe this was the enclosure intended for the Chinese dragon? The one his mom was transporting here when she disappeared?

The kraken waved her tentacles at Logan, pointing at the enclosure and then back beyond him.

Logan held up his hands helplessly in the universal *I'm sorry, I have no idea what you're talking about* gesture.

The kraken sank a little, then perked up, waving more frenetically this time. She held two of her arms out in front of her like a pouch and shook them up and down. Logan stared at her blankly. She wove two of her legs into a seated lotus position, then raised two more in a Zen-like pose.

Am I supposed to meditate?

Logan felt the water swirl around him as Zoe and Matthew swam up. He held up his hands in an *I'm okay* sign and Zoe mimed wiping sweat off her brow in relief.

Matthew pointed at a mound of orange seaweed that had been woven into a banner bordering the enclosure and wrote on his board: **Did the mermaids do that?**

Zoe shrugged.

The kraken poked their legs insistently. She went through the whole pantomime Logan had already seen. But the Kahn siblings looked equally flummoxed.

The kraken let out a series of noises, staring at them soulfully.

Bubble. Squerk. Wheek. Fwelk. Bubble.

What do you think she wants? Zoe wrote on Matthew's board.

No idea, Matthew wrote back.

He took the pail and a half of seaweed they had left and set about spearing them for the kraken. She slapped the water with her tentacles like she was sulking for a minute, before giving up and tackling the food.

Within a few minutes, the buckets were empty. The kraken's tentacles wrapped around the pails and she turned them over and shook them, then looked at Logan and Zoe reproachfully, as if to say *That's all?*

Logan spread his hands apologetically.

Matthew patted one of the kraken's tentacles and mimed *More tomorrow.*

"*Fwelllble,*" the kraken bubbled.

As they swam away, Logan turned once more to look at the kraken. She had sunk to the floor of the enclosure and was watching them mournfully. It could just have been Logan's imagination, but he thought she looked awfully lonely.

I wonder if krakens and Chinese dragons can play together. Trust me, kraken, if that's who you're waiting for, nobody wants to find him—and my mom—more than I do.

The return to shore went excruciatingly slowly. Logan's arms and legs felt like lead when they finally began to wade ashore.

He dragged himself out onto the sand and collapsed,

pulling the hippocamp rebreather out of his mouth and sucking in a mouthful of real air. Marco was flapping around him with a towel, but Logan was too exhausted to even sit up and take it.

"We can't do that again," Zoe said to Matthew, dropping her mask and rubbing her hair with one of the towels. "Every day? We're not cut out for it, and we won't have time for any of our other chores. What are we going to do if the merfolk keep acting like ASININE UNICORNS!" She yelled the last bit at the lake and a few mermaids shook their fists back at her.

"Well," Matthew said slowly. "I might—know someone." He took the rebreathers and started drying them off, then packing them back in their case, with an oddly embarrassed look on his face.

"Know someone?" Zoe said. "Like who? Another mermaid?"

"No," he said. "Just someone I met at Tracker camp who might be able to help. I'll call—uh, her tonight and ask."

"OOOOOOOOOOOOOOOOOOOOOOOOOOOOH," Zoe said. "HER? Who is this HER?"

"Do not be an annoying little sister about this," Matthew said, throwing a towel at her. "If Elsie does decide to come, you must promise to act *normal.* By which I mean *normal as defined by most people.* There will be none of *that* face."

"I'm not making a face!" Zoe protested, scrunching her nose around like she was trying not to smile. "I'm sure *Elsie* will think we're perfectly normal."

Matthew rubbed his head. "This is a terrible idea," he muttered. He got up and stalked off to the golf cart, carrying the green case.

Zoe sat down next to Logan and poked him in the ribs. "Thank you for your help down there."

"No," Logan wheezed, "problem."

"You should probably go take a nap," she suggested.

He managed, barely, to tilt his head toward her. "Why?"

"Because we're going to be up all night, remember?" she said. "Hanging out in the Dark Forest, waiting to catch your dad." She bit her lip and started wrestling off one of her flippers. "Although he might not come tonight. I wonder what he'll tell us if he does come. Will he help us stop the Sterlings? By Tuesday? Sorry, I shouldn't be piling all my worries on you."

"It's all right," Logan said, but he couldn't help worrying himself about what was going to happen that night. Was he hoping to catch his dad sneaking into the Menagerie or not? Did he want to know what Jackson Wilde had been doing on his earlier trips over the wall?

Was Logan ready to finally find out the truth?

TWELVE

Zoe didn't usually lie to her parents, but she decided the whole hide-in-the-Dark-Forest-to-catch-a-saboteur plan was a need-to-know thing they didn't need to know. For one thing, she wanted to know what Mr. Wilde was up to before telling her parents about him. And for another, she had a feeling they'd get all frowny and irrational and try to stop her.

Besides, they had enough on their minds after spending the whole day either fighting with mermaids or strategizing about the Sterlings with the SNAPA agents. There'd been one long conversation about whether the properties of kraken ink would hold up if it were baked into, say, a friendly neighbor's apple pie. There were also a lot of snide comments from

Runcible about Ruby and her poor taste in people. Everyone had looked very stressed out by the time the SNAPA agents went back to their motel, and Ruby was too busy sulking to even come down for dinner.

So really, it was better for all involved if Zoe just waited until her parents were asleep, then tiptoed down the hall to Blue's room.

Still, she paused for a moment to feel guilty about it before she lightly tapped on his door.

Blue and Logan silently slipped out and they all crept down the stairs. Zoe was wearing a black shirt and black jeans with a black hoodie over top. It had a few holes nibbled in it by baby griffins, but it should hide her in the dark. She took a flashlight from the kitchen drawer but didn't turn it on yet.

"What'd you do about Captain Fuzzbutt?" Logan asked.

She sighed. "I suggested he have a sleepover with Mooncrusher, in the ice garden. You'd think I told him to go back to the cloning lab your mom rescued him from. He moped the whole day."

"Oh," Logan said. "That's what the big sad face at dinner was about."

"Yup," Zoe said. "Poor Fuzzbutt." The mammoth had pointedly sat across the room so he could give Zoe his most tragic eyes all through dinner. But really, how was she supposed to sneak out with a curious mammoth on her heels? She could just imagine the sound of the Captain's big shaggy feet tramping merrily down the stairs after her.

They crept out into the Menagerie and hurried past the Doghouse. Zoe heard one of the hellhounds growl, but he must have smelled her scent, because none of them barked.

How did Logan's dad get around the Menagerie without being noticed by the hellhounds? Zoe wondered. She glanced at Logan. The moon was shadowed by thin gray clouds, so it was hard to see his face, but his shoulders were hunched and he seemed focused on the ground in front of him. *He must be even more nervous than I am.*

They soon reached the large wooden fence that separated the Dark Forest from the rest of the Menagerie. DARK FOREST, said the sign on the door. DID YOU BRING NOSE PLUGS?

Blue tapped the sign and looked at Zoe. "Well?" he said. "Did you?"

"Why do I always have to remember everything?" she demanded.

"Because you always *do*," he pointed out, maddeningly. "So no one else bothers."

"Well, if we don't disturb Guava, he should leave us alone," Zoe said, "and then we won't really need nose plugs."

"Famous last words," Logan said. His voice was a little wobblier than usual, but he was clearly trying to sound cheerful and unworried.

Zoe lifted the latch and they all went through. Large

damp leaves smacked them in the face as soon as they were inside the fence. Zoe felt her sneakers sink slightly into the marshy undergrowth, and she could hear the quiet buzz of insects all around them.

"Whoa," Logan said, pushing his hood back. "How is it so warm in here?" He reached out and brushed one of the enormous fan-shaped leaves with his fingers. "These aren't evergreens."

"Guava and Mochi need an environment more like a jungle to live in," Zoe said. "So we had to hire those." She pointed to the nine small balls of light that were zipping madly through the trees toward them, as if they were racing—which, in fact, they were. Each was a slightly different color, but they were all about the size of a tennis ball and glowed like they were made of an unearthly fire.

The blue one reached them first. It seemed to skid to a halt in the air, where it turned in a slow circle, and then it darted up to Zoe's face, then Blue's, then Logan's. In front of Logan it jumped a bit—recognizing that he was someone new—and then did a little wiggly happy-dance.

"It's a will-o'-the-wisp," Zoe explained. "Sometimes called elf-fire, although not by actual elves, who get all offended and are like, 'Ahem, our fire is no different from your fire, and we have nothing to do with these attention-seeking flame balls.' "

"It's really cool," Logan said. "Will it burn me if I touch it?"

"No, but it won't let you touch it," Zoe said. "They're fast.

And just so you know, right now it is trying very, very hard to hypnotize you."

Logan blinked at the blue fireball, which was slowly bobbing up and down before his eyes, wobbling its little flames around as eerily as it could.

"Don't stare at it for too long, or it might work," Blue added.

"Why would it hypnotize me?" Logan asked, covering his eyes. "What does it want?"

"To lead you far astray into the marshy swamp," Zoe said in a spooky voice, "where you will be lost forever."

"Whoa," Logan said. "Really?"

"Poor things," Blue said. "They haven't completely wrapped their tiny fire-minds around the fact that there is no 'lost' in here, or that their purpose now is warming up this mini-jungle for other creatures, instead of leading travelers to their doom."

"Doom?" Logan echoed. "Are they evil?"

"No, that's just what will-o'-the-wisps do," Zoe said. "Like if fireflies could give you malaria, but they wouldn't be doing it on purpose. They're no more evil than bugs."

Five more little fireballs arrived in the clearing at once, colliding with each other as they darted frantically around examining the visitors. Their flames all shot upward excitedly as they discovered Logan, and in a minute he had six will-o'-the-wisps floating in front of him, jostling and bumping each other as they tried to get his attention and look mysteriously mesmerizing at the same time. The effect was not terribly menacing.

"Anyway," Zoe said, "now that you know what they're trying to do, it won't work on you. And the scarab would protect you from them regardless. Just ignore them and they'll give up soon."

"Okay," Logan said. "You know, I thought my nose was starting to recover from the basilisk, but—"

"That's Guava," Zoe said with a sigh. "Our mapinguari." The giant sloth smelled like a mountain of rotting mangoes, no matter how many baths he got. She was kind of used to it by now. "I'm still on bath duty for glitter bombing Matthew and Agent Runcible, so I *know* he had a bath yesterday, but it never seems to help. On the plus side, he weirdly loves baths. Just try not to breathe through your nose."

"It's actually not much worse than it's been all day," Logan said with a shrug.

"It is for *me*," Blue protested, holding his nose.

"Come on," Zoe said, tugging on Logan's sleeve. "I figure we'll hide near the camera that caught your dad coming in."

She led them to a swathe of thick bushes halfway between the mapinguari's hut and the wall. They crouched down below the leaves and Blue made a disgruntled noise.

"How long are we going to wait?" he asked.

"Yeah," Logan asked. "What if he doesn't come tonight?"

"I think he will," Zoe said. "He did the last time you slept over."

"That's really weird," Logan whispered. "That he was here at the same time as I was, but neither of us knew it, and we both have these huge secrets we've been keeping from each other." He fell silent.

"I'm sure he has his reasons," Zoe said softly.

"What do we do if he does come?" Blue asked. "Tackle him? Did you bring the griffin net? I'm kidding, Logan, don't have a heart attack."

"I think we should follow him," Zoe said. "Is that okay, Logan? So we can see what he's doing?"

"We could just ask him," Logan said slowly. "I think he'd tell me the truth, especially if we catch him here, like this." He glanced at Zoe. "But if you want to follow him first, I guess we can see where he goes."

Poor Logan. He doesn't want to watch his dad do something to the Menagerie. If his dad is the saboteur, and if the saboteur is the one who rigged the fire extinguisher to blow a hole in the Reptile House . . . well, I wonder if Mr. Wilde gave him that scarab because he knew the basilisk might be loose today. She decided not to float this theory to Logan.

Rustling and harrumphing sounds came from Guava's hut. "Shh," Zoe whispered. "Let's be really quiet so Guava won't come out to investigate."

"But he's a vegetarian, right?" Logan whispered. "I remember your dad saying that."

"He is," Zoe agreed. "But most mapinguaris will happily eat any humans they can catch. Ours is pretty tame, but he hasn't had to deal with many strangers. I wouldn't want to see him riled up."

Logan mimed locking his mouth with a key, pulled his hood up, and sat with his arms wrapped around his knees. The will-o'-the-wisps kept trying to entice him with flares of colorful flame and uncanny behavior, but after a while they gave up and flitted away, bumping each other crossly as if they were all saying, "You are such a failure at being eerie! I'll have you know I won 'most mesmerizing fireball' at the Elflympiad! He would have followed me if you hadn't been so annoying! Now he'll never drown in a creepy swamp!" And so on.

Zoe's phone buzzed softly and she glanced at it.

Are merboys allowed to date human girls? said the text from Jasmin. Zoe smiled at it.

Have you ever ridden a dragon? said the next text, followed by: **Can I ride a dragon?**

Yes, no, and no, Zoe texted back.

YES?!!!!!!!! came the response.

Allowed to, yes, Zoe typed. **Smart enough to, I'm not sure.**

LOL. What is he doing right now? What is he wearing right now? Also, then what CAN I ride?

Zoe glanced at Blue.

"What?" he whispered.

She shook her head and typed, **Nothing.**

The response came quickly. **He's wearing NOTHING???????**

Ha-ha-ha gross, Zoe typed back. **Dark blue coat, jeans, sleepy expression. We're on a mission in the mapinguari's habitat.**

??? OK, you got me on that one. I'm looking it up.

I bet Capt. Fuzzbutt would let you ride him, Zoe typed.

Mapinguaris sound dangerous, Jasmin wrote back. **You need a BFF sidekick with a totally menacing tennis racket.**

Do not sneak out of your house right now, you lunatic, Zoe typed. **We are fine. I will update you in the morning.**

SIIIIIGH, Jasmin responded. **OK. Call me first thing.**

Good night.

Don't let the chupacabras bite. OMG, you don't have those, do you?

Stop making me laugh! The mapinguari is sleeping.

OK, OK. I'm off to delete all evidence of this conversation. Good night!

"I'm guessing from your face that that was Jasmin," Blue whispered.

"She's amazing," Zoe whispered back, trying to wipe the grin off her face.

"Yeah," he agreed. "I mean—for you! Amazing—friend—type—person." He coughed and punched Logan's shoulder.

"Shhh," she scolded him. "Don't wake up Guava."

Zoe, Logan, and Blue sat quietly for a long time, staring at the wall. It was very high and made of stone, but on this side Zoe could see that a lot of the vines had grown up along it, creating an easy crisscross web to climb down. They'd have to fix that. She wished she had her notepad so she could add it to her to-do list.

Stupid dragons, she thought, shaking her head with frustration. Why had they let Mr. Wilde in—not just once, but three times? She hadn't had a chance to question them yet because of all the chaos of the merfolk strike. She knew Scratch had neglected his guard duty to go out hunting sheep a few times, but she'd checked the log and both Clawdius and Firebella had ignored Mr. Wilde's trespassing as well. And if they were willing to ignore him, they could have ignored anybody. For all she knew, the Sterlings could have been climbing in and out of the Menagerie for months without a single dragon saying boo about it. After all, they hadn't so much as snorted when Jasmin came into the Menagerie.

She hugged her knees, thinking of Jasmin. She'd wanted to bring Jasmin into the Menagerie and show her all the animals for practically her entire life. It had seemed wildly unfair to her when Jonathan got to meet them instead, just because he was Ruby's boyfriend. And it had been even *more* unfair when Jonathan betrayed their trust and the rules got even stricter.

For a while, she'd started to think she'd never have any friends but Blue, possibly ever again.

And then she'd found Logan in her unicorn stables, holding a griffin cub.

She glanced sideways at him again. He'd changed everything. Now she had him, and Marco, and, most miraculous of all, she had Jasmin back. But it had all started with Logan.

"I don't think your dad's coming," Blue half whispered, half yawned. "Maybe we could go back and just watch the security monitors."

"Right. Which, in Blue-speak, means *I* could watch the security monitors and *you* could nap on the couch," Zoe said.

"Well, if you insist," Blue said with a grin.

"Wait," Logan whispered, touching Zoe's knee. He pointed to the top of the wall, where a small beam of light was skimming the treetops on the other side. It blinked out, and then there was a quiet scraping sound.

Like someone leaning a ladder up against the wall.

Zoe could feel the tension humming through Logan. She realized she was a tiny bit terrified. She was sure Logan's dad wouldn't hurt them—but she was also sure he wouldn't be happy to see them.

Maybe I should have told Mom and Dad about this.

She rubbed her damp palms on her jeans and felt for the flashlight in her pocket.

Bump. Bump. Bump. Footsteps climbing the ladder.

They didn't have night vision without the security camera, but the moon cast enough light that they could see the shadowy head that slowly rose up above the wall. A tall, lanky figure swung himself over and carefully climbed down. He glanced around and took a couple of steps into the trees.

The will-o'-the-wisps came shooting through the woods and surrounded him, bobbing and weaving frantically. In the light they cast, Zoe could clearly see Logan's dad's face. He was smiling at the little fireballs.

Logan drew in his breath. His dad held out one hand and let the will-o'-the-wisps dance around it for a minute. His smile slowly faded, and then he dropped his hand and started toward the fence with a serious expression on his face.

"HRRRRRMMMMMGGRRRRR." A growl shivered through the forest. The hairs on Zoe's arms stood on end. She whirled and saw the enormous shadow of the mapinguari come shambling out of his hut.

"RRRRRRRRRAAAAARRRRGH," Guava roared. He stood up to his full height and roared again. The moon reflected off his long, sharp, shiny claws.

Logan's dad had frozen in place when he heard the first growl. Now he took a tentative step back toward the wall, which was closer than the fence.

The mapinguari swiveled its head toward him . . . and charged.

THIRTEEN

"Dad!" Logan screamed. He threw himself out of the bushes just as his dad went hurtling past, running for the wall. They crashed into each other and sprawled into the dirt.

"HRRRRRRAAARRRRRR," the mapinguari roared again, taking another slow, stomping step toward them. Logan sat up and scrabbled inside his shirt for the scarab. It must have protected his dad from the creature before. It would protect him again . . . Logan hoped. He pulled it out and held it up.

"Guava, stop!" Zoe cried. She tossed the flashlight to Blue, ran up to the giant sloth, and shoved its belly with both hands. "Behave! Bad mapinguari! No eating people! Bad!"

The mapinguari stopped and grumbled loudly. Blue got the flashlight switched on, and in its beam Logan could see that the overgrown sloth was giving Zoe a very reproachful look.

"I don't care what your venerable furry ancestors ate," Zoe said, putting her hands on her hips. "Like me and Dad, you are a respectable vegetarian. If you go back to bed right now and leave this nice trespasser alone, tomorrow I will bring you that eggplant thing from Veggie Monster that you like so much."

Guava grumbled again and reached his claws toward Logan and his dad.

"Right. Now," Zoe said firmly. "Or there will be NO BUBBLES in your next bath."

The giant sloth sighed enormously, rattling the leaves on the trees. He dropped to all fours and slowly shambled back inside his hut.

Logan twisted around and found his dad sitting up, rubbing his head, and looking rather stunned.

"See?" Logan said. "I told you Zoe was pretty cool."

His dad smiled weakly.

"Also," Logan said, "how dare you give me your scarab and then sneak in here with no protection? Do you know how mad I would be if you got eaten by a mapinguari?"

"Not as mad as I would be if you got stomped by a dragon," his dad answered.

"They're not very stompy," Logan said. "More . . . fire-breathy. And actually fairly chill if you don't bother them."

"Why are you cavorting with dragons?" his father demanded. He climbed to his feet and hauled Logan up, too. "That is exactly what I was afraid of. Anything could happen to you in here, especially since—since—" He fell silent, glancing at Zoe.

"Since you sabotaged us?" Zoe said challengingly. "Since you deliberately let the griffins escape and blew a hole in the Reptile House and framed Scratch for murder?"

Logan studied his dad's face and felt a surge of relief. There was nothing but confusion there.

"What?" Dad said. "What are you talking about? Who's Scratch?"

"Why else have you been sneaking into our Menagerie?" Zoe asked.

"Because you have Abigail!" Logan's dad burst out. He turned and gripped Logan's shoulders. "The Kahns have your mother, I'm sure of it. I've been looking for her all over this place, but there are areas I haven't gotten into yet. And then I was so worried they'd take you, too—but now they'll wipe our memories—and then who—who will rescue Abigail—" Dad broke off and rubbed his eyes.

"No, no, you've got it all wrong," Logan said, putting his hands over his dad's. "Zoe's family is as worried about Mom as we are. They're good people, Dad. Mom was friends with them. If she told you about this place, didn't she tell you that?"

"Yes," Dad admitted. "But she could have been tricked. There was a clue. . . ." He trailed off again.

"Mom wasn't easily fooled," Logan pointed out. "You know that."

"I think, if you guys don't mind, that maybe we should go talk to my parents," Zoe said. "I double-triple promise we won't kraken ink you, Mr. Wilde. I'm sure they'll want to meet you. And then we can tell you what we know about Abigail's disappearance."

Logan looked up at his dad, who hesitated for a long minute, then finally nodded. A thrill of hope ran along Logan's skin. Maybe if they put together everything they all knew about how Mom disappeared—maybe then they'd figure out where she was . . . and how to get her back.

Mr. and Mrs. Kahn were surprisingly calm about being woken up in the middle of the night to meet Logan's dad. But then, they were pretty calm about everything, as far as Logan had seen. They sat and listened with mugs of tea in front of them, bathrobes over their pajamas, as if strangers scrambled over their walls and accused them of kidnapping all the time.

Dad, understandably, had said no to tea, or anything else that might have kraken ink in it.

Logan sat next to his dad, in the warm yellow light of Zoe's living room, with Zoe and then Blue on his other side.

It was surreal, but also felt somehow right, having everyone together and talking about everything at last.

"I hired a private investigator," Dad said intently, tracing his finger along one of the grooves in the heavy wooden dining room table. "He said Abigail was last seen renting a car in Cheyenne, but someone else returned it—a young man. I thought perhaps that was your son."

"Matthew," Mrs. Kahn supplied. "No, we didn't know about the rental car."

Logan caught Zoe looking at him. Was she thinking what he was thinking? *Jonathan Sterling?*

Zoe's mom went on. "We got a call from her after she left Cheyenne—she said she was on her way with the Chinese dragon and would be here in about two hours. Usually with Abigail's driving that means more like one and a half, but we waited and waited, and she never showed up. We called her a hundred times, but she never answered."

"Same here," said Logan's dad. "But she did get to Xanadu that night. My PI said the last signal from her cell phone came from somewhere around here, before it went dead. That's why I thought she must have made it to this place." He waved one hand at the Menagerie around them.

"But why would you think we kidnapped her?" Mr. Kahn asked mildly. "We were getting the Chinese dragon anyway. Why would we want a Tracker locked in our cellar, when she could be out finding and saving more creatures?"

Logan saw his dad's eyes dart around the room, as if he was looking for a hidden cellar door, before he caught himself. With a sigh, he reached into his inside coat pocket and pulled out a wrinkled white rectangle.

Logan recognized it immediately. It was the last postcard his mom had sent them. The only postcard Logan hadn't wanted to put in his box of postcards from her. He'd read it about three thousand times that first week and then, when it still refused to make any sense, he'd thrown it out. He hadn't realized his dad had kept it; he must have salvaged it from the trash.

"Abigail sent us a postcard after she disappeared," Logan's dad explained. "It's all nonsense, doesn't sound like her at all. She says we won't see her again—that's crazy. She would never, never in a million years leave Logan. She's told me every day since he was born that he's her heart and soul."

Logan stared down at the table, blinking hard. He remembered her saying that, too.

"I wish she'd told me what she really does," he mumbled. His dad reached over to put one hand on Logan's shoulder.

"She was planning to," he said. "According to SNAPA rules, she had to wait until you turned thirteen. Then she was going to tell you everything. She even had this crazy idea that you might want to go to some kind of mythical creature tracking summer camp."

"Camp Underpaw!" Zoe chimed in. "He does! He should! He'd be perfect for it."

Logan's dad gave her a curious smile.

"Can I see the postcard?" Mrs. Kahn asked. She studied the front of it—a bland "Greetings from WYOMING" banner with a silhouette of a cowboy on a horse below it. It was nothing like the kinds of postcards Mom usually sent: sweeping vistas of Costa Rican rain forests, or Indonesian elephants giving themselves a shower on a beach, or Japanese monkeys swinging over a sunlit koi pond.

Mrs. Kahn flipped it over and slid it sideways so Zoe's dad could read it at the same time. Logan could remember the words as clearly as if he'd read them yesterday.

> *Hello my dear wild boys,*
>
> *I am so sorry about this, but a new job opportunity has come up that I can't say no to. It means I can't come home—in fact, I probably won't see you again. I know it's sad, but the silver lining is that you won't have to worry about me anymore. Just know I am on the kind of grand adventure we used to have with Roberto, Louise, and Fanny. I love you both. Take care of yourselves.*
>
> *Love, Abigail*

"Wow," said Mrs. Kahn. "That doesn't sound like Abigail at all."

"Agreed," said Mr. Kahn, shaking his head. "Someone made her write this."

Logan's chest ached with guilt. He hadn't even questioned the message. He'd just assumed that his mother meant everything she'd said. He'd been so mad at her all these months, thinking she'd left him and that she didn't really care about him at all. But the Kahns had known right away that it was all fake. His *dad* had known, too.

"You could have told me," Logan said to his dad. "I thought it was real."

"I wasn't sure which would be worse," his dad admitted. "If you thought she left, but was okay, or if you knew she'd been kidnapped."

"What made you think kidnapped?" Mrs. Kahn picked up the postcard and frowned at the top right corner.

"And what made you think it was us?" Mr. Kahn asked again.

"Roberto and Louise," said Logan's dad, pointing at the card. "I think she's hinting at Robert Louis Stevenson. *Kidnapped* was one of the books Abigail bought after Logan was born, for his future library."

"What about Fanny?" Logan asked. "Is that a real name? Who is it?"

"That, I don't know," his dad said. "If it's a clue, I haven't figured it out. But then there was something—"

"Under the stamp?" Mrs. Kahn guessed.

He nodded and took a small bag out of his pocket. Unzipping it, he tipped the contents onto the table: a tiny microchip, smaller than one of Logan's fingernails. Logan peered at it, trying to figure out what it was. He wished *he'd* noticed there was something under the stamp. It made him feel like his parents were both kind of secret agents, sending each other hidden spyware and messages in code.

"Aha," said Mr. Kahn. "I see. It all makes sense now."

"Aha what?" Zoe asked. "What aha?"

"It's the chip from Abigail's Tracker ring," Mrs. Kahn said. "All Trackers have them—it's a kind of identification card to let them into places like the Menagerie, no matter what alarm system is in place."

"That's how you've been getting in," Logan realized. "This little thing makes the dragons think you're Mom?"

"Or at least some authorized SNAPA representative," Mr. Kahn said with a nod.

"And that's why you thought *we* had her," Mrs. Kahn filled in. "Because the microchip seemed like a clue about where she was."

Logan's dad nodded tiredly. "She'd explained her ring to me before, so I knew what this would do. I thought I was supposed to sneak in here and look for her. I don't know why else she would send it to me."

"There's one possibility," Mr. Kahn said gently. "She wanted *us* to trust *you*. She hoped if you came to us with her microchip and this postcard, then we'd know she wanted us to include you in our investigation."

Logan looked up at his dad. There was some kind of war going on behind his face, and Logan could guess what it was about. Should he trust these people he'd suspected for months? Were they right about Abigail's plan with the microchip? Had he been all wrong this whole time?

Worst of all, had he wasted the last six months looking in the wrong place because he'd misunderstood her message?

"It's okay, Dad," Logan said. "Now we're all together, we'll find her. I know it."

"I totally didn't know their rings did that," Zoe said. Logan guessed, gratefully, that she was deliberately distracting everyone from staring at Logan's dad.

"It's a fairly well-kept secret," said Mrs. Kahn. "We wouldn't want anyone to get the idea to steal one of them."

"It's a good thing Jonathan never found out, for instance," Mr. Kahn pointed out. "Or the Sterlings could have taken it and snuck in here anytime they wanted."

"The Sterlings?" Logan's dad jerked back in his seat. "What do they have to do with this?"

"Nothing for sure," Mrs. Kahn said quickly. "It's just a theory we have." She explained about the map in Mr. Sterling's study and about the kraken ink Jonathan was supposed to take but didn't.

"Ohhh," said Logan's dad. "Yes. Okay, Mr. Sterling showed me some plans for an amusement park in this area, but they weren't as specific as what you're describing. He wanted to talk about permits for a zoo from the wildlife department, but he didn't say anything about mythical creatures. Understandably, I suppose. But if they're planning to take over the Menagerie—surely you don't think they were involved in Abigail's disappearance?"

"I find it hard to imagine the Sterlings as kidnappers," Mr. Kahn said doubtfully. "It's not like they need to hold anyone for ransom; they have more money than J. K. Rowling. And if they were going to use Abigail to blackmail us somehow, why haven't they done anything about it in the last six months?"

"Maybe it was an accident," Zoe suggested. "Maybe they tried to grab the Chinese dragon and ended up getting Abigail as well. Maybe they've been trying to figure out what to do with her. They have to be careful, knowing we could kraken ink them if they showed their hand too early."

"Dad," Logan said suddenly, sliding the postcard back in front of him. "Look! Here where she talks about the silver lining—what if that's a clue? Sterling silver? Maybe she's trying to tell us that the Sterlings are the ones who kidnapped her."

But his dad was shaking his head. "I thought of that," he said. "I did. I investigated just about everything having anything to do with silver in this town. But my PI checked into the Sterlings and they were out of town skiing in Colorado when Abigail was here. Not only that, they're in the spotlight all the time. When they're not at home, they're almost always at campaign events out in public. He trailed them for three days and they didn't go anywhere where someone could be hidden away, let alone someone and a Chinese dragon."

"They could have henchmen," Zoe pointed out. "People to carry out their evil deeds for them."

"Minions," Blue offered sagely.

"Let's not get carried away," said Mrs. Kahn. "The Sterlings are hardly supervillains. I mean, Mrs. Sterling runs the PTA bake sale every year, for goodness' sakes."

"But we do think they must have someone working with them," Logan said. "Right? Whoever is really sabotaging the Menagerie? Since now we know it wasn't my dad. Maybe that person is also the one who grabbed my mom and the dragon for them. Maybe he's the one who brings her food and stuff, so the Sterlings can look clean and aboveboard."

"Did SNAPA find out *anything* from Miss Sameera or Pelly?" Zoe asked her parents.

Mr. Kahn sighed. "Pelly said she never saw her abductor. She was knocked out by the tranquility mist when she was taken from the Aviary, and she woke up in a cabin in the woods somewhere. She screamed bloody murder, as you can imagine. Miss Sameera, meanwhile, apparently spotted a young man driving a van out into the woods and followed him—don't ask me why. She didn't know him, that much is clear. But when she heard Pelly screaming, she went in and got her. That's all the agents told me."

"We could have shown her pictures!" Zoe cried. "Maybe she would have recognized Jonathan! Or led us back to the cabin!" She ran her hands through her disheveled hair. "Our best source and they wiped her. I can't believe they did that."

"They didn't want her out in the world with any mythical creature memories," her dad reminded her. "They have a job to do, remember. And this morning they didn't know anything about the Sterlings, the map, or a saboteur."

"We'll find our answers some other way," Mrs. Kahn said reassuringly.

"Will we?" Zoe said. "By Tuesday?" She stopped, looking guilty.

"Tuesday?" her mom echoed. "What do you mean?"

"Um," said Zoe. "Well . . . let's just say I have reason to believe that Mr. Sterling is planning to expose the Menagerie on Tuesday, at his election night party."

"What?" Mr. Kahn cried.

"Let's just say a bit more than that," Mrs. Kahn said firmly. "What 'reason'?"

Zoe scrunched up her face. "A . . . reliable source?"

"Zoe." Mr. Kahn's tone was ominous. "You know we've always trusted you more than Ruby. Don't make us wrong about that."

"Okay," Zoe blurted. "I just—hadn't figured out what to do about it yet—and this may not be the best time to tell you this, but . . . Jasmin kind of sort of knows about the Menagerie now, too. As of this morning. But in a totally fine, I-trust-her, she's-nothing-like-the-rest-of-her-family kind of way."

Her parents stared at her in disbelief.

"It was an accident?" Zoe offered.

"It was," Logan chimed in. "She came over here, and then the basilisk escaped, and it was all chaos after that."

"All right," Mrs. Kahn said slowly.

"I suppose it's no worse than the rest of her family knowing," said Mr. Kahn. "If we have to kraken ink them all, she'll end up getting it, too."

"But maybe we don't have to kraken ink *her*," Zoe protested. "She's on *our* side. She warned me about her dad's election night plans. And she'll help us, I know she will."

Her parents exchanged a look and Mrs. Kahn lifted one shoulder. "Let's see what happens," she said. "I always did like Jasmin much more than the rest of them."

"So what do we do next?" Logan asked. "To find Mom? What can Dad and I do?"

But he knew before the Kahns even shook their heads. They had no idea. No one knew how to catch the saboteur or track down Mom's kidnappers.

They were at a dead end.

FOURTEEN

Snuffle. Snuffle. Snuffle.

Logan drifted slowly up from the depths of sleep.

Was I dreaming? Did I have nightmares? He had a vague sense that kelpies and basilisks and masked kidnappers had all been lurking in his dreams, but that they'd all been vacuumed out suddenly, leaving him to the most peaceful night of rest he'd had since Mom left.

He kept his eyes closed for a moment, wishing he could stay in that serene darkness just a little longer.

Something was gently poking his head. It felt squashy and warm and a little furry, like Captain Fuzzbutt's trunk. The mammoth must have come to visit him on the floor of Blue's room—and he should probably sit up before he got accidentally stepped on.

Logan opened his eyes and found himself nose to nose with an animal that was decidedly not Captain Fuzzbutt. It was a lot smaller, for one thing, only about the size of a Saint Bernard. It looked like something he'd once seen in a zoo—a tapir, he thought, kind of a cross between a pygmy hippopotamus and an anteater—except that this had soft, teal-blue fur and claws like a tiger's.

"Snuffle," the creature declared calmly. It poked his head with its long, wobbly snout. Its eyes were tranquil pools of dark green. It didn't look like a man-eating monster, but then, neither had the kelpie, at first.

"Blue," Logan whispered, trying not to startle it. "Blue, am I about to get eaten?"

"Hmmmrmf," Blue answered helpfully.

"Seriously! Blue!"

"Yeah, sure. Whenever I get around to it," Blue mumbled in his sleep.

Logan felt around on the carpet with the hand farthest from the animal until he found something he could throw at Blue's head, which turned out to be a paperback copy of *Holes*.

"OW," Blue protested, pulling the comforter over his head. "Duuuuuuude. Uncalled for."

The creature wiggled its snout at Logan as if it was

amused. Or possibly preparing to suck his brains out through his ears.

"There's something in here," Logan said urgently. "Something with claws."

Blue poked his head back out and squinted at the furry blue tapir. "Oh," he said. "That's just Mochi."

"And on a deadliness scale from qilin to basilisk," Logan asked, "where does he fall?"

"Completely not deadly," Blue said, burrowing back into his pillows. "They eat nightmares, that's all. Go away and let me sleep."

Reassured, Logan held out his hand to the little animal. "Hey, Mochi," he said. "Is that what you were doing here? Eating my crazy nightmares? Is that why I slept so well?"

Mochi blinked again, slowly, then turned and snuffled at the door, where Logan spotted the shadow of two feet. He got up and opened the door to find Zoe on the other side.

"Oh, hey," she said, as if standing in the hallway in her pajamas was totally normal. "I see you met our baku."

"Yes, he's great," Logan said. He paused, then tilted his head at her. "Did you send him in to eat my nightmares?"

"Well," Zoe said, fidgeting with the hem of her pajama shirt. "I thought maybe . . . after yesterday . . . well, there were more than a couple things you might be having nightmares about."

"Thanks," Logan said, smiling at her. He felt completely

different from how he'd felt last night. He wondered if the baku had gobbled up his worries and despair along with his nightmares of a basilisk tongue in his ear. Suddenly he had 110 new ideas about how to start looking for his mom. If he could track missing griffin cubs and a qilin, he could find a kidnapped Tracker with a Chinese dragon. He could do this. He *had* to do this.

"I want to talk to Nero," he said. "And Scratch. And the unicorns." He grabbed his sweatshirt from the floor. "And maybe Ruby knows more than she realizes. And maybe Jasmin can find something we can use. And—"

"We need to make a list!" Zoe said excitedly. "I'll get my notepad. Meet you downstairs." She darted off to her room with the baku ambling behind her.

Logan got dressed quickly and headed downstairs. It was early, probably not even eight o'clock in the morning yet. Out in the Menagerie, near the unicorn stables, Keiko was doing some kind of martial arts maneuvers by herself. Logan could also see the golf cart zipping around the lake toward the Reptile House, so someone else was up and probably on their way to feed the pyrosalamanders. He wasn't sure what the Kahns had done to contain Basil while they fixed the hole in the wall, but he hoped it was something incredibly secure.

Logan's dad was asleep on one of the couches in the living room, stretched out under an eggplant-colored blanket with his feet sticking over the edge of the couch. It was kind of awesome that he'd agreed to stay over. Logan hoped that meant he'd decided to fully trust the Kahns.

A small snuffling sound by the stairs made him turn around. Mochi was descending slowly on his little tiger paws.

"Hey," Logan said, beckoning. Mochi wandered up to him and wuffled around his shoes. Logan pointed into the living room, at his dad. "Do you think you could help him, too? I bet his nightmares are as bad as mine."

Mochi's eyes lit up and a little pinkish-gray tongue slipped out of his mouth to lick his nose. The baku prowled quietly across the pillows and books scattered around the big room. *That's what the tiger paws are for*, Logan guessed. *So it can sneak up without waking the sleepers.* It reached Logan's dad and gently began feeling his head with its snout.

"I wish I could take a picture," Logan whispered to Zoe as she came down the stairs. "Dad has never looked sillier."

She grinned and went into the kitchen. Grabbing two bananas and her shoes, she led the way out through the garage and into the Menagerie.

"Just in case the sliding doors woke your dad," she said once they were outside, handing Logan one of the bananas.

"Thanks," he said. "Who can we talk to first?"

"The unicorns will be asleep right now, after their usual midnight run," Zoe said. "And they will be EXTREMELY unhelpful if we wake them up. We could try Nero, but it might not work—he's calmed down a bit, but he still bursts into flames any time we bring up the night Pelly was abducted."

"Maybe we could get Marco over to do some birdish bonding with him," Logan suggested. "He is kind of the closest thing we have to a bird expert, right?"

Zoe pushed her hair back behind her ears. "He is going to start thinking we only like him for his rooster side," she said.

"I'll tell him Keiko is awake already," Logan said, pulling out his phone. "That should make up for it."

"Tell him to meet us at the dragons," Zoe suggested. "We can talk to Scratch while we wait. Maybe I can even brush his teeth, since the SNAPA agents seemed *really* serious about us doing that." She wrinkled her nose.

The dragons lived in a set of caves in the cliff at the back of the Menagerie. Zoe stopped first at a small shed near the base of the cliff and brought out a green toothbrush that was taller than Logan, with curved bristles that looked designed to get around the dragons' fangs. She also pulled out a giant silver tube marked DENTAL HYGIENE—FOR DRAGONS ONLY and passed it to Logan to carry.

They did not stop for fireproof suits, Logan noticed. For someone who worried about almost everything, Zoe was unexpectedly not concerned about a dragon setting her on fire.

As they started up the rocky path, Marco texted back: **Save the day AGAIN? Oh, all right, if I must. This better involve pancakes.**

Awesome, thanks, Logan texted back.

His phone buzzed again: **I'm dead serious about the pancakes!**

And then again, a minute later: **Ask Zoe if Keiko likes blue or red better.**

"Tell him Keiko likes running in the woods at night, ripping the heads off of birds, and hypnotizing dopey middle schoolers into doing anything she wants," Zoe said.

Red, Logan guessed.

They were halfway to the dragons when a hideous noise suddenly split the air.

"DDAAAAAAAAAAAAAAAAAAAAAAAAAAAAA
AAAAAAAAAAAAAAAAAAAAAAAAAAAAAA
AAAAAAAAAAAAAAAAAAAAAAAAAAAAAA
AAAAAAAAAAAAAAAAAAAAAAAAAAAAAA
AAAAAAAAAAAAAAAAAAAYYYYYYYYYYYY
YYYYY!!!!!!!!"

"Oh no," Zoe said, stopping with a grimace. She sat down on a rock and covered her ears. "You'll want to do this, too!" she shouted.

Logan copied her, but the caterwauling was so loud that it didn't seem like anything could block it out.

"BROKEN ARE THE CLOUOUOUOUDS! RISEN IS THE SUUUUUUN! ARIIIIIIIIIIIIIIIIIISE ALL YOU BEINGS OF MUUUUUUUUUUUUD! GREETING THE DAAAAY IS FIREBELLA! SINGING UP THE

DAAAAWN IS FIREBELLA! SOON TO BE CRUSHING AND EATING HER FOES IS GLOOOOOOOOORIOUS THE FIIIIIIIREBELLAAAAAAAA!"

"Hey, did she say something about crushing and eating someone?" Logan shouted at Zoe.

"Ancient dragon tradition," Zoe yelled back. "They sometimes sing a dawn song to announce to the world how menacing and magnificent they are, and they're as loud as possible to show they're not afraid who hears them. Firebella's the only one of our three who still does it sometimes."

The piercing, ear-rattling noise went on for another minute, then finally ended with another dramatic "DAAAAAA AAAAAAAAAAAAAAAAAAAAAAAAAAAAAAAAA AAAAAAAAAAAAAAAAAAAAAAAAAAAAAAAA AAAAAAAAAAAAAAAAAAAAAAAAAAAAAAA AAAAAAAAAAAAAAAAAAAAAAAAAAAAAAAA AAAAYYYYYYYYYYYYYYYY!!!!!!!!!!!!!!!!!!!!!"

Several moments later, Zoe slowly took her hands away from her ears. "I think it's safe," she said. "Firebella usually makes up for her volume by at least being succinct."

"How," said Logan, "in the name of dragons have your neighbors never heard that? I'm fairly sure my neighbors in *Chicago* just heard that."

"It's our thing," Zoe said with a little shake of her head. "You know, Bob." She started up the path again.

"Wait—it has a name?" Logan said. "I thought your thing

was a machine, like some kind of cloaking device."

"We shouldn't talk about Bob," Zoe said. "She doesn't like it."

"Who doesn't like it?" Logan asked. "Bob? Bob is a girl?"

"Do you have your questions ready for Scratch?" Zoe asked, as if she hadn't heard him. "Dragons are notoriously difficult to interview. They absolutely cannot stay on topic."

You should talk, Logan thought, but he was already starting to forget what he'd asked about. With enormous mental force, he dragged his mind back to their conversation and thought, *Bob. Bob. Bob. This must be its power; it's a creature with some kind of magic that keeps people from noticing it, talking about it, or remembering it. And it works on the whole Menagerie, probably because if its home is safe, it'll be safe, too. I've never heard of a mythical creature who could do that . . . well, oh, right. That's the whole point of its power.*

Firebella, the enormous black dragon, was sitting on the edge of the cliff, staring out at the Menagerie. Her wings were spread and smoke spiraled slowly from her nostrils. She looked like she was waiting for someone to come challenge her to a fight.

Her vast, SUV-sized head turned toward them, catching Logan and Zoe in her yellow glare.

"Good morning, Firebella," Zoe said. "Your dawn song was beautiful, as always."

The dragon regarded them with slitted eyes.

Zoe elbowed Logan.

"I liked it, too," Logan said quickly.

"Quaking with fear are the foes of Firebella," the dragon mused, sliding more smoke out her nose. "Brimming with cowardice are the foes of Firebella. Wheeling about us are the stars in endless time and more-time, and yet never coming are the foes of Firebella." A dark forked tongue slipped in and out of her huge, sharp teeth. "Ever so dismal and moreover-so thwarted for the lack of crushing and eating is Firebella."

Logan wasn't entirely sure he'd understood that right, but he was pretty sure he didn't like the sound of it.

"Firebella, a friend is coming to the Menagerie in a few minutes," Zoe said, glancing at her watch. "His name is Marco Jimenez, and you've met him before—we cleared him to come to the jury selection for Scratch's trial. So please don't set off the intruder alert when he comes in, all right?"

There was an unsettlingly long pause.

"Unfamiliar with this medieval torture device is Firebella," said the dragon unexpectedly. Logan realized that her malevolent gaze was trained on the toothbrush Zoe was holding. "But sensing are we all of the sinister plan of it. Dark is the nefarious purpose of yon bristle stick. Fooling Firebella are you not. Full grim is the outlook for she who approaches teeth of Firebella for any other reason than being eaten." The dragon thought for a moment. "Grim also for those who approach to be eaten, truth is."

"Don't worry, I'm not going to brush your teeth," Zoe promised. "This is Scratch's toothbrush. Yours is purple. I'm sure Dad will show it to you one day."

"Hmmmmm," said Firebella. "A more noble color is purple, yet near the teeth of Firebella shall bristle stick never come, even of regal hue. Full warned are puny humankind."

"Okay," Zoe said. "I feel full warned."

"Me too," Logan agreed fervently.

"So," Zoe said. "You're all set for Marco? Then we'll go brush Scratch's teeth now."

"Hmmmmmmm," Firebella said again. Logan could feel her gaze pricking along his spine as he climbed up to the next cave, where Scratch lived.

The rust-colored dragon came bounding out of his cave, beaming with delight at the sight of them.

"Favorite visitors of Scratch!" he declared happily. "Friends of small stature and smart eyes! Saviors of Scratch! Beholden is Scratch for ever and evermore! Even forgiving is Scratch for unfortunate return of nasty honk-bird!"

"We did have to bring her back to prove you were innocent," Zoe pointed out. "The two were connected."

Scratch waved this away with a dismissive claw. "Mountain-soaring high is the heart of Scratch. Gratefully committed to earth are talons of Scratch. Safe forevermore from Scratch are vast tragically wasted hordes of fluff on legs."

"That's good," Zoe said. "Nice work not sneaking out and

eating sheep, although not that you could anyway, now that your restraints are fixed and your electric collar is working and we'll be checking them every night."

"Thoroughly unnecessary these precautions of dragon attendants," Scratch said with dignity. "Ever and ever-so good will be Scratch for always."

"Sure, okay," Zoe said. "Logan has some questions for you."

Scratch inclined his head graciously toward Logan.

"We're trying to figure out who let you loose," Logan said. "Like you said, you were set up. Someone broke your chain and disabled the electric collar so that it would look like you killed Pelly. They wanted you to go on trial and—uh—" He paused, not wanting to remind Scratch of the Exterminator. "Well, they were trying to disrupt the Menagerie, clearly. They did the same thing with the griffin cubs and the basilisk, making sure they were able to get out. So we need to figure out who it is, and we're hoping you can help."

"Yearning to help is Scratch," said the dragon, "but not so rotund with wisdom is Scratch."

"Just tell me what you remember," Logan said. "Like who visited you the day your ankle chain broke."

"Broke itself boom!" said Scratch. "Down and off clank! Curious and delightful the day! Er, for young and foolish the dragon that was Scratch of yore."

"It's all right," Zoe said, pulling out her notepad. "Just tell us what you remember. It must have happened after the SNAPA agents first came through for inspection, because I know they both checked your anklet and it was fine then."

"Indeedness," said Scratch. "Day the following it was. Awake in the star-time and alert for guarding was Scratch when sound of freedom went CLANK in the night."

"So who was here in between?" Logan asked. "Anyone unusual?"

Scratch furrowed his brow thoughtfully and started tracing grooves in the dirt with one claw. "Elder female attendant first."

"My mom," Zoe filled in. "Maybe don't ever tell her you call her that."

"Young Tracker student next."

"Matthew?" Zoe said. "Why was he up here?"

"Wielding same barbaric device came he," Scratch said, pointing at the toothbrush with a small growl. "Having none of that was I."

"Oh," Zoe said, "that's right, that was after the agents gave us their stern instructions about dragon tooth brushing, which must be a crazy new thing SNAPA has come up with. Matthew did tell me he gave it a wildly unsuccessful shot."

"Anyone else besides Mrs. Kahn and Matthew?" Logan asked.

"Two the creatures of fish smell," Scratch said, nodding.

"What?" Zoe said, dropping her pen in surprise. "Mermaids? Why would mermaids come all the way up here? Do you mean Blue?"

"Not the boy of half-fish smell," said Scratch. "Older and more snappish were these. Came only to stomp and complain and scribble notes about grand all-mighty dreadful and dangerous the dragon presence."

"Did they go anywhere near your chains?" Logan asked.

"Poked them yes," said Scratch. "Much hullaballooing about insufficiency of security restraints. Tremendous the annoyance. Tempted to eat fish-smellers was Scratch. But NOBLY REFRAINED, did Scratch."

"Tremendously annoying," Zoe said. She wrote something down. "That does sound like mermaids. But if this entire thing turns out to be a long mermaid con to get themselves moved to Hawaii, I am going to BOIL THEM IN THEIR OWN FISH OIL."

"Was that it?" Logan asked.

"Sadly the no," said Scratch. "Also furball the huge and, later, the human of numbers and frowns."

"Furball the huge must be Mooncrusher cleaning out the caves. But numbers and frowns?" Zoe rubbed her forehead with the hand holding her pen, accidentally leaving a blue streak over her left eyebrow. "Who the heck?"

"Many the buttons?" Scratch offered. "Stern the face?

Displeased the expression always? Beloved much of long flapping papers?"

Zoe looked at Logan with a mystified expression.

"Well, who else is there?" he asked. "You, your parents, Blue, the mermaids—"

"Melissa!" Zoe said. "Blue's mom! Is that who you mean? Melissa?"

"Asked many the question for paper with small boxes," said Scratch.

"Yup. Melissa," Zoe said. "Well, that would have been procedural stuff related to the SNAPA visit. If that's it, then it must have been the mermaids—"

"And finally, furball the small," Scratch interrupted conclusively. "All visitors all. Surprisingly busy the day. Hardly time for stretching. No wonder it is that boom clank happened not until night."

"Wait, what?" Zoe asked. "Who's furball the small?"

"A griffin cub?" Logan guessed.

"Amusing the idea," Scratch said. "No, secret the furball friend of Firebella. Beloved of dragons. Decidedly not causer of trouble for Scratch. No need for furball the small on list the scribbly."

"But who is it?" Zoe asked. "Firebella has a secret furball friend? What ARE you talking about?"

Scratch clamped his mouth shut and shook his head vigorously.

"Oh dear," Zoe sighed.

"Put 'furball the small' for now," Logan said, "and we'll figure it out later." He heard scrambling and puffing noises from the cliff path and turned to see Marco hastily scooting past Firebella, who ignored him.

"Hey hey hey," Marco said with a huge grin as he reached them. "Meet us at the dragons! What is up! How awesome is the world that I am now getting texts like that?"

"I hope you deleted it," Zoe said, frowning slightly. "In case anyone ever gets ahold of your phone by accident."

"Oh, we're all doomed if that happens," Marco said. "Or else whoever finds it is going to look at my photos and be like, 'Um, is that a moose in his house? Why is that owl yelling at that squirrel? How many pictures of doughnuts can one guy take?' I should have mentioned, by the way, that I will also accept payment in doughnuts, if pancakes are not available."

"I'm sure we can muster pancakes," Zoe said, rubbing her temples again.

"We can head over to the Aviary now, right?" Logan said.

"I should at least *try* to brush Scratch's teeth again," Zoe sighed. "Everyone stand back."

"What?" Marco declared with glee. "That's a dragon TOOTHBRUSH? That is MAD CRAZY AWESOME."

"Exceptionally not thrilled is Scratch," the dragon pointed out. "Gorgeous and lovely the fearsome teeth as is."

"I know," Zoe said. "But we do want to keep SNAPA

happy, right? You especially should want to make them happy. Ahem."

Scratch sighed out a long stream of smoke.

"And that's the dragon toothpaste?" Marco guessed, pointing to the tube Logan had set down on a boulder. "Do dragons have mint-flavored toothpaste? Or is it, like, beef-flavored like Aidan's dog's toothpaste? Don't say chicken-flavored, by the way, let's all be sensitive here."

"I have no idea," Zoe said, swinging the toothbrush around and propping it against the rock.

"Let me help." Marco sprang over to the tube and opened the top. "Hmmm," he said, sniffing the contents. "Wow. It smells kind of like cheeseburgers. Or bacon. Can I taste it?"

"Why would you want to do that?" Logan asked, amused, but Marco was already squeezing a glob onto the toothbrush and swiping a bit on one of his fingers.

"Marco, you goof, we don't know what's in——" Zoe started to say.

Marco stuck the toothpaste in his mouth.

"Whoa, totally bacon," he said. "Maybe even ba——"

He stopped. His eyes rolled up in his head.

And he collapsed to the ground.

FIFTEEN

"MURDER!" shrieked Scratch. "TOOTHPASTE OF DEATH!"

"He's not dead!" Zoe cried, feeling her heart burst into overdrive. Logan knelt beside Marco, checking his pulse. "Right? Logan? Tell me he's not dead!"

"He's alive," Logan said, "but what happened? What's wrong with him?"

"I don't know!" Zoe said in a panic.

"MURDEROUS MURDERY TOOTHPASTE! CONSPIRACY OF DOOM!" howled Scratch. He ran in a small circle, flapping his wings frantically. His invisibility glamour was fading parts of his body in and out.

Zoe scrabbled her phone out of her pocket and called her dad.

"Hey, Zoe," her dad answered. "Just checking out the Reptile House. These repairs are not going to be cheap."

"Dad," Zoe cried. "Something's happened to Marco! We're up by Scratch and Marco tasted the dragon toothpaste and now he's collapsed and he's not moving and I don't know what to do!"

"I'll be right there," her dad said.

"Why so hating of Scratch is the world?" Scratch moaned, throwing himself down on the rocks and covering his head with his talons. "All the tragedies of the universe falling upon head of Scratch. Family exterminated! Accusing-face of honk-bird consumption! And now poison-bedecked toothpaste! Determined on death of Scratch is world!"

"It's not poison," Zoe said, trying to calm herself down. "It's probably just a sedative. A sedative isn't terrible. Although why would there be a sedative in the toothpaste?"

"Wait," Logan said. He was trying to roll Marco into a more comfortable position, but he stopped and stared up at the dragon. "Scratch, your family was exterminated?"

"Mother and sister both," said the dragon with a sigh. "Tragic the life of Scratch."

"That is really sad," Logan said, glancing at Zoe. "I didn't know dragons were exterminated that often."

"They're not!" Zoe said, puzzled. "I had no idea, Scratch. I thought SNAPA hardly ever exterminates dragons if they can help it. Two in one family has to be stratospherically rare."

"Nearly three," Logan pointed out, nodding at Scratch.

Zoe's mouth fell open. "There's no way that's a coincidence!" she said.

"As intoned Scratch long ago," said the dragon. "CONSPIRACY."

Could he be right? Zoe didn't know what to think. Why would anyone have it out for Scratch? He was dopey, but not a bad dragon. He'd been shipped here from another menagerie five years ago and he'd never gotten in any trouble until this sheep thing.

"We'll have to look it up. What were their names?" she asked Scratch.

"Sister Scritch, mother Lacewing," Scratch answered. "Scales now forever resting in the star-time." He heaved an enormous sigh.

"Here comes help," Logan said, pointing down the mountain.

Zoe's dad was sprinting up toward them; some distance behind him, Matthew was leading Captain Fuzzbutt along the path. The mammoth kept stopping to eye the drop below him and Matthew had to keep nudging him forward.

"Dad!" Zoe called.

He stopped to give her a quick hug and then hurried to Marco's side. "Tell me what happened."

Zoe explained again about the dragon toothpaste. "Is there something in it?" she asked her dad.

"DEATH, such as for instance?" Scratch suggested.

Her dad cautiously sniffed the tube. "Maybe SNAPA puts a sedative in to make it easier to brush their teeth without upsetting the dragons. I'm sure it's something innocuous, but let's get Marco back to the house and make sure he's all right."

"Thanks for your help, Scratch," Logan said.

"Entirely right about sinister bristle-stick were we," muttered Scratch, stomping back into his cave. "Never and also never and moreosever NEVER to be brushed shall be teeth of Scratch."

Logan helped Zoe's dad sling Marco over his back to get him down the twisting path to where Firebella sat, scowling. Captain Fuzzbutt reached the black dragon's level at the same time and stood there with a deeply anxious expression, twisting his trunk into worried loops.

Together, Zoe, Matthew, Logan, and her dad were able to get Marco up on top of the mammoth so that he was flopped out like a sloth on the Captain's shaggy brown back. Zoe took the mammoth's trunk and led the way carefully back down the mountain, while the others stayed close around Marco to make sure he didn't fall off.

At the Reptile House, they bundled Marco off the mammoth and into the golf cart, and Zoe and Logan rode back to the house with him and her dad. Marco let out a few snores, but didn't wake up at all. Zoe felt her phone buzzing but ignored it.

Logan's dad was standing outside the sliding doors, blinking at the Menagerie and rubbing his arms. He saw Mr. Kahn carrying Marco up to the house and his eyes widened in alarm.

"Don't worry," Logan said quickly. "He's just drugged. He got knocked out by something in the dragon toothpaste."

"Oh, right," said Mr. Wilde, raising his eyebrows. "Doesn't sound worrying at all."

They tumbled Marco onto one of the couches in the living room and Zoe tucked a blanket over him.

"I'll call SNAPA," her dad said. "Just to make sure whatever this is won't do anything weird to humans, like give them a tail." He hurried off into the kitchen.

"I *think* he's kidding," Zoe said to Logan's startled expression. Her phone vibrated again and she pulled it out. "Oh, it's Jasmin! Hang on a minute."

She answered the phone as she stepped outside. "Hi!"

"Hey, Zo!" Jasmin sang. "I have been totally snooping, it's excellent. Everyone is at church, so now I'm in Dad's study. And I have shocking news to report. Did you know that grown-up papers are INSANELY BORING?"

"Don't get caught, Jasmin," Zoe said anxiously.

"Oh, they won't be back for ages," Jasmin said. "Seriously, Zoe, all I can find from the last six months is campaign stuff and this one new company he bought. K-N-O-H? Maybe it's Russian. The N looks all squiggly on one end, you know, like that Russian kind of И? I'll take a photo and send it to you."

"Doesn't seem familiar," Zoe said as her phone buzzed with the incoming photo. "Jasmin—" She hesitated. How could she ask her best friend if her parents might have her other best friend's mom hidden away someplace? *By the way, hypothetically, if your parents were kidnappers, where might they keep a famous Tracker and a small dragon?*

"I wish I could invite you over tonight," Jasmin said. "My parents are having one of their massively boring dinner parties for big donors. I figured I'd lock myself in my room and watch *Frozen* like eight times in a row. Want to sneak in and join me?"

"That sounds like the most fun terrible idea ever," Zoe said with a grin. "Hey, listen, if your parents do have a, um, mythical creature to show to the cameras on Tuesday, where might they be keeping it? Do you have any idea? Could it be in your house somewhere?"

"No way," Jasmin said. "The cleaning people scrub every corner of this place from top to bottom once a week. Maybe our new summer cabin, the one on the lake? We haven't been out there since August."

"If it's the creature I'm thinking of," Zoe said, "then they've had it since the beginning of May. Maybe since your skiing trip? Do you remember that?"

"To Vail?" Jasmin asked. "You mean our skiing trip that was supposed to be all about family bonding and tradition, except Mom spent the whole time on her cell phone and Dad left early to do campaign stuff? I do remember that, yes, unfortunately."

Zoe was silent for a moment, her mind racing. Mr. Sterling had left the ski resort early? Did Mr. Wilde's private investigator know about that? Had Jasmin's dad snuck back here to kidnap Abigail?

"Well, there definitely weren't any weird-looking creatures at the cabin this summer," Jasmin said. "Sorry, I'll keep thinking about it."

"Thanks," Zoe said. Summer cabin on the lake . . . could that be where Pelly was taken? "Do you have any pictures of your cabin? Can you send me one?" Maybe Pelly would recognize it.

"Um . . . sure," Jasmin said. "Give me a few minutes. Oof, that is not a flattering campaign photo, Dad."

"I don't think you should be in his office," Zoe said nervously.

"Here's what I want to know," Jasmin said, clearly ignoring her. Zoe could hear papers rustling on the other end of the phone. "Why hasn't Jonathan gone back to college yet? He's been here, like, over a week, and he's obviously not leaving today because his stuff is still scattered in every room in the house, and P.S., why HE isn't getting yelled at for that is

ANOTHER mystery. Isn't he missing classes? He's so lame, maybe it doesn't make a difference."

"He's probably sticking around for the big reveal on election night," Zoe said.

"WHAT?" Jasmin said. "Jonathan is in on it, too? My family is so totally sinister."

Oh, Jasmin, Zoe thought. *I'm so worried they are, and I don't know how to protect you.*

"Whoops, that's Cadence on the other line," said Jasmin. "She wants to rehash the whole party, which, like, whatever, it wasn't even that fun after Blue left. Poor Cadence. She's no substitute for you, Zoe."

"No one's ever been a replacement for you, either," Zoe said, holding the phone tighter.

"But I should take this anyhow. Talk to you soon, okay?"

"Okay." Zoe stared at her screen for a minute after she hung up, wishing she could run over to Jasmin's house and check on her right now.

Her mom slid open the doors and leaned out. "Hey, kiddo. Up for a pancake?"

"*Mom,*" Zoe said.

"No lectures," her mom said, waving a spatula at her. "I know we're in the middle of yet another world-ending epic crisis, but we'll have a better chance of solving it on happy stomachs. Agreed?"

Zoe sighed and followed her mother back to the kitchen,

past Logan and his dad watching something on Logan's phone. Blueberries were scattered all over the counter, some of them half-buried in little mounds of spilled flour. The air smelled like maple syrup and melted butter. Zoe began collecting silverware and napkins for the big table.

"Morning," Blue said sleepily, wandering through.

"Nice of you to join us," Zoe said. "So far today we've interrogated Scratch, added mermaids to our sabotage suspect list, discovered there was something wonky in the dragon toothpaste, and carried Marco down the mountain on a mammoth because he tasted it and got knocked out. He's on the sofa, by the way."

"Cool," Blue said, propping himself against the counter. "Can I have whipped cream on my pancakes?"

"Mermaids, Blue!" Zoe said, banging forks and cups around. "Mermaids were poking around Scratch's chains the day they broke! They could totally be the ones sabotaging the Menagerie!"

"That seems pointless and unlikely," Blue observed calmly. "They could do that just by going on strike, the way they are now." He tipped his head toward the window. A number of merfolk were patrolling the lake again with their signs, splashing furiously up and down.

"Boy, I hope Matthew's friend is here by noon," Zoe said, swiping one hand through her hair.

Logan came into the kitchen and exchanged casual boy

nods and grunts with Blue. He went over to the cabinet and got down two glasses. Zoe liked that he knew where they were; she liked that he felt like a natural part of her home now.

"Oh!" she said, remembering. "Mom! I have a question for you."

"Oh dear, yes?" said her mother.

"Scratch told us his mother and sister were both exterminated," Zoe said. "Isn't that totally weird? I didn't even realize he had a sister. What are the chances they'd both have to be exterminated—and that Scratch nearly was, too?"

Logan put down the water pitcher to listen. Her mother studied her with a puzzled frown. The pancakes on the griddle were starting to bubble around the edges, but she didn't notice.

"That is odd," Mom said slowly. "I knew about what happened to his sister . . . but his mother, too? How very strange."

"What happened to his sister?" Logan asked. "He said her name was Scritch."

Zoe's mother turned back to the pancakes. "I didn't want to worry you, Zoe," she said.

"I'm already worried!" Zoe said. "All the time! Just tell me everything!"

"Okay," her mom said. "Scritch was the dragon at the Amazon menagerie."

It took a moment before everything that meant hit Zoe. "The one who went crazy and killed someone?" she said with a gasp. "That was why they closed the place down, wasn't it?"

"Right," said her mom. "Your father and I—well, we thought Scratch wasn't that kind of dragon, but I must admit we were concerned, briefly, after what happened to Pelly. We thought perhaps he had gone bad like his sister."

"Does anyone know why she went crazy?" Logan asked.

Zoe's mother shook her head. "There was no chance to talk with her or find out what set her off. She was on a rampage and had to be stopped . . ." Her voice trailed off, and she swiped at her eyes with the back of her hand.

Zoe sometimes forgot how much her mother loved all the animals. Mom had devoted her whole life to protecting and caring for mythical creatures. Although she hid her worries better, she must be just as anxious and heartbroken as Zoe was.

Zoe wrapped her arms around her mother from behind and gave her a hug. "It'll be all right, Mom," she said, trying to convince herself, too. "You'll see. SNAPA will help us stop the Sterlings, I know they will."

Zoe's mom turned and hugged her back.

The doorbell rang.

"Whoa, again?" Blue said. "That's just weird. I can't say I'm a big fan of this doorbell thing."

"I'LL GET IT!" Matthew bellowed, charging out of the living room and nearly running Logan over. "NO ONE ELSE TOUCH THAT DOOR!"

"Oooooooooooooooooooooooh," Zoe said. "It's Matthew's mystery Tracker camp girlfriend! The one who can mysteriously help with mermaid things! Quick, Mom, think of something wildly embarrassing to say."

"Oh, I'm sure it'll come naturally," her mom said with a grin.

Matthew skidded into the front hall, shot a stern look at the faces peeking out of the kitchen at him, smoothed down his hair, and opened the door.

It was not a mystery friend from Tracker camp.

It was Miss Sameera, the school librarian. The one whose mythical creature memories had been entirely wiped the day before.

"Hello!" she said brightly, beaming from ear to ear. "I'm here to see the unicorns!"

SIXTEEN

"Holy smokes," Matthew said.

Logan glanced at Zoe, but she looked as flabbergasted as he was. In fact, everyone looked as though they'd been smacked in the face with a mapinguari.

"Do I smell pancakes?" Miss Sameera sailed past Matthew, shrugging off her squashy neon pink coat to reveal a resplendently bright lime-green dress covered in yellow sunbursts. Gold tassels draped from the wrists and the hem where it brushed her toes. Her normally disheveled dark hair was smoothed back into a twisted updo. She noticed Matthew staring and twirled around, holding out her skirt. "Oh, yes, I dressed up! For the *unicorns*." She clasped her hands together with a dreamy sigh and then wafted into the kitchen.

"H-h-hi, Miss Sameera," Zoe stammered.

"Good morning," the librarian sang. "Oh, I would love a pancake. Perhaps it'll settle my stomach; I've been too excited to eat since yesterday."

"Yesterday?" Mrs. Kahn said carefully. "What happened yesterday?"

"I was released from my interrogation cell!" Miss Sameera said. "Sinister men-in-black types had been asking me questions for *ages*. And then they tried to wipe my brain and turned me loose, and here we are! Hello, Blue. Hello, Logan." She patted them lightly on their heads. "Shall I bring the syrup to the table?"

"Wait," Logan said. "They *tried* to wipe your brain, but it didn't work?"

"Well, some things are gone, but it'll come back to me eventually," she answered airily, waving one hand at her head. "I'm used to little holes in my memory here and there. They've done this before, you know. Like I told the other Free Rangers, I'm on to the government's tricks now. I even offered to teach a seminar once on Preserving Your Memories by Keeping Your Faith in Unicorns, but nobody signed up. And they claim to be dedicated to the cause of freeing mythical creatures everywhere! Between you and me and the bookshelves, those people never respected me enough. It's as though they think I'm *making this all up*. Can you imagine?"

"Somehow, yes," said Blue.

"But how do you remember us?" Zoe blurted.

"I just fix on the one thing that's most important to remember, and instead of trying to hold on to the memory, I connect it to a book in my mind," Miss Sameera said. She closed her eyes and whispered, "Zoe, *The Last Unicorn*, Zoe, *The Last Unicorn*, Zoe, *The Last Unicorn*." Her eyes popped open again and she smiled. "So no matter what else is gone, when I woke up today, I immediately knew I could come here and see unicorns. That's a wonderful book, by the way," she added as an aside to Logan. "You should read it. I'll put it on hold for you."

"Um, okay, thanks," he said.

"You've also probably built up some immunity to the kraken ink," Mrs. Kahn said. "From taking it so many times. Also, it only erases real supernatural memories, so anything you just imagined or hoped for would probably still be there."

"Wow," Zoe said.

"It didn't help me at all in Parkville," Miss Sameera said with a sigh. "By the time I got back to where the unicorns were supposed to be, they were all gone. And as usual, nobody listened to me. You're not all going to disappear suddenly, are you?"

"That might depend on a few things," Zoe said. "Such as how well you can keep a secret."

"Dazzlingly well," the librarian said promptly.

Logan and Zoe exchanged dubious looks. He remembered

what she'd said earlier—"If we can't wipe Miss Sameera's memories, what do we do with her?" He wondered if SNAPA had ever dealt with a problem like this before . . . and what their idea of a solution was.

"All right then," said Mrs. Kahn. "Another place setting for breakfast, Zoe."

"Come meet my dad," Logan said to the librarian, picking up the glasses of water he'd poured for himself and his dad. She trailed him into the living room, where Logan's dad was trying very hard and very unsuccessfully to talk sports with Mr. Kahn.

"Oh!" said Mr. Kahn, startled by the sight of Miss Sameera, or possibly just by her dress. "Hello! Good heavens."

"This is the school librarian, Miss Sameera Lahiri," Logan said. "Kind of a long story."

"Are you here to see the unicorns, too?" she said to Logan's dad, pumping his hand up and down.

"No way," he said. "Not if the rumors about them are true."

A little bewildered wrinkle appeared between her eyebrows, then vanished again quickly. "Is that Marco Jimenez?" she asked Mr. Kahn. "May I ask why he's snoring on your couch?"

"We're not entirely sure," Zoe's dad answered, turning to include Zoe in the conversation as she set the table. "Agent Runcible said he hadn't heard anything about adding sedatives to the toothpaste, but Agent Dantes thought it could have been mixed into this batch by accident. She's telling SNAPA to issue a recall."

"Or maybe somebody mixed it in after it got here," Zoe suggested. "Like whoever is causing all the rest of the trouble."

"That's an awfully weird choice of sabotage, though," Logan pointed out. "Making dragons sleepy is hardly going to disrupt the Menagerie. Sounds like it would make things more peaceful, actually."

"Unless the idea was to drug them so someone else could get past the intruder alarm," Zoe said. "AHA!"

"Speaking of which," said Mr. Kahn. "Matthew! Could you please run up to the dragons and tell them not to yell about our current visitor when she steps into the Menagerie?"

Matthew appeared in the doorway of the kitchen and made a forlorn face. "But pancakes!" he said.

"They'll be here when you get back," his father said implacably.

"Unless Marco wakes up," Logan chimed in. "Then all bets are off."

"And what if Elsie shows up while I'm gone and you're all super-embarrassing?" Matthew paused, then got a wicked look on his face. "I think Ruby should have to do it."

"If you can get her out of bed," said Mr. Kahn, "then you have my complete support."

Logan could hear Matthew chuckling gleefully all the way up the stairs.

"I didn't understand any of that," Miss Sameera said blithely. "But I assume I will once all my memories come back. We're all very good friends, aren't we? Although I have this feeling there's someone here I'd rather avoid. I suspect there's some connection to the new mountains of nibbled pillows at my house."

"We'll steer clear of the Aviary," Logan promised, guessing that Pelly wouldn't be too pleased to see Miss Sameera, either, given how willing the librarian was to part with her. He glanced at Marco, wondering how long the sedative would last. Maybe they should go ahead and interrogate Nero without him.

"Breakfast!" Mrs. Kahn called. "Where's Melissa?"

"Talking to SNAMHP about the merfolk situation," Mr. Kahn said. "She'll be a while, we should start."

"All right. Keiko!" Mrs. Kahn shouted at the stairs. "Breakfast!"

"I'm not hungry!" Keiko shouted back.

"It's blueberry paaaaaaancakes!" Mrs. Kahn sang.

"I hate blueberry pancakes!"

"I suppose I could have seen that coming," said Zoe's mom. "Everyone, sit, sit, sit."

"So what do you remember?" Zoe said, steering Miss Sameera into the chair next to hers. "You said you followed someone into the woods and that's where you found Pelly. Do you remember that?"

"Nope," Miss Sameera said cheerfully. "Who's Pelly?" She paused suddenly, and a dark cloud seemed to cross over her features. "Oh dear. I think something is coming back that I might prefer not to remember."

"If you could think really hard," Zoe begged. "It's so important. We need to figure out who you followed into the woods. Or where the cabin was. Or *anything* that could give us a clue about who took Pelly."

"Pancakes will help," said the librarian. "And seeing a unicorn, of course." She smiled at Logan as he passed her the platter of pancakes.

Zoe sighed. Logan could tell that sitting through breakfast was like torture for her right now. He looked around at the others eating and thought, *I wish my mom could be here, too.*

"Can I just show you one thing?" Zoe said, flipping through pictures on her phone. "Does this cabin look familiar? Could it be the place where you found Pelly?"

Miss Sameera studied the building in the photo Zoe had up on her screen. After a moment she said, "Well, goodness. I've definitely been there. I don't remember who this 'Pelly' is. But I have a feeling I did some kind of daring rescue—this window gives me a kind of 'I crawled through that' vibe."

"Really?" Zoe turned to her dad. "That's the Sterlings' cabin," she whispered to him and Logan. Logan took her phone and looked at the elaborate two-story structure, which was bigger than any house he'd ever lived in.

"So they *are* working with whoever's sabotaging the Menagerie," he whispered back. "Because they couldn't have gotten in to get Pelly or set up Scratch, right? It must have been someone else doing their dirty work for them."

"I hope Pelly ruined all their stuff," Zoe said furiously.

Ruby came storming down the stairs with Matthew right behind her. Her short blond hair stood up in little spikes and she was wearing a chunky red sweater over her pajamas. "Why do *I* have to go talk to the stupid dragons?" she demanded, flouncing into the living room. "Oooh, pancakes. Are those organic blueberries?"

"You may have some after you go see the dragons," Mr. Kahn said, smoothly moving the plate out of her reach. "Which you have been chosen to do because we said so."

"Because you're in trouble," Zoe offered. "Because you did something way way *way* worse than I have ever done."

"You know nothing about love!" Ruby declared passionately. "None of you do!"

"Perhaps the dragons will shower you with all the understanding and affection you've been lacking," her mother said. "Better take a jacket, it's cold out there."

"And wear a flameproof suit," Mr. Kahn added.

"I bet I can eat all of these before she gets back," Matthew said, sliding into his chair and eyeing the stack of pancakes.

"Don't you dare!" Ruby cried. She dashed into the hall, grabbed her coat, scarf, and boots, and ran out the back door.

They watched her sprint down the hill, trying to put everything on at once.

"When does she start the OOPSS course?" Matthew asked his mom.

"Over her winter break," said Mrs. Kahn. "I'm afraid she won't be home for Christmas this year."

"That is a terrible shame," Matthew said impassively.

Logan turned back to his plate and spotted something small and furry near his foot. Carefully he leaned a little bit to the side, pretending he was reaching for the syrup while looking down out of the corner of his eye.

He was pretty sure it was the tiny creature he'd seen eating marshmallows the day before. Now it was sitting against the leg of the table, picking up crumbs and eating them delicately with long, slender fingers. It looked a lot like a slow loris or a lemur with no tail—its face was all giant eyes and its fur was the color of caramel, except for dark patches around its black eyes that made them look even bigger. Unlike a slow loris, though, it had two little wings that folded between its arms and its body like a bat's.

"Zoe," Logan whispered, testing a theory. "Is there a creature under my chair?"

She gave him a baffled expression but didn't even look down. "I doubt it," she said.

It's the deflector, Logan guessed. *Bob. I bet I can see her now because of the scarab.* He touched the lump of the insect necklace under his shirt. *That's why her deflective power isn't working on me anymore.*

He cut off a piece of his pancake, glanced around to make sure no one was paying attention to him, and casually dropped it beside his chair.

Swoop! A small hand darted out and snatched it.

If nobody can see her or even remember she's there most of the time, then nobody feeds her, Logan realized. He remembered the disappearing candy bar on Halloween night. *Obviously she can take care of herself.* He dropped another piece of pancake, and again it vanished in a flash.

He took the next bit of pancake in his fingers and slowly lowered his hand until he was holding the pancake just under his chair. Conversation swirled around him, but he barely listened; his attention was focused on the slightly sticky crumb he was holding.

A long moment passed.

And then he felt tiny fingers brush his as the little creature tugged the pancake out of his hand.

Yes, Logan thought with excitement. *We'll be friends in no time, Bob.*

"—con cheeseburgers," Marco said suddenly from the couch. He sat up, blinking and shaking his head. "Whoa. How did I get here?" Logan saw a blur of motion as Bob zipped out of the room.

"Oh, thank goodness," Zoe said with relief. She twisted

around in her chair to look at Marco. "I was worried you'd sleep through school tomorrow."

"Yikes, Ma would have such a fit if that happened," Marco said. He hopped off the couch and wobbled a bit on his way to the table, but made it into a chair. Logan pushed the plate of pancakes toward him.

"Hi, Marco!" Miss Sameera said brightly.

Marco stared at her for a minute with his fork halfway to his mouth. "Did I miss something?" he said. "Isn't this the same librarian who chased me down the hall with a stapler just a few days ago?"

"*Did* I?" Miss Sameera said with avid curiosity. "I don't remember that at *all.*"

"She has a few holes in her memory," Logan explained.

Marco apparently decided not to volunteer that he'd been a rooster at the time. He shrugged and went back to eating pancakes.

But that reminded Logan of what they'd found that day on the librarian's computer while she was distracted with Marco.

"How often do you talk to the other Free Rangers?" he asked. "You haven't told them anything about this place, have you?"

She sat up indignantly and waved her fork at him. "Those troglodytes!" she cried. "I could probably send them a photo of me riding a unicorn and they still wouldn't believe me!"

"Neither would anyone," Zoe said with a frown. "Unicorns absolutely refuse to be ridden. You should hear them gripe about their 'delicate bone structure.'"

"I found the most appalling thing when I got home yesterday," Miss Sameera said, reaching around to fish in her coat pockets. "Look at this! A letter from Mr. Claverhill—finally, after all the letters I sent to him!—and what does it say? It says 'Please stop ensnaring us in these elaborate hoaxes'! HOAXES INDEED."

She slapped the letter on the table and Logan leaned over to look at it.

"Cease and desist!" the librarian yelped, stabbing at the letter with one finger. "Cut off all ties with our organization! Take your harebrained nonsense to the *Inquirer*! Leave the serious mythical-creature investigating to the truly dedicated cryptozoologists! WELL. The joke's on THEM, isn't it? Now I'm going to be the first Free Ranger to befriend a unicorn and *they'll never even know.* Ha!"

"That's great," Zoe said with relief. "You're right, they didn't appreciate you. You're way too smart for them, Miss Sameera. Never speaking to them again is definitely the way to go."

"And the ridiculous thing is," Miss Sameera went on, "if they had just *listened* to me and sent backup six *months* ago when I followed the lady with the little furry dragon here, they could have been in on all these amazing discoveries, too. But NO. Roll their eyes at ME, will they?"

Logan's father dropped his fork with a clatter. Logan felt his own heart stop in his chest.

Miss Sameera rolled to a halt, realizing that everyone was staring at her.

"What did I say?" she asked. "I promise I won't really go to the *Inquirer*."

"Lady with a furry dragon?" Logan's dad said in a choked voice.

"Oh yes," she said brightly. "I spotted her in an airport in Los Angeles. At first when something moved in her pocket I figured, you know, illegal monkey smuggling or something. But then I caught a glimpse of its face. SO adorable, clearly a furry dragon, just like you might see in a Chinese painting. I changed my flight right away, of course, so I could follow her. To Denver, then Cheyenne, and then out to Xanadu, as it turned out, although I nearly lost her when I had to argue with the rental car people. So what if I didn't have a reservation? Do you think all the cars in Cheyenne were booked? I mean, really."

"You followed her all the way to Xanadu?" Logan said. "Did you see what happened to her?"

"Nothing happened to her," Miss Sameera said in surprise. "Oh, well, she got pulled over, but the police officer didn't give her a ticket or anything. Probably because her friend showed up and talked to the cop. I don't know what he said, but she ended up switching to his fancy black car and leaving her car on the side of the road."

"Her friend?" Logan's dad asked. "What kind of car did he have?"

"The fancy kind," she said confidently. "It was definitely black."

"Where did they go after that?" Logan asked.

"I don't know," she said. "That's when I lost her, I'm afraid. I stopped to try and snoop in her car, which was silly of me. I thought maybe she'd left the dragon in there, but it must have gone with her."

Logan reached out and took his dad's hand. This was the closest they'd ever come to finding out what happened to Mom. Miss Sameera might have been the last person to see her before she disappeared.

"This 'friend' she drove off with," Logan's dad said slowly, as if he was afraid the librarian would suddenly leap up and bolt away. "Can you describe him?"

"Well, sure," said Miss Sameera. "But I don't really have to. His picture is all over town. It was that nice man who's running for mayor."

SEVENTEEN

There was an electric pause.

"Jasmin's dad?" Zoe whispered.

"That's right," said Miss Sameera. "He's very charming, isn't he?"

Before Logan could regain control of his breathing, his father stood up, knocking his chair over, and headed for the door.

"Wait," Mr. Kahn said, scrambling after him. "Jackson, wait. Storming over there isn't going to do any good. They'll just lie. You won't get her back that way. Stop and think about this."

"The Sterlings kidnapped my wife," Logan's dad shouted.

"What is there to think about? I'm going to get her back."

"We need a plan," Mrs. Kahn said. "If you go charging in there shouting accusations, they'll probably have you arrested. Mr. Sterling is close friends with the sheriff. Without proof—"

"We've got her," he said, pointing at Miss Sameera. "She can tell them what she saw."

They all looked at Miss Sameera again, and Logan had to admit to himself that she didn't seem like the *most* reliable witness. He believed her, but he doubted the police would.

"Uh, guys? There's a girl in the Menagerie," Marco said suddenly. He pointed out the glass doors.

A teenage girl, about fifteen years old, with skin as dark as Logan's, tight coppery-brown curls, and a small snub nose was wandering across the grass with her hands in her jeans pockets, studying the mermaids in the lake below. She had a large beaded bag the color of lava slung over one shoulder. Shambling along at her heels was some kind of perfectly ginormous wombat.

"Elsie!" Matthew cried.

"All of you go, please," said Mrs. Kahn. "We need to talk to Mr. Wilde. Except you, Sameera, we might have more questions for you."

Logan had a feeling they'd let him stay if he asked, but he needed to escape that room. He needed to wrap his spinning brain around the image of his mother getting into Mr.

Sterling's car and disappearing into the sunset.

Had she gone with him willingly? Why would she do that?

"Elsie!" Matthew called as he slid open the doors. "Up here!"

The girl turned and waved, grinning. "Hiya," she called. "I hear you've got something of a mermaid problem." She had some kind of accent—Australian, Logan guessed—and a dazzling smile. The wombat looked over its shoulder at them, too, blinking sleepy eyes, and Logan realized that its front two feet were actually giant flippers. Its fur was short and gray but sort of lavender when the sun hit it. It was as tall as the girl's waist and probably big enough for her to ride if she wanted to.

"Why didn't you come to the front door?" Matthew asked as they met on the hill.

"Don't care for doors," Elsie said with a shrug. "And I wanted to check out the famous Kahn Menagerie. It's quite wild, really. I'd love to meet your yeti; our sasquatch is such a bore, always going on about how things were better before the end of the last ice age, like anyone believes he's that old or cares."

"Thank you for coming to help," Matthew said. He waved one hand at the picketing merfolk and several of them made rude noises at him.

"Mermaids are such nimrods, aren't they?" Elsie said, rolling her eyes.

"Ahem," Blue said. "Not *all* of them."

"Nah, all of them, sorry, mate," Elsie said. "Matthew, I heard about your epic Tracking of the qilin. You're, like, such a legend now."

"Oh," he said, blushing furiously. "Well, I had help."

Elsie raised her eyebrows at the others. "From a were-rooster, a half merman, your little sister, and a regular human?" She stopped and shook her head, blinking. "Wait. No way. You're not—who are you?" she asked Logan.

"GWORP," said the creature at her feet. It had a deep, flat voice that was startlingly loud.

"That's what I thought!" she said to it. "But what are the chances of that?"

"GORNORG," it said, and started munching grass as if no further discussion was necessary.

"That's Logan," said Matthew. "And these are Zoe, Marco, and Blue."

"That was crazy. How did you know I'm a wererooster?" Marco asked.

"Are you any relation to Abigail Hardy?" Elsie asked Logan, ignoring Marco.

Logan shivered as though ice water was running down his back. "She's my mom," he said.

"Ah, right, you so look alike," she said, nodding. "She came to Tracker camp one year to do a presentation on barangs. I am going to *be* her when I grow up. Do you know where she is? My theory is she's on some really extra-top-secret Track-ing mission, like, some animal we've never even heard of, right? And maybe nobody even knows about it, but when she comes back riding the world's only winged bandicoot-panda, everyone will just shut up and feel stupid for all the completely stupid things they've said about her. Because she is amazing, right? Like, my own personal hero, no joke."

Logan glanced back at the house. Maybe he shouldn't have left his dad in there. Maybe he should go back and join the argument. He kind of wanted to march over and accuse the Sterlings right now, too. But were the Kahns right? Was there a smarter way to get his mom back?

If so . . . what was it?

Marco pointed at the flippered wombat. "What is that?" he asked.

"This is Uluru," Elsie said. "He's a bunyip, obviously."

"Whoa," said Blue. "I've never met anyone with a pet bunyip before."

Uluru stopped munching and looked up at Blue with steely distaste.

"He is *not* a pet," Elsie said scornfully. "He is my friend, or you might say, my sidekick."

"SORGBORG," the bunyip rumbled.

"Yeah, all right, it's possible I'm *his* sidekick," she said. "Although Mum originally wanted him to be my bodyguard. She's a bit overprotective." Her hand tightened on the strap of her shoulder bag, and Logan glimpsed something brown, sleek, and furry inside.

"It's almost noon," Zoe said to Matthew.

"Are you up for kraken feeding?" Matthew said to Elsie. "How do you feel about kelpies?"

"I wrestle them every day," she said. "I was born to tame kelpies! They're really just misunderstood hell-horses of death who want to eat you, you know."

"There's a zaratan, too," Zoe said. "Once you feed the three of them, that's it."

"Wait—by herself?" Logan asked. He had kind of expected "Matthew's friend" to (a) be older and bigger and (b) bring along a gang of helpers.

"Uluru and I can handle it, no worries," Elsie said, giving Logan a crinkly-eyed smile. Her wide brown eyes were just a tiny bit too close together, but still, she was really pretty. He could see why Matthew was trying and failing to stop beaming like a dork at her.

"Where should I change?" she asked Matthew.

"Up at the house?" he suggested. "Or the unicorn stable is closer to the water, if you'd prefer that."

"Yeah, that should work," she said, eyeing the stable. "Come on, Uluru."

"Oh, no no *no*," yelled a voice from the lake. Blue's cousin Sapphire pushed the other mermaids aside and came storming out onto the shore, wearing a bright yellow bikini top and matching shorts. Her long blond hair streamed wetly down her back. She threw herself in Elsie's path. "What do you think you're doing?" she demanded.

"Something you're apparently too lazy to do," Elsie said. "But then, that's typical mermaid, isn't it? Oooh, no, we can't do our jobs, we might accidentally be useful for once."

"You can't help these humans," Sapphire said. "You'd be betraying water folk everywhere!"

"BURGS," said the bunyip placidly.

"There's no need to be rude!" Sapphire shrieked. "You should stand with us in solidarity! All we want is basic rights!"

"Living in Hawaii is not a basic right," Zoe said, crossing her arms. "Your king made an agreement for you all to live here, but if you want to go back to the ocean and fend for yourselves, you can take it up with SNAMHP."

Elsie smirked. "If you do, say hi to the sharks for me. And by the way, I'm not helping humans; I'm helping a few perfectly nice sea creatures who deserve to have their lunch without a bunch of flipperbutts shrieking up and down all over their habitat and neglecting them. So get out of my way, mermaid."

"We're not letting you past," Sapphire said, putting her hands on her hips. "We'll stop you! We're not afraid of any—"

The bunyip suddenly opened its mouth and let out the most bloodcurdling scream Logan had ever heard. It echoed and echoed around the Menagerie, louder even than the dragons' intruder alert. And it didn't end; Uluru seemed calmly prepared to make that awful noise for as long as necessary.

Elsie regarded Sapphire with a face like, *Well, you asked for it. Your move.*

Sapphire clapped her hands over her ears. "All RIGHT!" she yelled. "FINE! MAKE IT STOP!"

Elsie touched the top of Uluru's head gently with her fingertips. He snapped his mouth shut and the scream abruptly cut off.

"I'm complaining to—to—to someone about this!" Sapphire yelped. "It's not fair!" She whirled around and stomped back to the lake, where the other merfolk were booing and hissing and throwing small fish in Elsie's general direction.

"NORGBLOG," Uluru observed.

"I *completely* agree," said Elsie. They headed off to the unicorn stable.

"So," Matthew said, smiling from ear to ear. "That's Elsie."

"She's *way* out of your league," Zoe said sympathetically.

"I know!" he said. "But she's here! And she knows about the qilin. You heard her. I'm a *legend* now."

"Wow, I can't wait to hear about that forever," Zoe teased. "Logan, how are you doing? Are you okay? I mean, about all that stuff about your mom?"

He shrugged, hoping he looked more okay than he felt. "We sort of guessed the Sterlings might have her. But is she still in Xanadu? If Dad's PI never saw them visit her, who's helping them take care of her?"

"Maybe whoever is helping them sabotage the Menagerie," Zoe said.

"Still not me," Matthew said. "Just so we're clear."

The door of the unicorn stable opened and the bunyip ambled out, followed immediately by a sleek, beautiful brown seal.

"Ohhhhhhhhhhhhhhhhhh," said Marco knowingly. "A wereseal. I get it now."

"She's not a wereseal, doofus," Matthew said. "She's a selkie."

"Right," he said, nodding. "That's what I meant. A selkie." Behind Matthew's back, Marco made a face at Logan like, *What? No idea! Never heard of it! You?*

"They're seals who can take human form," Zoe explained. "They come out of the water and shed their sealskin, then keep it somewhere safe until they want to put it back on and go back in the water. Usually not the hugest fans of people, so maybe she does really like you, Matthew."

"Maybe," he said dreamily.

The seal and the bunyip slipped into the water and vanished into the depths, past the protesting merfolk. On the other side of the lake, the zaratan lifted its head hopefully, as if sensing the selkie's arrival. A swirl of ripples near the kraken's enclosure indicated that she'd noticed her as well.

If it weren't for the Sterlings, the Chinese dragon would be out in that lake right now, swimming and playing peacefully.

And if it weren't for the Sterlings, Logan could be standing here with his mom.

"Logan," Zoe said, pulling his attention back to reality. "Listen. Here's what I know about Chinese dragons. They get really attached to people they like. I bet this one refused to leave your mother, and she wouldn't abandon it, either. She'd insist on staying with it to make sure it was all right, even if the Sterlings offered her a boatload of money to vanish."

She took Logan's hand. "And here is what I know about Abigail Hardy. The only thing in the world that could keep her from going home to you would be protecting a mythical creature. It's not just a job to her."

Logan understood. He more than understood. He knew what he was willing to do for Squorp or any of the griffin cubs.

"We're going to find her," he said, trying to convince himself.

Before Tuesday, he thought. *Or they'll put the dragon on TV, expose the Menagerie, and endanger the lives of every mythical creature here.*

EIGHTEEN

It was agony to do all the other regular Sunday chores, but as Zoe's parents said, they still had to be done. Griffins needed feeding, hellhounds needed exercising, unicorns needed to be brushed and told they were magnificent. Just the essentials, though; Zoe managed to get out of doing the mapinguari's bath, thankfully. And Ruby was sent off to do all the worst chores, with Mooncrusher looming grimly over her to make sure they were done right.

Miss Sameera turned out to be the perfect passionately devoted worshipper the unicorns had always wanted. Zoe's mom didn't think it was safe to just send her back into the world, and they didn't want to try kraken ink again in case they needed her for finding Abigail. But the librarian seemed perfectly happy to camp out on their couch indefinitely, if it meant she got to see unicorns every day.

Logan and Zoe took Marco to the Aviary to try to interview Nero. The phoenix was strutting around, deliberately getting just close enough to Pelly's nest for her to see him but out of her snapping range. She had her head under her wing but kept poking it out to glare at him.

"Hey, Nero, can we talk to you?" Zoe asked.

"ME?" he said with delight. "You need to talk to MEEEEEE?"

"It's really important," Logan said.

"Let's find somewhere more PRIVATE," Nero said, shooting a significant look at Pelly. "So no one will EAVESDROP on our PRIVATE IMPORTANT CONVERSATION. With MEEEEE." He puffed up his chest and strutted ahead of them to a secluded corner of the Aviary.

"This is Marco," Logan said.

"Wererooster," Marco filled in. "Wow, *the* actual one and only phoenix. I'm a big fan."

Nero preened, fluffing out his tail feathers. "You're quite rare yourself," he said. "I've only met three other wereroosters in my lifetime."

"Please don't explode into flames," Zoe said, "but we want to ask you about the night Pelly was abducted."

Nero flung his wings wide. "DANGER!" he shrieked.

"VIOLENCE! In my VERY HOME!" He paused, and then settled his wings back down. "Although if she was going to steal someone, I don't know why she wouldn't have picked ME, the TRULY exceptional and most UTTERLY UNIQUE creature in the WHOLE MENAGERIE. Taking Pelly is more like doing the rest of us a favor. If only she hadn't sent her back!"

"She?" Zoe said sharply. "It was a woman? Did you see her?"

Nero hesitated. "No?" he tried.

"Buddy," Marco said, crouching beside the beautiful bird. "We don't want to put you in any danger, but you are the only one who can help us, you know? Literally the fate of the entire Menagerie is riding on *your* wings."

"OOOOOOOOOOOOOOOOOOOOOOH," Nero said, enchanted. "LITERALLY!"

"Depending on what you can tell us," Zoe said. "Weren't you knocked out by the tranquility mist, too, like the other birds?"

"Oh no," said Nero. "It must have gone off while I was still in my egg, being reborn. By the time I crawled out, all the other birds were asleep—except Aliya, who I could smell had been knocked out by a tranquilizer dart. JUST IMAGINE the TERROR I felt! A newborn phoenix chick, utterly defenseless! Woe is me!"

"So who did you see?" Zoe asked.

"Save the day now, my friend," Marco said.

"Fate of the Menagerie," Logan added.

Nero leaned closer to them. "WELL," he said, and paused.

Zoe's pulse was racing. Did he really see someone? Were they about to find out who the saboteur was?

"It was . . ." Nero paused again, took a dramatic breath, and said, "IT WAS . . . a WOMAN."

Zoe and Logan exchanged glances. "A woman?" Zoe asked. "Any particular woman? Anyone you know?"

"Well," he said again. "It was . . . a TALL woman!"

"Taller than Mom?" Zoe asked. "How tall?"

"Taller than YOU," he said.

"Everyone's taller than me." She frowned at him.

"I'm guessing most people seem tall to Nero," Logan said in a low voice.

"But you'd never seen her before?" Marco prompted.

"I . . . may have," Nero said. He stared up into the trees with a deep, thoughtful expression.

"Nero! Did you or didn't you recognize her?" Zoe demanded.

"Well," he said slowly. "My eyesight was not . . . completely sharp yet."

Zoe sighed. "You mean you had newborn baby bird eyesight," she said. "So you couldn't see her very well at all, is what you're saying."

"I know it was a woman!" he said, bristling. "She made an

enormous mess of that goose's nest and then absconded with her! She smelled of anxiety and lies and fire! Oh wait, the fire part might have been me." He poked his beak under one of his wings and sniffed.

"Can you tell us anything else about her?" Marco asked.

"Please?" Logan said.

Nero ruffled his feathers and eyed them with an indignant expression. "I think I have told you PLENTY," he said. "Just because you don't APPRECIATE it, doesn't mean I haven't been ENORMOUSLY HELPFUL. I know nobody loves me! But you could at least show a speck of gratitude! I am so very long-suffering!"

"All right, calm down," Zoe said, pulling out a box of chocolate-covered jalapeños. "I brought you these. But don't you dare give one to Pelly like last time. I was bringing her honey tea for weeks."

"Oooooooooooh," Nero said, distracted and delighted by his favorite treat. He wrapped his wings around the box and strutted off into the foliage.

"That didn't help much," Logan said, sounding discouraged. "A woman?"

"One of the mermaids," Zoe guessed. "Who else could it be?" She hesitated. "Unless it could be Ruby . . . but she wasn't in town at that point, that we know of. And she's awful, but I believe she didn't know what the Sterlings were up to. She wouldn't help them ruin us." She was at least 95 percent sure of that. She thought.

Logan and his dad went home soon after that. Zoe was worried about him. He'd barely said a word while he was helping with the chores. He'd been distracted even when he was covered in a pile of bouncing griffin cubs.

Marco went home, too, but Matthew went and pulled out a sleeping bag for Elsie, setting up a space for her in the living room, next to the bed they'd made for Miss Sameera on the couch.

The selkie girl emerged from the lake toward evening. Zoe was at the dining room table, extremely reluctantly doing homework because her parents had insisted on it, with Captain Fuzzbutt snoozing beside her. Elsie and Uluru came through the sliding doors, bringing a gust of chilly night air with them. Elsie was scrunching her curly wet hair with a towel. Her sealskin was back in her shoulder bag, which dripped damply across the floor.

"Hi, Elsie," Zoe said. "Dad's making dinner, Mom is out in the Menagerie with Sameera, and Matthew is up in his room studying. I have no idea where Keiko is. Can I get you anything? How'd it go?"

"Great," Elsie said, tossing her towel on the back of a chair. "They're all very sweet. My mum said I can stay as long as you need help."

"Thank you," Zoe said sincerely. "We'd be in trouble without you."

"Is Keiko the kitsune?" Elsie said. "I saw her on her way up to the dragons."

Zoe blinked at her. "No way. Keiko hates the dragons."

Elsie shrugged. "She went up about an hour ago and hasn't come back down yet."

Is Keiko "furball the small"? Zoe wondered. Was Keiko secretly friends with Firebella? On the one hand, they had almost the exact same personality, so that sort of made sense. On the other hand, why would Keiko pretend she and the dragons hated each other? Why keep their friendship a secret?

So she wouldn't have to do any dragon chores, she answered herself. *We never send her up there to clean out the caves or anything because we thought there was a major dragon-kitsune feud going on. Very crafty.*

Or was it sinister? Was Keiko up to something?

"GORM," the bunyip observed.

"I know, I remember," Elsie said to him. "Where's Abigail Hardy's kid?" she asked Zoe, pulling out a chair to sit. Uluru flopped to his belly on the floor beside her. Captain Fuzzbutt looked at him askance, eyeing the bunyip's damp fur, and sidled a bit closer to Zoe.

"He went home," Zoe said. "There's a whole thing going on with his mom—you know she's missing—well, she may have been kidnapped, and we think we know who has her but not where."

"I have a message for him," Elsie said. "Maybe it's connected."

"A message?" Zoe said, sitting up straight. She closed her math book. "From who?"

"From the kraken." Elsie reached over and grabbed a few carrot sticks from the bowl in the middle of the table. "She says she's been trying to tell him for a week now. But you know krakens. Her idea of trying could be waving the occasional tentacle at him from the lake as he walks by. Krakens always think everyone is paying much more attention to them than we really are."

"Why would the kraken have a message for Logan?" Zoe asked.

"Someone's been sending it to her through the water. She broadcast an image at me." Elsie pulled a napkin toward her and sketched out a small head with long wiggly lines coming out of it. "Someone like that? Sorry, I can't draw at all, I know it's kind of terrible."

Zoe blinked at it. It was beyond terrible; she couldn't even tell if it was supposed to be human. Was that a mustache?

"Um . . . maybe Matthew can help. He's a great artist," Zoe said. "Matthew! Elsie's back!"

She heard her brother's door open and he came pounding down the stairs. His feet stopped running right outside the living room, and then he wandered in nonchalantly. "Oh, hey," he said. "How's everything?"

"Elsie got a message from the kraken," Zoe said.

"But you know krakens," Elsie said again, shrugging apologetically. "It's all images and everything has this blurry underwater quality and you can hardly figure out what they're trying to say at all."

"Right," Matthew said. "Except no, we never get images from her, or messages of any kind. It must be a fellow sea creature thing."

"Can you figure out what this is?" Zoe asked, nudging the napkin toward him. "This is who the message is coming from, she says."

Matthew studied the scribbled drawing seriously, his mouth twitching.

"All right, go on and laugh," Elsie said, shoving him.

"No, I'm not! It's a good—well, the effort is—it's clearly a—huh."

"I have other skills," Elsie said amiably.

"Maybe I can draw it. Can you describe it to me?" he asked. He pulled a sketchbook off one of the bookshelves and a pencil from the emergency drawer and sat down next to her.

"It's small, and sort of reddish, with these long whiskers—"

"So it's a creature," Matthew confirmed. "Not a mustachioed Picasso person."

"Of course it's a creature," she said. "Uluru, I think he's making fun of me."

"GROBAGOG," the bunyip observed without moving from its prone position.

"All right, settle down," she said. "I've never seen one before myself, but the picture looked like a blurry Chinese dragon, maybe."

"What?" Zoe jumped to her feet. "The Chinese dragon? The one with Abigail? It sent a message to the kraken?" She covered her mouth to keep more questions from pouring out and took a deep breath. "Tell us everything she said."

"It wasn't much, right?" Elsie said apologetically. "The dragon is probably sending a kind of distress signal whenever it gets to be in water, and if it's in something where the streams or underground rivers or whatever connect back to this lake, then the kraken is picking it up. It's not a conversation, exactly. The kraken can't send a message back or anything."

"Still," Matthew said. "What was the distress signal?"

"It's four images," Elsie said. "Its own picture first." She tapped Matthew's sketchbook, where he was doodling a beautiful little Chinese dragon. "Then a picture of Abigail Hardy—I recognized her, of course, which is why I figured the message should go to Logan. Then a picture of a box with bars across it—I think that's just to signal that they're trapped or imprisoned somewhere. And finally, Jabba the Hutt."

Zoe and Matthew stared at her.

"It's probably not actually Jabba the Hutt," Elsie amended. "Now that I think about it."

"More description?" Matthew asked. "Maybe?"

"It's gray and kind of a triangular shape with a big round head at the top," she said, leaning closer to him to watch his pencil sweep across the paper. "Two closed eyes, a human nose, squiggly things on the top of the head—no, not antennae, you loon. Like little circles, like a hat with a dome on top of that. There might be hands in the middle of the triangle. And it's up on a short flat stone pedestal."

As Elsie kept describing it, Zoe came around to the other side of Matthew to watch. Something about the drawing was starting to look familiar. She closed her eyes to think. Could it be a statue? A big stone statue? She opened her eyes again and saw it.

"I know what that is," she said. "Matthew! That's the giant stone Buddha in the Sterlings' backyard!"

"What?" he said, stopping to study it.

"Whoops," Elsie said. "I was just really culturally insensitive, then, wasn't I?"

"Why would the dragon send an image of that statue?" Matthew asked. He looked up at Zoe with a small puzzled line between his eyebrows.

"It's a clue," Zoe said, feeling excitement rising up through her chest and shooting out to her fingers. "Think about it.

The dragon is trying to tell us—*that's* where the Sterlings are keeping him and Abigail."

"That makes no sense," Matthew argued. "It's a statue, not a building."

"I'm going over there to check it out," she said.

"You are definitely not," Matthew said. His hand shot out to catch her wrist before she could charge off to the front door. "Zoe! The Sterlings are having a massive campaign dinner right now. It's so big, even I know about it. There are cars parked for miles along the street, almost all the way to our house. That garden will be swarming with people. There's no way you'll be able to sneak over the wall and poke their statuary tonight."

"Besides," Elsie pointed out, "you should probably get Logan to go with you, yeah?"

"Tomorrow, then," Zoe said. "First thing. We're getting into the Sterlings' backyard and we are going to shake that statue until Abigail and the dragon fall out."

She went over to the window, twisting one hand around the other wrist.

I hope I'm right.

I hope they're there.

Because if they're not . . . I have no idea what we're going to do.

NINETEEN

Monday morning dawned cold and chilly, much colder than usual for early November, according to all the chatter on the car radio. Logan and his dad drove in silence for the first five minutes, listening to the local Xanadu station newscasters talk about the mayoral election the next day, which Mr. Sterling was predicted to win by a landslide. He'd been profiled in *Time* magazine as a small-town political star with big ambitions and a bright future, so the buzz around town was that a national news network was coming to cover his victory speech.

"He's always been such a benefactor to this town," gushed one of the radio DJs.

"I just hope we get to keep him for a few years before Congress snaps him up!" said the other with a laugh.

"I heard he's going to make a big announcement tomorrow night," said the first one. "Something that will put Xanadu on the map."

"And bring in lots of jobs, let's not forget!" said the second. "An economic boom for everyone, that's what Mr. Sterling has promised. We'll all be millionaires in three years if his plans are even half as successful as he's predicting they will be."

"Of course, the election's not over yet. There's also . . . the other candidate."

"Right. Anything could happen, after all—"

Logan's dad reached over and switched the radio off. "He's going to look like quite an idiot," he said calmly, "when everyone is standing there ready to hear his big announcement and he doesn't have that little dragon to show them."

Logan shot him a smile. Whether his dad was faking it or not, his confidence was incredibly reassuring.

"Or Pelly," Logan said. "I guess they stole her for the same reason—to prove to the world that the Menagerie is real." He shook his head. Something still didn't fit about that theory. Why frame Scratch? Was there a connection to the deaths of Scratch's mom and sister? Why disrupt the Menagerie so much at all? Why not just go on TV with the Chinese dragon?

He also didn't understand how telling the world about

the Menagerie was supposed to benefit the Sterlings. Even if everyone knew about the unicorns and griffins, that wouldn't make the Sterlings any money—exposing it still wouldn't give them the right to turn it into an amusement park for their own profit—and from what he knew about the Sterlings, money was the end goal of everything they did.

He wrapped his cold hands in the ends of the scarf around his neck. It was a warm fiery red shot through with soft gray streaks. His mother had brought it back for him from one of her trips—to Mongolia, she'd said. He wondered which animal she'd been Tracking on that trip and whether it was in the Kahns' Menagerie right now.

"Listen," his dad said. "I don't want you getting the wrong idea about skipping school. I'll write you a note saying you were sick today, but this isn't going to happen again, understand? Special exception for rescuing kidnapped mom."

"Got it," Logan said, returning his smile. He knew his dad was trying to joke to break the tension, but he had to be feeling as anxious and keyed up as Logan did.

His dad parked in the Menagerie driveway and turned to face Logan. "But seriously, Logan, I'm worried about involving you in this."

"I involved *you*," Logan pointed out. When Zoe had told him about the message, he knew they could have kept it to themselves and investigated the statue without their parents. But he also knew he was done with keeping secrets from his dad, and he hoped the same was true in reverse. "I want to find her together, Dad."

"I know," his dad said. "Me too. That's why I'm letting you come along."

"That's why I'm letting *you* come along," Logan said, grinning but only half joking.

"Partners, then." His dad held out his hand and Logan shook it.

Zoe and her mom were standing at their front door as Logan and his dad got out of the car. Zoe was wearing a fuzzy white hat with little black eyes and ears so it looked like a yak. Her red hair stuck out under the earflaps and her face was pink with cold.

"No luck with Blue?" Logan asked, pulling his own plain gray wool hat down over his ears.

Zoe shook her head. "Melissa said he was not allowed to miss school just to go on 'some wild goose chase,' when we don't even know if we'll find anything, and plus there were quite enough of us 'wasting our time' already."

"Melissa doesn't handle disorder well," Mrs. Kahn said sympathetically. "It's the merfolk situation. She's in a bit of a state about Elsie's paperwork, and SNAMHP is supposedly coming to negotiate with Cobalt today. Zoe's dad has to drive all the way to Cheyenne with Agent Runcible to pick them up from the airport. Apparently one of them is a vampire and needs special transport during daytime travel."

Captain Fuzzbutt poked his trunk around the door and made a mournful noise.

"Shhh," Zoe said, kissing his trunk and then nudging it back inside. "You know you can't be seen out here. We'll be back soon, I promise." She pressed her hands together, squeezing her fingers nervously.

"Are you sure you want to do this?" Mrs. Kahn asked her. "You could get in trouble. Maybe you should stay here, or go to school after all."

"*You* could get in bigger trouble," Zoe pointed out. "Logan and I are just kids poking around a friend's house. You and Mr. Wilde could get arrested for breaking and entering. Maybe *you* should stay here."

It sounded so much like Logan's conversation with his dad that he laughed.

"All right," Mrs. Kahn said. "I guess we're all going."

They walked to Jasmin's house, stopping at the bottom of the long driveway to scan for the Sterlings' cars. Zoe pulled off her glove to check her phone.

"Jasmin says they're all gone," she reported.

"Someone is going to notice that you, me, and Jasmin were all out sick today," Logan pointed out.

"We'll have notes," Zoe said, nodding at her mom and his dad. "And I highly doubt anyone will get Jasmin in trouble the day her dad gets elected mayor." She stuck her phone in her pocket and put her glove back on. "Except maybe her own parents," she mumbled. "I told her she didn't have to stay home and help us."

"But she didn't listen," her mom said. "Because she's just like you two."

"Intrepid?" Zoe guessed as they headed up the drive.

"Resolute?" Logan offered.

"Heroic!" Zoe said.

"I was going to go with *stubborn*," said Mrs. Kahn. "But sure."

Zoe hesitated at the bottom of the steps, looking at them. "Remember, Jasmin doesn't know about Logan's mom yet. I've told her we're looking for our missing creature. I just—I didn't want to tell her her parents are kidnappers until we were sure."

From the grim look on his dad's face, Logan could tell *he* was pretty sure. But he didn't argue.

Jasmin threw the door open before they could knock. She was wearing the same fuzzy yak hat as Zoe. "Eeeeee!" she cried, pointing to Zoe's head. "I was hoping you'd wear it!"

"Well," Zoe said, "I decided if we could wear them when we were pretending to be Arctic explorers—"

"We could wear them to find a mythical creature on the coldest day in the history of the universe," Jasmin said. "Me too!"

Logan had met colder days, living in Chicago with the wind coming right off the lake. But there was an extra chill in the air today that wasn't about the weather; it was the danger of hope rising under the awful dread that all this could lead to nothing.

"This is my dad," he said. "Dad, Jasmin."

"Hello," his dad said awkwardly. "Thanks for your help."

"It's nice to see you again, Jasmin," said Zoe's mom, stepping forward to hug her.

"You too, Mrs. Kahn," Jasmin said warmly. "Where do you guys want to start looking?" She waved them inside. "I swear, I don't think it could be here, considering how people get into every nook and cranny of this house. Even last night, at least three different people wandered into *my* room during that awful party, claiming they were looking for the bathroom. I ask you, what bathroom says JASMIN in huge glittery letters on the outside of it? I mean, seriously."

"We think we found a clue," Zoe said. "Can we look at the giant Buddha in your garden?"

Jasmin wrinkled her nose at her. "Sure. I don't think it has any secret compartments, though. Remember how we used to climb up and sit on its lap?"

"And remember how your mom yelled at us for doing that?" Zoe countered.

"Oooh, good point," Jasmin said. "She freaks out whenever anyone goes in her Zen garden. Okay, let's check it out."

Logan had seen the Sterlings' yard up close once before,

the night he and Zoe and Blue snuck in to look for one of the missing griffin cubs. It had looked a lot more mysterious and creepy in the twilight. Now, in the pale morning, it just looked gray and a little trampled. There was a cover over the pool and a few champagne glasses were scattered around, abandoned on the poolside table and the edges of the wooden planters.

The stone Buddha was as tall as Logan and sat in the corner of the yard, near the towering white brick wall. It was surrounded by a neat square of white sand dotted with three piles of smooth black rocks. A small bonsai tree grew out of a miniature rock mountain beside it, and water trickled down a pebble fountain nearby.

"How do we avoid leaving footprints?" Logan wondered, looking at the sand.

"We'll rake it again after we're done," Jasmin said, pointing to an odd-looking fork thing leaning up against the wall. "I'm sure we'll do it wrong, and Mom will get all shouty, but you know what, somehow she'll live."

Logan stepped gingerly across the pristine sand and studied the statue. It looked fairly ordinary—huge, with an enormous flat pedestal at least four feet square, but not huge enough to hide a person inside, obviously. And it appeared to be solid stone all the way through. He tapped on it gently.

On the other side of it, Zoe and Jasmin were poking it

much more vigorously, tugging on its earlobes and trying to find something that moved. Logan's dad crouched to examine the base, while Mrs. Kahn glanced around the garden uncomfortably.

Logan stepped back to look at the statue from a distance again. He tried to imagine himself as a small whiskered dragon, looking at it. Why would it be such an important clue—a quarter of the dragon's whole message?

"Can I see the sketch Matthew and Elsie made?" he asked Zoe.

She pulled out a folded-up piece of paper and passed it to him. The drawing did look quite a bit like the statue in front of him, except there were strange wavy lines coming off the left side of it.

"What are these?" he asked, showing them to Zoe.

"I don't know, but Elsie was sure they were part of it," Zoe said.

Jasmin leaned over to look at the drawing and giggled. "They look like those motion lines you see in a comic book," she said. "You know? Like, ZOOM! When the character is running across the page. Except here it's my giant stone Buddha zipping off." She gave Logan a stern look. "If you tell anyone at school that I know anything about comic books, I will destroy you."

"She's kidding," Zoe said.

"I am absolutely not," Jasmin said.

"Maybe that's it!" Logan jabbed the paper. "Maybe the whole statue moves!"

"Let's try sliding it," his dad suggested.

Jasmin squinted at him, then turned to Zoe. "Remind me why he's here?" she whispered.

"I'll tell you soon," Zoe said. "I promise." She glanced at Logan. He knew this must be hard for her. But all he could think about was his mom and how close she might be.

Logan, Zoe, and his dad lined up on the statue's left side, found spots for their hands, and started to push.

The statue moved an inch. And then another inch. And then, suddenly, it slid smoothly to the side, revealing a trapdoor barely hidden under a thin layer of sand.

"YES!" Jasmin nearly shouted. "That is amazing! I can't believe I've lived here my whole life and had no idea that was there."

Logan's heart was pounding. Was his mother below that trapdoor? What would they find when they opened it?

His dad reached down, twisted the handle, and pulled up.

A square shaft descended into darkness, with an iron ladder bolted to one side. They couldn't see the bottom.

"Abigail?" Logan's dad called suddenly into the hole. "Are you down there?"

There was no response from below. Logan felt like he was about to throw up; his whole stomach was a giant knot of nerves.

Jasmin tilted her head at Zoe. "A mythical creature named Abigail?" she said. "That's totally weird. It's like naming your dog John."

Zoe started to stammer nervously.

"I'm going down there," Logan said, tucking his scarf into his jacket.

"Obviously I am, too," said his dad.

"I'll get flashlights!" Jasmin said. She ran back to the house, her long black braids flying out behind her.

Logan's dad didn't wait. He swung himself onto the ladder first and started descending rapidly. Logan stepped onto the ladder next.

"How are we going to close this up behind us?" Zoe worried. "What if Jasmin's parents come home and see the open hole in the yard?"

"We'll close the trapdoor," her mom said, "and hope they don't notice that the Buddha has moved."

"They shouldn't be home until this afternoon," Jasmin added, racing back up to them with three flashlights. "Last-minute campaign stuff. Even Jonathan has been drafted to, I don't know, make phone calls or something. I'm supposed to meet Mom here after school to get dressed for like the millionth boring dinner." She checked her watch. "Which gives us six hours. Come on, let's go!"

Logan took the flashlight she handed down to him, turned it on, and clipped it to his belt loop with the carabiner on the end. The small light lit up the ladder a few steps below him and the shiny top of his dad's head going down, but nothing below that.

He started to climb down.

And down.

And down.

He didn't know how much time had passed when his dad called up, "I've reached the bottom!"

A few minutes later, his sneakers hit the floor and he stepped away from the ladder, unclipping the flashlight. Now they could see a tunnel stretching off into the distance. It looked like it had been blasted and carved and chipped out of the rock. A small railroad-type track stretched along the center of it.

"I think it's an old mining tunnel," his dad said softly.

Zoe, Jasmin, and Mrs. Kahn hopped down beside them.

"Whoa," Jasmin whispered, shining her flashlight around. "This is crazy, Zoe."

Logan's dad set off down the tunnel, and they all followed without discussion.

"I thought the Menagerie was a huge secret," Logan heard Jasmin whisper to Zoe. "Why do Logan and his dad know about it?"

"His mom works for the agency who oversees us," Zoe whispered back. "She's a Tracker—they go out and find mythical creatures in the wild and bring them back to places like the Menagerie, so we can take care of them and protect them."

Jasmin whistled softly. "That sounds like the coolest job in the world."

"Yeah, but it can also be pretty dangerous," Zoe said. Her voice trailed off, and Logan knew she was thinking that Abigail had faced basilisks and dragons and manticores, but somehow Jasmin's own parents had turned out to be the one danger she couldn't overcome.

The tunnel went on for miles. Logan didn't think he'd ever walked so far in his life, but he didn't feel tired; he felt like he could walk three thousand miles if his mom was at the end of them.

After an hour and a half, they stopped for a rest.

"We should have brought snacks," Jasmin said ruefully, stretching her legs like a ballerina warming up. She and Zoe had both taken off their hats and coats and were carrying them. Logan had taken off his coat but left his scarf on, for good luck and because it made his mom feel close by.

"And water," said Zoe. "I didn't realize there'd be such a hike involved."

"They can't be doing this every day," Logan said, glancing at his dad.

"No, but if they had to, this way they could get in and out unseen," his dad pointed out. "Anyone watching would think they were still at home the whole time."

Like the private investigator, Logan thought.

"Still, they must have someone working with them," Zoe said, running her hands through her hair again. "Jasmin, have you seen anyone from the Menagerie talking to your parents?"

Jasmin shook her head. "But I probably wouldn't notice," she said. "Grown-ups talking? Yawn, I'm out. They always have a million people coming around for campaign stuff anyhow."

"And if it is one of the mermaids, you wouldn't recognize them," Zoe said. "They don't usually leave the Menagerie, but they *can* anytime they want, as long as they don't do anything weird to attract attention. We should make them sign out," she said to her mom. "So we can keep track of them."

"Great idea," said her mom. "They'll absolutely love that. And now seems like the perfect time to suggest it, too."

Zoe sighed.

Jasmin copied her sigh. "Oh, my troubled life with all its *mermaids* and *unicorns*."

"Shut up," Zoe said, shoving her affectionately. "You spend a day trying to convince a mer-king that he isn't actually ruler of the whole Menagerie and then get back to me on how lovely mermaids are."

"I hope everything's all right there," Mrs. Kahn said, rubbing her eyes. "I know Matthew and Elsie can handle themselves . . . and Ruby's there, too. . . ."

"That's a minus, if you ask me," Zoe pointed out. "Ruby is

not going to add responsibility and thoughtful decision making to any situation."

"Oh, but there's Melissa," Mrs. Kahn said. "She's very responsible."

"And Miss Sameera," Zoe reminded her. "She's very . . . enthusiastic."

"Wait, what?" Jasmin said. "As in, our school librarian Miss Sameera?"

"Yes!" Zoe said. "Turns out she's totally obsessed with unicorns and has literally spent her whole life trying to find them."

"Then someone really needs to talk to her about her color choices," Jasmin said. "Because if I saw her ensemble from last Monday coming at *me* through the woods, I'd absolutely run in the other direction."

"Let's keep going," said Logan's dad, who hadn't even sat down while the others rested, but paced back and forth around the tunnel.

They walked for another hour before they finally saw daylight glowing up ahead of them. Logan was sort of startled by it; he realized he had expected to come across a cage or some kind of dungeon. Not a light at the end of the tunnel.

"Careful," his dad said as they approached. The light was dazzling in their eyes after so long with just the dim flashlights. Cold air swept in along with it, and they all put on their coats and hats again.

They paused in the mouth of the tunnel, looking out over a rocky slope.

"What in the world?" Logan's dad said, bewildered.

Below them was a town straight out of the Wild West. An empty corral stood at the end of a dusty street lined with ramshackle wooden structures. Saloon doors creaked in the wind. Hitching posts for horses stood empty next to the sheriff's office and a post office. A watering hole connected to a small stream next to the corral. There was even a tumbleweed rolling slowly along between the buildings.

Nothing else moved. The place was deserted—a ghost town.

"Did we go back in time?" Logan asked. In a world with griffins and krakens, it kind of didn't seem *that* unlikely.

"Oh my gosh," Zoe said in awe. "It's Wild Wild Xanadu."

"Dad forbade me to call it that," Jasmin said. "It's Old Silverado in our house or no dinner for you. How totally weird of him to have a secret tunnel from our house to here. Although, actually, it's kind of classic Dad."

"This was Mr. Sterling's original theme park idea," Mrs. Kahn said to Logan's dad. "An old ghost town, like from the mining days, where people could pretend they were cowboys. It was . . . not a success," she finished politely.

"I didn't realize it was still out here," Zoe said.

"What else was he going to do with it?" Jasmin asked. "I guess it's a good place to hide something, though. What are we looking for? A griffin? A hippocamp? A pegasus?"

"Not exactly," Zoe said.

"Let's split up and search," Logan suggested.

They scrambled down the slope, past a few crooked wooden signs with arrows showing the way to A GENUINE OLDEN DAYS GOLD MINE! Logan's dad pointed to the saloon and Logan nodded, watching him go.

But he knew the first place he wanted to check. He remembered the third image the dragon had sent.

Slowly he climbed the steps to the boardwalk in front of the sheriff's office and jail. His heart was thundering like a creature trying to escape his chest. The old wooden door creaked when he pushed it open.

Inside, someone was lying on the cot behind bars in the Old West jail cell.

As Logan stepped closer, she sat up and saw him. A slow, familiar grin spread across her face.

"Well, howdy, pardner," said Abigail Hardy.

TWENTY

"Mom!" Logan cried, running up to the bars. His mom got up and wrapped her hands around his.

"I had this weird feeling it would be you who found me," she said. Her smile was as bright as the sun. Her normally short hair had grown out into a small Afro like a dark halo around her head, and she was wearing a dark-green sweater he'd never seen before.

"Dad's here, too," Logan said. "And Zoe, and Mrs. Kahn."

"All my favorite people," she said, but the way she was looking at him, it sounded like she meant *You. You are my favorite person that has ever existed in all the world.*

"I missed you." Logan's voice wavered. "Are you okay?"

"I'm absolutely fine," she said. "I have a friend here who needs some help, though." She nodded sideways at the gray blanket on the cot. Something small was moving underneath it.

"The Chinese dragon?" Logan asked.

She looked delighted and a little sad at the same time. "Did your dad tell you everything? About what I do and the Menagerie and the Kahns?"

"Sort of," Logan said. "I found out a lot of it myself. By accident. There was a griffin cub under my bed—it's a long story."

"I was looking forward to showing it all to you," she said wistfully, squeezing his hands. "I wanted to see the look on your face when you met Captain Fuzzbutt."

"It was something like this," Logan said, making a casual *oh yeah, right, whatever, one of those* expression.

His mother laughed. "I missed you *so much*," she said.

Logan rattled the door and turned to search the walls. In the movies, there was always a useful ring of keys hanging just out of reach of the prisoner, but he couldn't see anything like that here.

"My charming captors take them away with them," his mom said, guessing what he was looking for. There was a small growling sound from the blanket.

"I'll get Dad, hang on." Logan ran outside and yelled, "She's in here!"

His dad came barreling out of the saloon and tore across the street toward Logan. He took two steps inside the sheriff's office, saw Abigail behind bars, ran over, and kicked the locked door so hard that it slammed open.

"Well, I could have done that," Abigail said, putting her hands on her hips.

Logan's dad was already inside the cell. He wrapped his arms around her and lifted her right off her feet, which was an accomplishment since they were almost the same height. Mom hugged him back for a long moment, and then she reached out and pulled Logan in to join them.

She didn't leave us, Logan thought, closing his eyes. *She does love us. She meant it when she told me she'd always come back.*

The door banged open and Mrs. Kahn came in, followed by Zoe and Jasmin.

"Holly!" Logan's mom said, spotting them over Logan's shoulder. Logan and his dad let her go and she ran over to hug Mrs. Kahn. "I am so sorry I never showed up with Xiang. You must have been so disappointed in me."

"Try *worried*," said Mrs. Kahn. "We knew something must have happened."

"Just a minor kidnapping," Abigail said with a shrug. "Nothing awful."

Jasmin had been staring at Logan's mom with enormous confused eyes. "Wait," she said now. "What?" She whirled around to look at Zoe. *"Kidnapping?"*

"We weren't sure," Zoe said quickly. "I didn't want to freak you out."

"Then you failed, Zoe Kahn," Jasmin cried. "I am INCREDIBLY FREAKED OUT. Kidnapping, are you *serious*? Of a *person*? Of *his mom*?" She jabbed one finger toward Logan.

"Oh, it was accidental kidnapping, really," said Abigail. "They just wanted Xiang. They thought I'd take the two million dollars and disappear, but I'm afraid they got the wrong Tracker. I wouldn't leave him, so they were stuck with me." She turned and whistled a low, shivery series of notes. The creature under the blanket rolled over with another growl.

"But couldn't you have pretended to take the money?" Mrs. Kahn said. "And then come to us for help?"

"I couldn't risk leaving Xiang—we might never have found him again. And he needed taking care of." Logan's mother crouched and whistled again.

A tiny, lionlike face poked out of the blanket. It had bushy white eyebrows, long curling whiskers, and small horns like antlers on the top of its head. A shaggy white lion's mane surrounded its gentle face, and as it crept forward, Logan could see shimmering reddish-pink and gold scales all along its serpentine body. Sharp little talons dug into the mattress nervously.

"Oh," Jasmin whispered, pressing her hands to her chest.

"It's all right, Xiang, these people are all safe," Abigail said quietly.

Xiang looked up at Logan, who tried to hold very still.

With a small ripple of motion, the dragon threw aside the blanket and flowed off the bed, scurrying across the floor into Abigail's arms.

"His pearl," Mrs. Kahn breathed. She knelt down beside Logan's mom. "Oh no. How did they know?"

Logan's mom expertly held the dragon in a way where he looked comfortable and she could tilt him to show Mrs. Kahn his chin. "They must have done their research," she said. "They took it first thing, before I could stop them. You see why I couldn't leave."

"Of course," Mrs. Kahn said.

"I don't," said Logan's dad.

Abigail brought the dragon over to show him and Logan. "Chinese dragons normally have a pearl here, fitted below his chin," she said. She pointed to a small depression under the dragon's jaw. "It's the source of their power—with it, they can be any size, they can call down storms from the sky, they can walk on clouds, and they can bring luck and protection to their friends. Without it, they lose all their magic."

Xiang made a sad cooing noise.

"It's all right," Abigail said gently. "I don't need luck. I have a brilliant husband and son, see?"

"So they took his pearl?" Logan said.

"And I couldn't leave him like this, with all his power gone," Abigail said. "He's been so sad."

"*They*," Jasmin interjected. "You mean the Sterlings. *My*

parents. My parents kidnapped you and stole this dragon's pearl?" She turned to Zoe. "So they could expose your Menagerie to the world and turn it into an amusement park?"

Zoe twisted her fingers together. "We think so. I'm sorry, Jasmin."

Jasmin turned and walked out, letting the door slam closed behind her. Zoe glanced at her mom, who had worry lines all over her forehead.

"I'll go talk to her," Zoe said. She pulled open the door and ran out after Jasmin.

"Poor kid," Abigail said. "I'm not sure I'd know what to think if I found out my parents were like hers."

"Jasmin seems fairly resilient," Mrs. Kahn said. "But I hope they don't find out she helped us."

Logan glanced at his watch. "Then we should hurry to get back," he said. "So we can make sure she's home by three thirty."

"I don't think we need to go back the way we came," said Mrs. Kahn, pulling out her cell phone. "If I can find service, I'll call Matthew to pick us up." She shook her head. "I don't know how we're going to get that pearl back, though."

"Um," Logan said. "I—I have a sort of half idea. It might be crazy, though."

"A crazy half idea is better than none," Mrs. Kahn said.

"Maybe we could use one of the Menagerie creatures,"

Logan said. "Can he bring Nira with him?"

"Who's that?" his dad asked.

"The mother griffin," Logan said. "She's pretty fierce. I bet she could help."

Mrs. Kahn gave him a quizzical look. "All right, I'll ask." She held up her phone, checking for a signal. "Let me go try outside."

Left alone again, Logan and his mom and dad looked at each other and broke into matching grins.

"I'm so proud of you for figuring out my message," Mom said to Dad.

"Well, sort of," he said, rubbing the back of his head. "Some of it took me a while."

"But you got here," she said. "I was afraid I'd been too clever with the Fanny reference."

"Right," he said. "Because she was . . . ?"

"Robert Louis Stevenson's wife!" she said. "He went on a honeymoon with her to an old ghost town and wrote a book called *The Silverado Squatters* about it! Come on, everyone knows that."

"Literally nobody knows that, Mom," Logan said, hugging her again.

She shook her head. "Too clever. I knew it. Then what brought you to Old Silverado?"

"Xiang sent a distress signal and the kraken picked it up," Logan said.

"Oh, aren't you clever," she said admiringly to the little dragon. "I'm so glad I convinced them to let you go swimming, then. See, even without your pearl you're full of wisdom."

"Qrrrrrrr," said the dragon, nudging her shoulder with his nose.

"He doesn't want to leave without his pearl," she said. "I've tried to talk him into escaping before. But it's everything to him."

"We'll get it back," Logan said. "Come with us, and we'll get it back together. Today. All right? I don't know exactly how, but we will." He imagined another night creeping around the secret staircases in the Sterling mansion and wondered where in that enormous house they could be hiding a magic pearl.

The little dragon leaned over and reached out one of its talons. Logan gently touched it with his fingertips.

"It has to be today," Abigail agreed. "The Sterlings are planning something big and I think it's happening soon."

"It is. Tomorrow," Logan said. "They're planning to expose the Menagerie at the election victory party. But if they don't have the dragon—"

"Doesn't matter," Abigail said, shaking her head. "If they have his pearl, they can compel him to come to them. He'll have to go if he senses his pearl is in danger. I'm sure they know that."

Logan felt his heart sink.

They'd rescued his mom.

But if they didn't find that pearl . . . then they were still going to lose the Menagerie.

TWENTY-ONE

Zoe sat next to Jasmin at the bar in the saloon. A dusty chalkboard overhead offered root beer floats and sassafras something-smudged. The mirror across from them reflected Jasmin's face, but Zoe couldn't read it, and that was only partly because of the dirty glass. Jasmin seemed to be staring into space, her hands holding up the sides of her head. She hadn't said a word as Zoe explained the whole story—from Jonathan trying to steal the jackalope to the kraken ink to Logan and the griffin cubs to the map and Miss Sameera seeing Abigail drive away with Jasmin's dad.

Zoe finally trailed off. "Did—did all that make any sense?" she asked.

"No," Jasmin said at last. "Would it make sense to you if you found out your parents kidnapped someone else's mom?"

"No," Zoe admitted.

"Zo—are my parents going to go to jail?" Jasmin asked, unable to look at her. "I mean . . . you said there was a government agency involved. When we bring Logan's mom back, how much trouble will they be in?"

"That's not how SNAPA works," Zoe said. "They'd rather keep everything quiet than deal with trials and jail. Jasmin, it's going to be okay, I promise. Now that Abigail is safe, we can give your parents and Jonathan kraken ink, and they'll forget all about the Menagerie. Everything can go back to normal."

But Zoe couldn't get the worried note out of her voice. *Except . . . except . . . except . . .* her brain kept chiming. *Except we still don't know who helped them sabotage the Menagerie or why they targeted Scratch. Except we have no idea how to give them kraken ink. Except we still have to find the dragon's pearl before tomorrow night. Except . . .*

"They're not bad people," Jasmin said. "Not even Jonathan. Although he did sneak his laundry in with mine and turned my new jeans pink, that jerk." She threw Zoe a weak smile. "If you need someone to lock up in a secret prison guarded by dragons, I volunteer him."

"We'll just wipe his memories," Zoe said. "He'll probably be very confused for a while."

"So, no different than usual," Jasmin said wryly.

Zoe started giggling. "You know, every time I've seen him in the last few months, he's had this vaguely spaced-out expression. I thought it was the kraken ink and the holes in his memory, but now I've realized—that's just his *face*."

Jasmin laughed. "I know exactly the look you mean." She thought for a moment and the smile slowly drifted away.

"You're right, they're not bad people, Jasmin," Zoe agreed. "They've done some bad things. But I know they've done good things, too, like all their work on wind energy, and I know they love you. And we can fix this."

"Yeah, we can," Jasmin said, flipping her braids back and squaring her shoulders. She gave Zoe a determined look. "I know where that pearl is."

"You do?" Zoe cried.

"If it's enormous and sort of golden, then yes. It's in my mom's new necklace," Jasmin said. "She never takes it off. She's been wearing it *all the time* for the last six months. That's why I noticed—I was like, 'Mom, hello, what happened to a little variety in our accessorizing?' and she was all 'Simple elegance is always in style, especially if it's wildly expensive.' You know. Mom."

"Do you think she's wearing it now?" Zoe asked. *How on earth are we going to get it if she is? Maybe Mom and I can put on masks and mug her. And then Mr. Sterling can give an ironic speech about crime in Xanadu and how he'll put a stop to it when he's mayor.*

"I'm sure," Jasmin said. "Still, knowing where it is is half the battle, right?"

"Absolutely," Zoe said, throwing her arms around Jasmin. "Thank you. Let's go tell the others."

Jasmin stopped her as Zoe hopped down from the stool. "If my parents do get in trouble—" she said. "Will you help them?"

"I will help *you*," Zoe promised. "Whatever it takes."

They went back out through the swinging doors and found Zoe's mom sitting with Logan and his parents on the fence of the corral. The dragon was coiled around Abigail's shoulders, stretching its tail in the sun and glittering gold-pink-red. It was pretty crazy-cute. Zoe wondered what Captain Fuzzbutt would think of it. Sometimes he got a little jealous of other creatures Abigail brought in, especially if they were adorable. But she hoped they'd end up friends.

"Matthew's on his way," Zoe's mom called. "We'll get you back in time to meet your parents, Jasmin."

"Oh," she said, glancing at her watch and then at Zoe. "That's right. Hey, maybe while I'm with them, I could grab the pearl."

"No way," Zoe said, alarmed. "Jasmin! Don't be crazy. We can't let you do something dangerous like that. I don't want them to have any idea that you're helping us." She told the others about Mrs. Sterling's necklace.

"Oh!" Logan said. "I saw it! She was wearing it the night of the Halloween party."

"So how are we going to get it back?" Mrs. Kahn asked.

"Logan has an idea," Abigail said with a smile.

"I'm still thinking about it," he said. "Let me figure it out a bit more."

"He's a natural Tracker, Abigail," said Zoe's mom. "You'd be so impressed. He's as great with the animals as Zoe is."

Zoe looked down at her shoes, feeling her face get warm. Her parents didn't usually have time to stop and tell her she was good at anything.

"Someone's coming," said Mr. Wilde, pointing at a cloud of dust in the distance.

Zoe rubbed her wrists, sending up a small prayer that it wasn't the Sterlings. There had been piles of food, a microwave, and a small refrigerator stuffed in the jail cell with Abigail, so clearly they didn't come every day. Zoe was hoping they weren't planning to return for the dragon until right before the victory party tomorrow. In the best-case scenario, they'd never discover he was missing because they'd be all kraken inked by sunset tonight.

Matthew rolled up in the Kahns' dilapidated van. "Hey there, vagrants," he said. "Sorry, my mom says I'm not allowed to pick up hitchhikers."

"Ha-ha," said Zoe's mom, leaning in the window to kiss his forehead.

"Hi, Ms. Hardy," he said. "I'm glad you're okay."

"Of course I am," said Logan's mom. "I wasn't exactly captured by wendigos, was I? And it's Abigail, you goober."

Matthew grinned. "Yes, boss."

As Zoe, then Jasmin, then Logan, then Logan's dad squashed into the second row of seats, they heard a thump from the back of the van.

"What was that?" Jasmin asked, her eyes wide.

"Part of the plan to get the pearl back," Logan said. "I hope. We just need to catch your mom alone."

"Aren't you meeting her back at your house?" Zoe asked. She glanced at her watch. "At three thirty, right? It's one o'clock now."

"Will your dad be there, too?" Logan asked.

"Let me check." Jasmin took out her phone and flipped to the calendar. "It looks like he's booked all afternoon, although it just says 'Meeting.' That's informative, Dad."

"Okay," Logan said. He leaned forward to Matthew. "Can we go to the Sterlings' house, then?"

"Sure," Matthew said.

"And can we stop for lunch on the way?" Abigail asked from the front seat, where she was sitting between Matthew and Zoe's mom. "I am STARVING. And so sick of microwave burritos and PB and J, you have no idea."

The little dragon on her lap chirped vigorously as if he agreed.

"I don't care what it is, as long as it's french fries and a cheeseburger," Abigail added.

"QRRRRURP!" the dragon concurred.

"And we should drop you off at school," Zoe said to Jasmin. "You can tell them you were helping your dad in the morning, and then go home after school like normal."

"But what are you going to do?" Jasmin asked Logan.

As they drove back to Xanadu, Logan explained his plan. At the end he added, "So I don't think we all need to go in. Me and Nira and maybe one other person?"

"No, no," Zoe said.

"Absolutely not," said Mr. Wilde.

"ME!" cried Abigail, all at the same time.

"They don't know you or your dad are involved," Zoe argued. "You shouldn't show your faces if you don't have to. But Mom and I are obviously a part of it. It should be us."

"And me," Abigail said firmly. "Absolutely definitely me. I have some things to say."

So that argument took up the rest of the drive, but by the time they'd dropped Jasmin at school, everyone had agreed. It was Abigail, Zoe's mom, and Zoe who hopped out of the van in the Sterlings' driveway. Zoe looked up at the imposing mansion and felt a weird thrill of fear.

"We'll be right outside," Matthew said, leaning out the window. "Call us if anything goes wrong."

"Be careful," said Logan's dad.

"Careful is my middle name," said Abigail. "No, wait. It's the other one. The opposite of that." She winked at Zoe, then turned and passed the dragon to Logan. Xiang flicked his tail, inspected Logan's fingers carefully, and then curled up in Logan's lap and closed his eyes. "Take care of him till I get back. Jackson, stop *worrying*."

Zoe's mom glanced up and down the street to make sure it was deserted, then opened the rear doors of the van. Nira, the beautiful white griffin, lifted her head. The van was still full of pillows from transporting Pelly, and she was sprawled across them with her wings spread. She clacked her eagle beak at them.

Are we here? she said. **Do we have to be? That was the longest nap I've been able to have in months. Oh, hello, Abigail, nice to see you.**

"Hi, Nira," Abigail said. "Let's get you inside fast."

The griffin stretched her wings and legs and then hopped down from the van. She paced over to the Sterlings' garden wall, flew up to the top, and vanished inside.

"Now us," said Abigail, closing the van doors. She led the way around to a more sheltered spot—the same tree that Zoe had used to climb into Jasmin's garden more than once. Zoe could hear her mom muttering soft curses at the branches as they scrambled up, then over to the wall, and then dropped down on the other side.

"We should fix the Buddha first," Zoe remembered. She looked at her watch. Nearly two thirty. Mrs. Sterling might come back before Jasmin was due home. They'd better hurry.

Nira was prowling around the garden, sniffing the pool suspiciously. It felt like a hallucination, seeing one of the Menagerie's creatures *here*, in the Sterlings' yard in broad daylight.

Zoe and her mom shoved the Buddha into place while Abigail got the rake and smoothed out the sand to hide their footprints. They went in through the kitchen door and Zoe put the three flashlights back in the drawer where Mrs. Sterling always neatly stored flashlights, matches, candles, and takeout menus for the only two restaurants in Xanadu whose food she was willing to eat.

Shiny place, Nira observed, her voice echoing in Zoe's head. **Cold and glittery. Full of secrets and lies and whispers. I can see why Sage was interested, and then frightened of it.**

The littlest griffin cub had chosen this place to look for treasure, which was why Zoe and Logan had had to sneak in to find and rescue her. "Oh," Zoe said, turning to her mother. "I wonder if Sage was drawn here because she could feel the power of the pearl. Maybe she somehow knew the most valuable treasure in Xanadu was here."

Probably, Nira said complacently. I do have very precocious cubs.

"Should we wait in here?" Abigail asked, turning slowly to take in the gleaming cherrywood and silver.

"No, in case Jasmin comes back first. She needs to be able to say she had no idea we were here," Zoe pointed out.

"Upstairs, then," said Zoe's mom, and Zoe nodded.

Goose bumps prickled along her skin as they climbed the wide marble staircase to the upper balcony. The house was so still and perfect and chilly, like an abandoned museum with all its exhibits still intact. *This is breaking and entering,* she thought. *But then we could accuse them of kidnapping. Who would the police believe, though? And we're the ones with the biggest secret to keep. We're the ones who can't afford a public spectacle.*

She pressed her fingers together and then shook them out, taking deep breaths.

The master bedroom was on the same side of the house as Jasmin's bedroom; on either side of the doorway sat a jade frog with glittering diamond eyes. They slipped inside, into a room with wall-to-wall dark-gray carpet and black dressers. The king-sized bed was perfectly made as if it had been ironed into crisp even lines, with a light-purple-and-silver comforter and several of those small pointless matching pillows that Zoe had seen in magazines but never understood.

Nira's claws sank into the carpet. She turned in a small circle, then sat down facing the door and curled her lion tail around her claws. Her white fur was normally spattered with the various messes her cubs had made that day, but she must have cleaned herself up for this, because she glowed like a marble statue that utterly belonged in this room.

"Maybe they're vampires," Abigail said, glancing around. "I mean, do they actually sleep in here? Have they ever even been in this room? It's horrifyingly neat." She pulled open a door and found a huge walk-in closet. "Holy cats, it's all color-coordinated. And *who* needs *this many shoes?*" She crouched and picked up a pair of strappy red sandals with a heel as long as Zoe's pointer finger. "No," she said, waving them at Zoe. "Just no."

"It'd be so much easier if they *were* vampires," Zoe's mom sighed. "Then we could report them to SNAMHP and leave them to sort it out."

Zoe sat down on the bed and pulled out her phone. Abigail came and peeked over her shoulder as Zoe scrolled through photos.

"There's a nice one of Logan in here," Zoe said to her. "He'd been playing with the griffins and looks all funny and happy."

"I'm so glad you guys are friends," Abigail said. "Wait— go back. What was that?"

Zoe slipped her thumb across the screen. A picture of a

foreign-looking word popped up, and it took her a minute to remember it was the photo Jasmin had sent her, from one of the papers in her dad's office. K-N-O-H in Russian-looking letters.

Abigail tilted her head, frowning at it. "Zoe," she said, "why do you have a picture of the Russian word for 'clone' on your phone?"

Before she could answer, her phone buzzed with an incoming text. "Oh, Logan says they just saw Mrs. Sterling go by. She'll be here any second." Zoe leaped to her feet, feeling like every inch of her skin was trying to jump off her.

What are we doing? What are we doing? This is so dangerous....

"I'm going to sit right here," Abigail said, plunking herself down on the edge of the bed. She studied the perfect bed-spread for a moment, then knocked a few of the pillows to the floor. "Yeah, take that," she said.

Zoe stationed herself behind the bedroom door, and her mom stepped into the master bathroom. Nira stayed where she was, magnificent and regal, as if she were in a throne room awaiting her supplicants.

A few long, awful minutes passed. And then, suddenly, Zoe heard the front door below them open and close, fol-lowed by the jingling of keys as Mrs. Sterling set her purse down on the table in the hall. The sound of heels clopped across the floor and began coming up the stairs toward them.

Zoe could barely breathe. Across the room, Abigail caught her eye and made a face like, *Look scarier!* But Zoe couldn't get her facial muscles to obey her. They seemed very intent on staying within the lines of *terrified*.

Footsteps at the top of the staircase.

Closer.

Closer . . .

Mrs. Sterling stepped into the room. Her eyes were trained down on her iPhone. She tapped out something, then looked up, spotted Nira and Abigail, and froze.

"Hello," Abigail said pleasantly.

This was the most terrifying part. They had never, ever taken a mythical creature outside the walls and showed it to someone before. But as Logan had pointed out, if they didn't have to worry about secrecy, then something as tall as a grizzly bear and nine thousand times as scary could perhaps be useful in this situation.

Mrs. Sterling's eyes were fixed on Nira, and there was an awful gleam in them, as though she were calculating how much money she could make off her. Slowly, carefully, she started to lift up her iPhone.

"I wouldn't do that," Zoe's mom said, stepping out of the bathroom and snagging the phone from Mrs. Sterling's hand. "Flash photography sends her into a violent rage."

Doesn't look delicious, Nira grumped, ad-libbing. *I thought you said she'd be my best meal in weeks.*

Mrs. Sterling blanched, but before she could take a step back, Zoe closed the door and planted herself in front of it with her arms crossed.

"We're here to talk," she said.

"But if we *have* to feed our hungry griffin while we're here," Abigail said, "then that just means one less thing on our to-do list. I bet one of your ears would make a good snack."

Mrs. Sterling's hands jumped to her ears. "What are you doing in here?" she managed at last, shrilly. "You broke into my house! I could call the police!"

"True, but I don't think you want to," said Zoe's mom.

"Nira could *definitely* eat you before they got here," said Abigail.

The griffin clacked her beak menacingly. She looked as if she'd swelled up to twice her size, somehow, all outraged feathers and wickedly sharp talons.

"You wouldn't—you wouldn't actually—" Mrs. Sterling said.

"We're here for the pearl," said Abigail. She pointed to the gleaming chain around Mrs. Sterling's neck, where a pearl the size of a grape glowed softly in a gold-and-silver setting. "Hand it over and we'll go. Hand it over right now, and we'll even let you keep all your fingers."

But I love fingers, Nira said plaintively. Can't I have just a little one? Maybe a thumb? Those don't look important.

Zoe had to steel her face to look stern. Nira would never in a million years eat any part of a human, but she was acting the part of slightly unhinged deadly griffin to perfection.

Mrs. Sterling's face went blank, as though she was calculating something rapidly behind those sharp brown eyes. After a moment, she reached up and began to undo the clasp.

"All right," she said. "Let's all be reasonable here. Perhaps we can work out a deal."

"I think we just did," Abigail said calmly. She stood up and lifted the necklace out of Mrs. Sterling's hands, looking tall and imposing and fearless. "Xiang's pearl in exchange for your fingers. Seems fair to me, what do you think?" she asked Zoe's mom.

"We know what you're hiding," Mrs. Sterling said, smoothing her burgundy suit. "We just want a piece of it."

Oh, certainly, why not. Like I just want a piece of you, Nira said, swishing her tail. **Which would you suggest? A foot? Your nose? I do like noses, very squishy.**

"It is not fair to hide what you're hiding!" Mrs. Sterling protested, stepping hurriedly back until she bumped into the wall. Her dark hair was starting to escape its neat helmet shape.

"Shouldn't we ink her?" Zoe asked. "While we have a chance?"

Her mom shook her head. "It won't do any good if her

husband immediately reminds her of everything, and we don't want her to end up like Miss Sameera." *Resistant to kraken ink*, Zoe translated in her head. "We have to do them together."

"It's not going to work," Mrs. Sterling hissed. "You can't keep a secret like that forever."

"We've made it over a hundred years so far," Zoe's mom said, bristling. "I don't think a couple of selfish millionaires are going to bring us down now." She started for the door. "We're done here."

"You'd better stay away from me, the dragon, and my family from now on," Abigail added. "Or else we'll invite Nira to visit you in the middle of the night sometime."

Oooh, can I? growled Nira, flexing her giant lion's paws. **I love midnight snacks. I love biting into something while it's still asleep. I love sneaking into places after dark, prowling up the stairs, sniffing for fresh meat . . .**

"All right!" Mrs. Sterling said, waving her hands frantically in front of her face. "I understand. We'll leave you and the dragon alone."

"Great," said Abigail.

"And stay out of the Menagerie," Zoe chimed in.

She opened the bedroom door and heard the front door opening downstairs. Quickly she shut the door again and leaned against it, listening.

"Mom?" Jasmin called from downstairs. "Mom, are you home?"

Mrs. Sterling opened her mouth and then looked at the griffin.

Mmmmmm, said Nira. **Dessert.**

"Act normal," Abigail said. "Tell her to go to her room."

Mrs. Sterling cleared her throat. "I'm up here!" she called. "Just getting dressed. Go take a shower and I'll come help you pick an outfit in a minute."

"Oh, I don't think so," Jasmin's voice answered. They could hear her stomping up the stairs. "If I want to look like I'm six and on my way to a pageant, maybe. I can pick my own 'outfit,' thanks."

"Don't argue with me!" Mrs. Sterling called. "Just do as I say! Your father is waiting for us!"

"I'm not arguing!" Jasmin shouted back. "And I'm not your American Girl doll! You're so annoying!" Her bedroom door slammed.

There was a pause.

Mrs. Sterling rubbed her forehead and looked at her watch. "That should give you at least ten minutes of sulking to get out without her seeing you." She held out her elegantly manicured hand. "May I have my phone back?"

"In a minute," said Zoe's mom.

Zoe opened the door and checked the hallway. She knew Jasmin knew not to come out until they were gone, but of course she was nervous anyway. Quickly she sprinted down the stairs, texting Logan as she went.

The van was pulling into the driveway as the others came down, with Nira's sharp eyes trained on Mrs. Sterling the whole time. Matthew jumped out and opened the back doors.

The griffin paused at the foot of the stairs and regarded Mrs. Sterling for a moment.

It wouldn't take me long to eat her, she observed. **I promise not to make a mess.**

"No, Nira," said Zoe's mom. "We're going to leave this one intact."

For now, mused the griffin.

"If we promised not to expose your secret zoo," said Mrs. Sterling, "would you promise to leave our memories alone? And keep your wild monsters away from us?"

Nira's eyes narrowed.

"You would promise that?" Zoe asked. "After everything you've done?"

"Of course," said Mrs. Sterling, smiling with all her teeth. "We understand we can't end up with every acquisition we try for. You'll see, we're very gracious losers."

Zoe glanced at Abigail, who looked frankly disbelieving.

"I'll consult my husband and the agency," said Mrs. Kahn. "We'll get back to you."

Nira stood up, arching her back like a cat. **This is very disappointing,** she pointed out. **I'd better really** get to eat the next one. She marched out the door and climbed gracefully into the back of the van, folding her wings and circling before settling down. Matthew closed up the doors as Zoe went around to get in.

"Something doesn't feel right," Zoe said to Logan, who was crouched on the floor so Mrs. Sterling wouldn't see him through the window. The dragon was perched on his knees, its nose and whiskers twitching eagerly. "It's like she gave up just a little too easily."

"Wouldn't you agree to pretty much anything if Nira was snapping her beak at you?" Logan asked. "Maybe they didn't really think through that these are wild animals. Maybe she's realized that turning the Menagerie into an amusement park would be a lot more dangerous and difficult than they thought."

"Hmmm," Zoe said, twisting to look out the window. Mrs. Sterling was smiling and waving from her front steps as though they'd just dropped off a six-figure campaign donation.

Abigail hopped in the front and hung over the seat to pass the pearl to Xiang. The dragon reached up reverently to take it in his front claws. He snapped it out of the setting and then, with a happy murmuring sound, he tucked it under his chin and beamed around the van at everyone. The pearl seemed to shine a little brighter and a little more golden against his shimmering scales.

"We did it," Logan said, stroking the dragon's head between its horns. "We saved my mom and got Xiang's pearl back. Everything's going to be okay, Zoe. The Sterlings have nothing to show at the news conference tomorrow. They can't expose the Menagerie. You guys are safe."

Are we? Zoe wondered as they drove down the street toward home. Was it really over? She couldn't remember what it felt like not to be worried all the time. Imagine, she'd have time for homework and hanging out with Jasmin and maybe even watching TV with Captain Fuzzbutt. It sounded impossible.

They turned up the long driveway to Zoe's house.

Abigail leaned forward in her seat. "Did you guys change your front door?" she asked.

"No, what . . ." Zoe's mom trailed off.

Zoe lurched up to see out the front window.

The door to her house was hanging open, half off its hinges. The frame was cracked as though someone had smashed it with a sledgehammer—or as though something large had been squashed through the opening.

"Oh no," Zoe whispered. "Oh no, oh no—"

She didn't remember getting out of the van. It felt like the world was tumbling around her as she ran inside.

The house was a wreck. Side tables were overturned, books were knocked everywhere, vases were smashed, and one of the tapestries had been ripped right off the wall. The pillows in the living room had been trampled flat, some of them split so that feathers drifted out of them.

Lying unconscious on the living room floor was Miss Sameera, with a thin trail of blood trickling down her forehead.

He might be out in the Menagerie, Zoe thought frantically as she ran to the librarian. *Maybe he was with Mooncrusher. Maybe he was visiting the baku.*

But she knew. All the dread that had been lurking inside her, coiling and coiling like a snake, suddenly sprang up and grabbed onto her lungs so she couldn't breathe. She couldn't see straight. She couldn't think anything but one thought, over and over like a boulder thumping down into a dark ravine.

Captain Fuzzbutt was gone.

TWENTY-TWO

Logan remembered the first time he'd spoken to Zoe, the day he nearly ran into her with his bike. She'd told him she'd lost her dog—which turned out to be Menagerie code for "six missing griffin cubs"—and he'd wanted to do anything to help, to erase that devastated look from her face.

This was a million billion times worse. Of all the things that had happened in the last two weeks, nothing had crushed Zoe as badly as someone stealing Captain Fuzzbutt.

"What are they going to do to him?" she sobbed into her hands, crumpled on the edge of the couch. "What if they hurt him?"

"Let's not panic until we know exactly what happened,"

said Mrs. Kahn, but the tone of her voice was as close to panic as Logan had ever heard her. "Is Sameera all right?"

"She's coming around," Abigail said from where she was kneeling beside the librarian. Mrs. Kahn had propped a pillow under Miss Sameera's head and cleaned her cut with a damp washcloth; the wound was shallow and didn't look too serious.

The librarian's eyelids flickered and she slowly opened them. "The mammoth," she mumbled immediately. "Is he all right?"

Zoe let out another sob.

"He seems to be gone," Mrs. Kahn said gently. "I sent Matthew to check the Menagerie. Sameera, who did this?"

"Mr. Sterling," said Miss Sameera. "And his son. They came with a U-Haul and broke in—they moved so fast— they had a harness all ready for that poor little mammoth. They knew what they were doing."

"Did they take anything else?" Abigail asked.

Logan clenched his fists. A griffin cub would be a perfect adorable thing to pull out at a news conference to shock the world. If they had touched a hair—or a feather—on Squorp or any of the others—

"I don't think so." Miss Sameera shook her head and winced. "They just came through the house—and the mammoth fought them—I don't think they would have had time to go out into the Menagerie." She grabbed Mrs. Kahn's hand. "I tried to stop them," she said. "I really did."

"We can see that, don't worry," Abigail said.

Miss Sameera seemed to focus on her finally.

"Oh, the lady with the dragon," she said, managing a smile. "Hello."

"That's my mom," Logan said.

The doors to the Menagerie slid open and they all whirled around.

Ruby shuffled into the room in gold satin pajamas, a long puffy blue coat, and bright green bunny slippers. She stopped mid-yawn and blinked at the chaos around her.

"Sheesh," she said. "What happened here?"

"Where have you been?" Zoe asked murderously.

"Cleaning up Pelly's nest," Ruby said, bristling. "Remember? One of the MILLIONS of new chores I've been assigned as part of Mom and Dad's hideous nineteen-point punishment plan? And then we got talking about how life is so unfair and we're so misunderstood. Pelly really gets me. Unlike YOU people. Don't give me that look; *I* didn't wreck the house, if that's what you're accusing me of now."

"Captain Fuzzbutt has been kidnapped," Mrs. Kahn said. "I assume you didn't hear anything?"

"The mammoth?" Ruby raised her eyebrows and stifled another yawn. "What? Who would do that?"

"Who do you think?" Zoe yelled. "Your STUPID BOY-FRIEND, that's who!"

"Jonathan was here? And didn't say hi to me?" Ruby said, and then caught the looks on all their faces. "I mean—that's very bad. Are you sure it was him?"

"Ruby! He broke in here and stole Captain Fuzzbutt! How can you possibly defend him now?"

"You sound very angry," Ruby said, waving her hands at Zoe. "I read on the internet that too much negativity in the people around me could be what's causing my stress headaches. I'm going to go away and clear my chakras and let you calm down."

She fluttered up the stairs to her room. Zoe grabbed a pillow and screamed into it.

Mrs. Kahn took a walkie-talkie off the table and called Matthew. "I don't think anything else was stolen," she said. "I'm going back to the Sterlings'. Mrs. Sterling must know where they took him."

"I'm coming," Matthew's voice crackled through the walkie-talkie.

"I'd better call Robert. And SNAPA." Zoe's mom started toward the kitchen, then stopped and scanned the room with a puzzled expression. "Wait—where's Melissa? Why wasn't she here?"

"I don't know," said Miss Sameera. "She got a call and went out."

Zoe lifted her head and Logan caught her eyes. Why would she have left the Menagerie essentially unguarded?

"The Sterlings must have known somehow," Logan said. "They planned this. They must have known you were all gone."

"That's why Mrs. Sterling didn't care that we took the pearl," Zoe said. "She already knew that her husband had a mammoth to show off instead."

Matthew came through the door, panting for breath. "Elsie's been in the lake the whole time," he reported. "She's fine. In case anyone else was worrying."

"Let's get back over to the Sterlings' with Nira and find out what we can," said Mrs. Kahn.

She ran out the door with Matthew and a moment later Logan heard the coughing rumble of the van starting. Zoe half stood up and then sat down again and pulled out her phone. She let out a little gasp.

"I got a message from Jasmin five minutes ago," she said. She held it out to Logan.

Mom's fre

That was all it said.

"I'm worried," Zoe said. "Something happened in the middle of her sending this. I don't know whether to text her back. What if her mom took her phone? Logan, what are we going to do?"

He sat down beside her and awkwardly rubbed her

shoulder. "Let's think about this," he said. "If they knew everyone was out, it must have been from their contact inside the Menagerie. Whoever has been sabotaging you."

"The mermaids," Zoe said halfheartedly. "Maybe?"

Or maybe someone else, Logan thought, not ready to put it into words yet.

"Oh my God," Blue said, bursting in the front door. "What happened? Zoe! Zoe, are you all right?"

"They took Captain Fuzzbutt," she said, tears spilling out of her eyes again.

"Oh no," he said. He sat down on the other side of her and put one arm around her. "Zoe, he'll be all right. He made it all the way here from Siberia when he was a baby. He's tough."

"Hey, Blue," said Abigail. "You've grown like six inches since I saw you last."

"You found her!" Blue cried. "Hi, Abigail. I'm glad you're okay."

"Me too," she said. Logan's mom got up suddenly and came over to them. "Zoe, let me see that picture on your phone again. The one in Russian."

Puzzled, Logan watched Zoe pull up a photo of a word in blocky dark letters, printed on the corner of stationery with other Russian words all over it.

"I've seen this before," Abigail said. "When I rescued the Captain from that cloning lab in Siberia. This is the same company."

"What?" Zoe said. "How? Jasmin said her dad just bought it . . ."

"Which means he's now officially Captain Fuzzbutt's original owner," Abigail said darkly. "I think I see where he's going with this. Logan, I have to talk to your dad for a minute." She got up and went into the kitchen, where Logan's dad had gone to make tea for Miss Sameera, who still seemed a little woozy.

"We have to figure out who's working with the Sterlings," Logan said. "They'll know where Mr. Sterling is taking the mammoth, don't you think?"

"But how do we do that?" Zoe said. "Blue, do you know if any of the mermaids have left the Menagerie recently?"

He shook his head slowly. "I'm not sure, but they usually don't once it's this cold out."

"Maybe we figure out the motive first," Logan said. "I have a really strong feeling that it all comes back to Scratch. Everything else was sort of easy—cutting a hole for the griffins to escape, or tampering with the fire extinguisher that set Basil loose. Even getting the mermaids riled up enough to strike, if that's connected."

"Yeah," Blue agreed. "That wouldn't take much effort."

"But the whole Pelly plan . . . making it look like she was dead and going to all the trouble of framing Scratch . . . why would someone do that?" Logan asked. "Why not just make the goose disappear, if they only wanted to cause trouble?"

"Can we find out more about Scratch's mom?" Blue said. "We know that Scratch's sister went crazy. Maybe she did, too."

"Or maybe someone made it look like she did," said Zoe. She wiped her eyes and stood up. "Let's see if Melissa's computer has any archives on Scratch's family."

They stepped around the mess of destroyed pillows and overturned chairs and went into Melissa's office, at the far end of the room.

It was neat and orderly as usual. Nothing indicated where she had gone off to.

"Do you know where your mom is?" Logan asked Blue, not quite as casually as he was trying to.

Blue shrugged. "I haven't heard from her today, but she's probably doing something for SNAMHP. Or SNAPA. Most likely it involves forms." He grinned at Logan and Logan tried to smile back.

Something small moved in the corner of his eye, and Logan turned to see the deflector creeping quietly into the office behind them. Bob clambered onto a filing cabinet in the corner and plucked a chocolate kiss out of a bowl of candy on top of it. She sat down, unwrapping the silver foil with slender, clever fingers, and noticed Logan watching her.

The huge dark eyes stared back at Logan for a long moment. Logan blinked first, then nodded, trying to convey *It's okay, I won't say anything.*

Bob turned the chocolate between her hands thoughtfully for a minute, looking ready to spring away. But when Logan didn't move, she slowly settled her paws in a yoga position and began to nibble contentedly on the kiss.

She's getting used to me, Logan thought.

Zoe sat down at the computer and started clicking on files. "Lacewing," she said. "That was his mom's name, right? Oh, here." She clicked on a folder labeled "DRAGONS" and then one inside that which said "SCRATCH." About a hundred documents popped up, and she started scrolling through them.

"There," Logan said, leaning forward to point. "Parental History."

Zoe clicked, and a newspaper headline filled the screen.

HIKERS KILLED BY FOREST FIRE OR MYSTERY ANIMAL?

The bodies of a young couple were found in a remote corner of the Rocky Mountains today, several miles from the nearest hiking trail. They appear to have been mauled by some large beast, perhaps a grizzly bear. Identification could take weeks, as the bodies were also apparently caught in a forest fire and are charred beyond recognition.

"What the . . ." Zoe murmured. She clicked on the next page, which turned out to be an internal SNAPA report on Scratch.

"Father unknown," she whispered, scanning through it. "Mother part of a trial program to allow hatching in the wild. A lot of dragon eggs don't make it in captivity," she said in an aside to Logan. "No one's sure why." She went back to reading. "Program canceled due to unfortunate fatal incident." She stopped with a small gasp. "Oh! That's so sad!"

"What?" Blue asked, craning around Logan.

"The animal in the woods—the one who killed those two hikers. That was Lacewing," Zoe said. "She was watching over her eggs . . . it says here she testified that the hikers came too close and she thought they were a threat. Oh, those poor people. And poor Lacewing."

Logan didn't want to imagine it, but the images filled his mind before he could stop them. A dragon in a secluded spot, curled up with her two eggs, thinking they were safe. Two hikers exploring the wild, coming around a bend, and stumbling over the nest by accident. The dragon, terrified and protective—the hikers, trying to escape but failing . . .

"So SNAPA exterminated her?" Logan said in a hoarse voice. "For protecting her eggs?"

Zoe pressed her eyes like she was trying to shove the tears back inside them. "It's SNAPA policy for any creature who kills a human," she said. "They have to, or the government might decide to exterminate all of the mythical creatures, just to be safe." She sighed. "But that poor dragon. Scratch and

Scritch must have been in those two eggs. No wonder he feels like the world is against him."

"And no wonder he chose invisibility for his glamour," Logan pointed out. "It *was* childhood trauma."

"How is this related, though?" Blue asked. "What does this have to do with Scratch now, or everything that's happening in the Menagerie?"

Zoe leaned forward and started scrolling through the files again. There was a series of forms and reports related to Lacewing's trial and extermination. And then another newspaper article:

DECEASED HIKERS IDENTIFIED

The hikers who were found dead in the woods three weeks ago have been identified as Brad and Missy Strong, a married couple from Albuquerque, New Mexico, who were known for their love of hiking off-trail and nature photography. Mystery still surrounds the incident, however, as they were apparently traveling with their only daughter, Brigid, age ten. No other bodies were found at the scene, and there have been no lost children found matching her description. Emergency crews are searching the surrounding areas, but there is little chance a ten-year-old could have survived on her own for this long, even one known to be an accomplished hiker.

The article went on, speculating about the bear and the forest fire, which was suspiciously confined to a small area.

Zoe frowned at the screen. Without saying anything, she clicked to another file—a report on SNAPA's own unsuccessful search for the missing Brigid. Lacewing claimed she hadn't seen the girl with the two hikers, but in her state of panic she could easily have overlooked her. They searched for months . . . but never found any trace of her.

"That's it," Logan said suddenly. Pieces were starting to fly together in his head.

"What's it?" Blue asked.

"Brigid." Logan pointed to the screen. His mind was racing. "That's your saboteur. She'd be in her thirties now. Old enough to come looking for revenge on the family of the dragon who killed hers."

"But how?" Zoe asked.

"You think she changed her name," Blue said, catching on. "And it's someone we know."

Logan hesitated, meeting Blue's eyes. How could he say this out loud? How could he point the finger at someone who was such a part of the Menagerie family?

How could he accuse Blue's mom?

"Miss Sameera?" Zoe guessed in a whisper. "Do you think she's been playing us this whole time?"

Logan slowly shook his head. "I—I think—"

"Wait, there's a picture," Zoe said, leaning toward the

computer. She clicked on an attachment under the article and a photo popped up of a smiling couple with a young, dark-haired girl. Brigid looked serious and a little worried, as if she sensed something terrible coming.

Logan stared at the screen.

Brigid did look familiar.

But she didn't look like Melissa.

Zoe sucked in a sharp breath. "I've seen this photo before," she said. She jumped to her feet, shoving the chair back from the desk in a violent clatter. "I know who Brigid is."

There was a knock at the office door, and the three of them turned to see Abigail standing there—with Agent Delia Dantes.

TWENTY-THREE

"It's her!" Logan and Zoe cried at the same time, pointing at Agent Dantes.

"What's me?" she said with alarm. She took a step back, her gray eyes wide and shocked.

"Mom, don't let her go," Logan said. "She's the one who's working with the Sterlings."

"What?" the SNAPA agent yelped.

"Delia?" Abigail said. "What are they talking about?"

"I don't know, I—" Agent Dantes looked up at Logan's mom for a tense, humming moment—and then turned and bolted across the room.

Abigail shot after her, but Delia didn't get far before

she tripped over a pillow and went sprawling. Logan's mom hauled her up and sat her firmly on one of the armchairs.

"That was a silly thing to do," she said, crossing her arms. "Now I know they're right."

"Why—I didn't—why would I—" Delia stammered.

"What's going on?" Logan's dad asked, coming in from the kitchen. Miss Sameera was also watching in bewilderment from her position on the couch.

"Wait," Abigail said, hearing the rumble of the garage door. "Holly and Matthew are back. They'll want to hear this, too."

Logan saw the desperate hope in Zoe's eyes as she turned toward the door. A moment later, Zoe's mom appeared. Her face was pale with worry, and it went even paler when she saw them all standing over the SNAPA agent.

"No sign of Mrs. Sterling or Jasmin or anyone at their house," she said. Zoe's shoulders sagged. "They've all vanished—probably hiding until the election party tomorrow. What—what's happening here?"

"Delia is the one who's been sabotaging us," Zoe said fiercely. "She helped the griffin cubs escape. She stole Pelly. She framed Scratch." Her hands were shaking, and Logan knew she was thinking of Captain Fuzzbutt and what he must be going through right now.

Everything was starting to click. Logan ran through the sabotage in his head. Agent Dantes could have done all of it—she'd had access to everything during that first inspection. She could easily have tampered with Scratch's anklet and his electric collar, and the fire extinguisher in the Reptile House. She could have talked to the unicorns about how they deserved their enclosure back; she almost certainly had told the mermaids they weren't safe so close to the basilisk and dragons, and she'd probably planted the idea that she could get them moved to Hawaii. She also could have picked up golden goose feathers at another menagerie to use at the scene of Pelly's "murder."

"The dragons wouldn't have set off the alert for her," he pointed out. "She knew she could climb in and steal Pelly, even if Scratch did stay on watch."

"And that's why she wiped Miss Sameera's memory so fast," Zoe added. "I bet Sameera *did* see her, and the story about following a strange young man in a van was a lie Delia made up."

Another realization hit Logan. "And she's probably responsible for what happened to Scritch, too. I bet if we check we'll find out she was inspecting the Amazon menagerie when Scritch's rampage happened."

Delia closed her eyes and shuddered, but didn't deny it.

"Why would she do any of that?" Mrs. Kahn asked, spreading her hands.

They all looked at Delia, who buried her face in her hands.

"It's Brigid, isn't it?" Zoe said. "You're Brigid Strong."

Everyone looked confused except for Logan's mom, who stared at Delia with dawning horror.

Delia nodded and her shoulders began to shake. "No one's called me that in so long," she said, her voice muffled by her hands.

"Were you there?" Abigail asked, dropping to a crouch beside Delia's knees. She put one hand gently on the agent's shoulder. "Did you see it happen?"

"I see it every night," Delia said in a cracked, hopeless voice. "Every night when I fall asleep, if I can sleep at all. Every night I see that dragon kill them." She sat up suddenly, brushing away tears. Her face was lit with anger. "I figured it out, you know. That dragon had a tag in her ear, like the kind for tracking endangered birds. Someone *knew* it was out there, running wild, ready to kill people. And then I read the papers and saw the cover-up. I knew someone was protecting that dragon." She said "dragon" the way most people would say "giant hissing cockroach."

"But how did you survive?" Zoe asked. "And how did you end up in SNAPA?"

"I made it as far as I could through the woods and got picked up by a woman who was living in a cabin, off the grid," Delia said. "She didn't care where I came from, and she didn't believe what I told her about the dragon, of course. But she took care of me for a while, until everyone had stopped looking for me. I learned to tell people I had amnesia, didn't remember my parents, couldn't remember where I came from. I wound up in the foster care system until I was able to get a scholarship to college."

She took a deep breath. "I read all the rumors. I wanted to find a way in, so I made myself into the perfect candidate. I majored in zoology and did my thesis on the potential link between the bones of extinct species and the tales of mythical creatures. I became an expert on wildlife protection, endangered animals, cryptozoology, anything I could think of that might make me the right person for a job with whoever was hiding dragons. And then it happened. SNAPA approached me, just as I'd planned."

"All of that," Logan's mom said, "your whole life, dedicated to getting your revenge?"

Delia lifted one shoulder, staring at her hands. "My parents were worth it," she said. "But once I was in, once I had access, I found out that the dragon I wanted was already dead." She frowned, then glanced out at the Menagerie. "So I went looking for the dragons who hatched from those eggs."

"Scratch and Scritch," Logan said.

"What did you do to Scritch?" Mrs. Kahn asked.

Delia hunched forward. She looked brittle and easy to snap in two. "I gave her a shot of a kind of dragon PCP. Like a drug to make her go crazy." She took another deep, shuddering breath. "But I didn't know how bad it would be. I didn't think she would . . . I didn't mean for her to kill anyone. That's why I came up with a new plan here," she added quickly. "Something safer. I just had to make it *look* like the dragon had escaped and done something bad. And I put a sedative in the toothpaste so he couldn't actually get free and hurt anybody." She passed one hand over her eyes. "Of course, I thought you would use it."

"I'm guessing *you've* never tried to brush a dragon's teeth," Matthew interjected.

Delia shuddered from head to toe as if she couldn't imagine anything worse.

"Did you also tamper with the fire extinguisher in the Reptile House? How is letting the most deadly creature in the world out of its enclosure a 'safer' plan?" Mrs. Kahn asked pointedly.

Logan's hands went to the scarab beetle under his shirt, his skin prickling at the reminder of how close to death he'd come.

"That was an accident," Delia said. "Honestly, I never meant for the basilisk to get free! I thought the damaged fire extinguisher would be up by Scratch's cave and if everyone thought he'd set it off, it would just be extra ammunition for having him exterminated. In all the chaos of the trial, I forgot to check on where it ended up."

"So the night Pelly was stolen—" Logan said. "You weren't monitoring Agent Runcible as a werewolf?"

She shook her head. "He just thought I was. I drove him

to the reserve, waited until midnight when he was definitely stuck in wolf form, and then came to get the goose."

Logan remembered the night he, Zoe, Blue, and Keiko had snuck into the woods to look for a werewolf—the night they'd seen Marco change into a rooster. There had been a car in the parking lot at the reserve that night. An empty car, where Delia should have been sitting, watching the tracking monitor to make sure Runcible stayed within the woods.

That was the night after Pelly was stolen, but he guessed she'd taken the same opportunity that night, while Runcible was furrily occupied, to sneak away, this time to check on her captive.

"So what does this have to do with the Sterlings?" Logan's dad asked abruptly, his deep voice from across the room startling Logan.

"They caught me," Delia said. "They've been monitoring you, too, for months. There are cameras hidden all through the woods around your property. So they saw me cutting the hole in the river grate, and they approached me with the proposal that we could . . . work together."

She turned to Abigail. "I swear I didn't know they had you, or the Chinese dragon. They didn't tell me everything." Her face went hard. "I didn't know about their plans for an amusement park, either, until you came and told us about the map you found. I've told them it's foolish and far too dangerous. I said I would help them expose the Menagerie, but only if they promised me that dragon wouldn't be allowed to live."

"I think we've heard enough," said Zoe's mom, looking sick.

"No, wait," Zoe said. "Delia, where did they take Captain Fuzzbutt?" She knelt beside Delia's chair, looking desperate. "Please tell us. If anything happens to him—I'm so worried. . . ."

Delia gave her a look that seemed genuinely sympathetic.

"I'm sorry, Zoe," she said softly. "They didn't tell me. I have no idea where they've taken him."

Logan watched Zoe's face fall and wanted to hit something. Finally they'd found the person they'd been looking for this whole time, but she couldn't tell them what they really needed to know.

The Sterlings had vanished along with the mammoth.

But there was one place they would definitely be . . . at the election party the next night, in front of a hundred cameras, at the Buffalo Bill Diner.

Which meant there might be one last chance to stop them before the Menagerie was exposed and destroyed forever.

TWENTY-FOUR

"I wish *I* could vote," Logan said grumpily, leaning against the side of the van.

"Me too," said Blue.

"Me three," Zoe said. She couldn't stand still. She hadn't been able to sleep all night; she just kept rolling over and looking at the empty floor where Fuzzbutt usually slept. Her chest ached as though the Sterlings had carved out part of it on their way out the door.

"I voted," Ruby said cheerfully from her perch on a nearby railing. "Except the other candidate seemed lame, so I just wrote in Miley Cyrus."

"I'm sure that'll help," Zoe said, rolling her eyes.

They were stationed in the alley across from the back of the Buffalo Bill Diner. There was only one set of doors big enough to fit a mammoth through—the big rolling service door at the back, where trucks delivered the food. Earlier it had been busy with staff getting ready for the party, but now it was quiet; the action had moved to the front of the diner, where guests were already starting to arrive. Zoe could see the flash of cameras going off like lightning. She twisted her hands together nervously.

Where were the Sterlings? Why weren't they here yet?

Was Jasmin okay?

Was Captain Fuzzbutt okay?

Was this going to be the night everything was ruined forever?

She squinted at Logan, distracted for a moment from her scurrying thoughts. "Logan, did your shirt just . . . move?"

"Don't worry about it," he said. "I brought backup."

"Okay." Zoe didn't know what that meant, but she couldn't add one more worry to her list right now. She looked at her watch. "The polls are about to close. Why aren't they here?"

"I think they are," Matthew said, hopping out of the van.

A U-Haul rolled slowly down the small street behind the Buffalo Bill Diner. It jerked to a halt, and then backed up to the delivery entrance. Jonathan Sterling jumped out of the passenger side, glanced around furtively, and hurried to the back of the truck. Ruby let out a small hissing sound. He hit the button for the diner doors and turned to roll open the U-Haul.

As the metal door of the diner rattled up, Zoe could see her parents and Logan's parents standing inside the loading area, waiting. Jonathan didn't notice them; he was busy pulling out the ramp that led down from the U-Haul.

But now Mr. and Mrs. Sterling were climbing out of the front of the truck, and they spotted the welcoming committee at the same time.

"We're not going to let you do this, Arnold," Zoe's dad said in a clear, ringing voice.

Mr. Sterling grinned in a way that made Zoe want to feed him to the kelpie. He sauntered toward the loading area, brushing off the arms of his suit jacket. He was wearing a white cowboy hat that matched Mrs. Sterling's impeccable jacket and skirt. They looked shiny and photogenic, tailormade for a national news conference.

"I don't rightly see how you're going to stop me," said Mr. Sterling. "After all, this mammoth is my property, as I am now the owner of the company who created it." He tipped his hat at Abigail. "And I happen to have security camera footage that shows you stealing it. Along with evidence that you've been harboring it in your little zoo there for some time now."

He made finger guns at each of Zoe's parents. "So here's what's going to happen. I'm going to announce my plans for a jim-dandy rooting-tooting tourist attraction right here in little old Xanadu that's going to bring in visitors from all over the world. And I am going to sue you for stealing this mammoth, and I'm going to win, and I'm going to end up with everything you own."

"Not if I have anything to do with it," said Mr. Wilde. "I'm a lawyer, in case you didn't know, and I can see several holes in your case from across the Grand Canyon. Not to mention the little matter of your kidnapping escapades."

Mr. Sterling shrugged this off. "I guess we'll see you in court then, my friend." His teeth were as big as mammoth toenails. "Because once we expose this little secret, I have a feeling a lot of people will be rooting for me. By the way, Robert, Holly—if you're not too disagreeable, I might let you stick around to show us the ropes. But if I have to get my own zookeepers in here, that's all right with me, too. Now excuse me, I've got a speech to give."

He made a commanding gesture at Jonathan, who had climbed up into the truck. Jonathan started forward, tugging on a rope. From her angle, Zoe couldn't see into the U-Haul— but she could see that he was holding a riding whip.

She couldn't stay back anymore, even though her parents had warned her to keep out of the way.

"Zoe, wait!" Logan protested as she launched herself away from the van and ran across the street. A moment later, she heard his footsteps behind her, and then the others as well.

"Captain!" she cried, darting to the back of the U-Haul.

The mammoth was at the top of the ramp, his ears drooping sadly, wearing a harness attached to the rope Jonathan held. When he saw her, Fuzzbutt's whole face lit up and he surged forward.

"Don't touch him!" Mrs. Sterling barked as Zoe reached out. She held up her cell phone, her thumb poised over the screen. "We have an email here ready to send to every major news outlet. It contains a press release along with an absolutely beautiful set of photos of a mammoth, a golden goose, and an exotic Chinese dragon. Of course, we would rather reveal our surprise out there, in front of the cameras, with Arnold's marvelous speech that he's practiced so much. But if you make one move to stop us, I will hit send right now."

Everyone was frozen in place. Zoe glanced up at Captain Fuzzbutt, now halfway down the ramp, and spotted Jasmin standing in the truck behind him. She had her arms wrapped around herself and she looked like she'd been crying.

Mrs. Sterling spotted her, too. "Oh, *Jasmin*," she snapped. "I told you it was a mistake to let her ride in the back with the animal," she said to Mr. Sterling. "Now look at you. Your hair is a mess, your dress is covered in fur, and what is wrong with your face? We don't have time to fix your makeup."

Jasmin wiped her eyes. "I'm sorry, Zoe," she said. "They took my phone. I couldn't do anything."

"It's all right, Jasmin," Zoe said. "It's not your fault."

Blue looked from the Sterlings to Jasmin, and then stepped over to the U-Haul. Mrs. Sterling raised her phone threateningly, but instead of going to the mammoth, Blue went over and held his hands up for Jasmin.

She blinked at him for a moment, then reached down and took them. He held on to her as she hopped to the ground. With a dark look at the Sterlings, he put one arm around her protectively.

"Well, great seeing y'all, but I'd better get out there," Mr. Sterling said, taking a step toward the kitchen door. "My public awaits."

Zoe's heart was pounding. There had to be *something* they could do. If she tackled Mrs. Sterling, could she knock the phone away before Jasmin's mom hit send? Was it too risky?

Jonathan led the mammoth to the bottom of the ramp. Captain Fuzzbutt stamped his feet and reached his trunk toward Zoe.

"Stay back," Mrs. Sterling warned again.

"You are such a liar!" Ruby yelled suddenly. She stormed past everyone and shoved Jonathan in the chest. "You horse-faced cow! You giant worm! I defended you! I trusted you! You were lying to me the whole time!"

"I wasn't!" Jonathan said in a voice that was almost a whine. "I love you, Ruby!"

"Oh YEAH?" she shouted. "What kind of boyfriend

steals mythical creatures from his girlfriend and ruins her family? What kind of boyfriend totally lies about giving his parents kraken ink? What kind of boyfriend doesn't even CALL ME BACK for an ENTIRE WEEKEND after I've left like THIRTY MESSAGES and then posts pictures on Facebook where he's dancing with some BRUNETTE?"

"I told you, she's nobody!" he protested. "My phone died! I was studying for an exam! I swear I was thinking about you!"

"You could have emailed!" Ruby smacked his shoulder and he reeled back. "You promised you would call me every day! Next you're going to tell me you can't make it to my play!"

"Um, Ruby," said her mother. "I think we're getting a bit off topic here—"

"We are OVER, Jonathan!" Ruby shrieked. "You are the WORST! I hope Captain Fuzzbutt stands on your foot AND BREAKS ALL YOUR TOES!" She stormed out of the garage and off into the night.

"Oh, Ruby," Zoe's dad sighed.

Where's Logan? Zoe suddenly thought. She blinked and looked around. He'd been right next to her . . . hadn't he? What was he—

She spotted him suddenly, creeping quietly up on the other side of Captain Fuzzbutt. He was holding something small and furry in his hands—something honey-colored, with big dark eyes. Its head was swiveled nearly all the way around so it could stare at Mr. Sterling, and it was shaking in a strange way that looked more like rage than fear.

Bob? Zoe thought.

"Come along, dear," Mr. Sterling said, taking Mrs. Sterling's free hand.

And that's when the deflector attacked.

TWENTY-FIVE

It wasn't exactly a plan. It was more of a desperate last-ditch quasi-idea.

They'd been on their way out to the Buffalo Bill Diner when Logan had thought of it. The deflector—if Logan could talk her into coming. How strong was her power? Could the deflector shield Captain Fuzzbutt? If Logan got her close enough, would the deflector's power be able to hide the mammoth from the news cameras?

He'd taken a bag of chocolate chips from the kitchen and gone looking for Bob. He'd found her draped peacefully over Keiko's pillow, snoozing, although she came fully awake as soon as Logan set foot in the room.

Logan didn't know how much Bob understood. But he had offered the chocolate, spread out his hands, and pleaded for help. He knew it could only possibly work if the deflector agreed to come willingly.

Shockingly, she had. Bob had crawled under Logan's shirt and munched chocolate chips all the way to the diner. Logan was a little worried that she'd be in a sugar coma by the time they arrived, but he could feel the deflector poking his belly button and playing with his scarab necklace even while the Sterlings and the Kahns were facing off.

So he'd taken advantage of the fight between Jonathan and Ruby to sneak up on the mammoth's other side. He had a vague notion that he might slip Bob onto Fuzzbutt's back and see what happened.

But the closer Logan got to Mr. Sterling, the more the deflector seemed to be freaking out. Bob scrambled up to the collar of Logan's shirt and wrestled her way out. She wrapped her long furry arms around Logan's neck and gripped Logan's chest fiercely with her toes. Her head swiveled back and forth between Mr. and Mrs. Sterling, staring at them with her giant black eyes.

"It's okay," Logan whispered to her. "They can't see you. They'll leave you alone."

Bob was pulsing weirdly now, as if something was going *DANGER! DANGER! DANGER!* inside her head.

And then, as Mr. Sterling took Mrs. Sterling's hand, the

deflector suddenly launched herself off Logan with a shriek of fury.

Logan stumbled back. Zoe screamed.

Mr. Sterling turned and caught the deflector in his hands like a football.

"What in the world?" he said. "Did you bring me a present?"

"How adorable!" Mrs. Sterling said, leaning on his shoulder.

Bob stared up at them . . . and a third eye slowly opened in the middle of her forehead.

The air between them crackled, *zzzzip zzzzzap*.

The Sterlings stood stock-still, as if they were being mesmerized. Their faces went slack. Their eyes seemed to reflect back a hundred swirling mirrors. Mrs. Sterling's cell phone clattered to the ground and Zoe leaped forward to swoop it up.

And then the deflector's third eye slowly closed, and it felt like color coming back into the world.

Bob sat up in Mr. Sterling's hands, looked around at everyone, and announced, "Much better."

Then she hopped down to the ground and loped calmly off to the Kahns' van.

The Sterlings blinked and blinked, dazed. Mr. Sterling rubbed his face. Mrs. Sterling touched her cheeks and then her forehead as if checking they were still there.

"Mom?" Jasmin said softly. "Dad? Are you okay?"

"Goodness me," said Mrs. Sterling. She smiled brightly around the room. "What an odd assortment of people. How are you all? What are we doing here? Jonathan, where did you get such a sweet furry elephant?"

"Uh—" Jonathan said hazily. "What just—"

"Are we in a garage?" Mr. Sterling said, scanning the room. "What's all the noise out there?" He jerked his thumb at the door to the kitchen.

"That's your victory party, Dad," Jonathan said. "Remember? You're going to show everyone this mammoth? During your victory speech?"

"Victory speech!" Mr. Sterling said with delight, as if someone had just offered him a person-sized candy cane. "What did I win?"

"The election!" Jonathan said. "Dad! For mayor! What happened to you?"

"Mayor?" said Mr. Sterling, his face falling.

"Oh dear," said Mrs. Sterling.

"That sounds like a lot of work," Mr. Sterling said. "Why would I want to do that?" He turned to survey the other people. "Oh, Jackson, why don't you do it? You'd be a much better mayor than I would."

"Uh—" said Logan's dad. "I'm not sure there's legal precedent for—"

"Gosh, I don't want to run Xanadu, do you?" said Mrs. Sterling to her husband.

"Not in the slightest," he said. "We wouldn't have any time for raising ponies and donating money to sick children in Africa."

"Or our family!" she said. "And family is so important. I want to take Jasmin to a spa with me next weekend."

"But I wanted to take her hiking!" he said.

"I guess we can let her decide!" Mrs. Sterling said brightly.

"Holy mother of Zeus," Jasmin said. "Who are these people?"

"There's our angel," said Mrs. Sterling. She went over and kissed Jasmin's head. Blue kept his arm around Jasmin, watching her mom warily. "Sweetheart, you look tired. Let's take you home and order pizza and watch *Frozen* eight or nine times in a row."

"I'll make the popcorn!" said Mr. Sterling, bounding over to them.

Jasmin started to giggle. "I think I could get used to this," she said. "Zoe, how long does it last?"

"I have no idea," Zoe said. "I don't even know what just happened."

"I think I do," Matthew offered. "But I thought it was a myth—I mean, *really* a myth. I read once that deflectors have a kind of 'nuclear option,' for when they're feeling extremely threatened, that renders their adversary completely non-threatening in every way forever."

"Forever?" Jasmin said with delight.

"But what am I supposed to do with this?" Jonathan said plaintively, waving his whip at the mammoth.

"Here's one idea," Matthew growled. He stalked over and grabbed the whip out of Jonathan's hands and then broke it over his knees. Jonathan shrank back, tripping over his own feet in his haste to get away, and fell off the loading dock into a waiting Dumpster.

"Oh dear, watch your step, honey," Mrs. Sterling called after him.

Zoe wrapped her arms around Fuzzbutt's neck. Abigail came over and helped her wrestle the harness off. Fuzzbutt shook his head vigorously as soon as he was free, letting his ears flap wildly.

"What do we do about the press conference?" Mrs. Kahn asked.

"I say we let them come up with their own story," said Mr. Kahn. "We'll think of some excuse for Mr. Sterling stepping down in the morning."

"I've got one!" said Mr. Sterling. "I need to focus on my cooking. I've always wanted to learn to make a perfect paella. Clearly I can't do that and be mayor at the same time."

"Um," said Mr. Kahn. "Let's keep thinking on that one."

"But for now, let's go home," said Logan's mom. She pulled Logan to her and gave him a huge hug. "Can you always be there to save the day?" she asked him. "How do you feel about traveling to Cambodia with me over Christmas break?"

He leaned against her, too exhausted and relieved and filled with disbelief to even joke.

Zoe took Captain Fuzzbutt's trunk in her hand and led him carefully back into the U-Haul. Mrs. Kahn steered the Sterlings over to the Menagerie's van.

"The world is a weird, weird place," Jasmin said.

"But an awesome one," said Blue. She smiled up at him, and he leaned down and gave her a kiss.

"Logan," Zoe called. "Want to ride back here with me and the Captain?"

"Sure," he said.

"Me too," said Blue

"Me too!" said Jasmin. "He's the sweetest mammoth I've ever met." She giggled.

Everyone headed out into the night, leaving Jonathan to scramble out of the Dumpster on his own. Jasmin waved good-bye to him as Logan pulled the ramp inside the U-Haul.

"But now what do I do?" Jonathan cried, picking discarded ketchup packets off his sleeves. "Hello? My parents are all weird and my girlfriend just broke up with me! And what about my great future? Hello? Anyone?"

Logan pulled down the door, shutting him out, and went over to sit between Zoe and Blue. They could give Jonathan kraken ink later. Captain Fuzzbutt flopped down in front of them with a relieved snort.

"I think we're going to be okay," Zoe said wonderingly.

"Like, really okay. Like, I might actually make it to thirteen without completely losing my mind."

"Oh, it might be too late for that," Jasmin teased.

Logan leaned his head back against the wall of the truck and closed his eyes. He felt the truck jolt forward. All the fear of the last few days was finally disappearing, leaving him room to breathe again.

The Menagerie was safe at last.

TWENTY-SIX

"You'd better not," Logan said, reaching out to stop his dad. Mr. Wilde froze with his hand halfway to the Kahns' doorbell and raised his eyebrows.

"Does it open a trapdoor to a pit of hellhounds?" he asked.

"No, it just kind of freaks them out. They're still not used to visitors." Logan knocked on the Kahns' brand-new front door instead.

"Ruby, can you get that?" he heard Mrs. Kahn call.

"I can't. I'm too depressed to get off the couch, remember?" Ruby yelled back.

"I've got it!" Zoe shouted as she pulled open the door. She

beamed at Logan and his parents. "Oh good, you're here. Is that banana bread?"

Abigail held out the fresh-baked loaf as they followed Zoe into the house. "I'd like to claim it's an old family recipe, but the truth is Jackson made it. We all know I'm a lump in the kitchen."

"But we appreciate your other talents," Logan's dad said, kissing her on the nose.

"All right, cut it out," Logan said jokingly. He didn't really mind his parents' displays of affection. They'd been practically inseparable all week, except for whenever his dad had to go run the town. Since Mr. Sterling didn't want the job anymore and the other candidate had withdrawn, the town council had agreed that Logan's dad could take over as interim mayor until they organized a special election.

Logan had a feeling his dad would be throwing his hat in the ring come election time. And if the Kahns and the Sterlings had anything to say about it, Logan's dad would be mayor in a snap.

But win or lose, Logan was sure his family would be in Xanadu for a long time.

"Morning, Holly," Logan's mom greeted Mrs. Kahn.

"Good morning!" Zoe's mom smiled at them all, brushing off her hands to give Logan's mom a hug.

"If you'll excuse me, I'm going to go pick Melissa's brain

about the budget," Logan's dad said. "I can't understand how a town so small can spend so much money on snow plows. You'd think every family had one." He strode off toward Melissa's office.

Logan caught a flicker of movement and turned to see Bob perched on top of the fridge. Logan winked at the furry deflector, who smiled serenely back. Looking around, Logan spotted some fresh strawberries and sidled over to them. He grabbed a handful and surreptitiously held them behind his back as he leaned against the counter. Bob's face lit up and she leaped down and began gently picking them out of Logan's hand.

"How's Fuzzbutt doing?" Logan asked.

Zoe turned to him, her eyes full of relief. "He's much better. Mom coaxed him into the house for the first time while I was at school yesterday. He's been refusing to come in until I get home, and even then he'd follow me from room to room. It certainly made showering interesting." Zoe blushed.

"My mom and I were going to visit the griffins this morning," Logan said to change the subject. "Want to come?"

"I'm going to exercise Fuzzbutt, but I'll walk you there."

Logan felt the last of the strawberries leave his hand. He followed Zoe into the living room, where his mom and Mrs. Kahn were chatting on the couch. "Mom, meet you at the griffins?"

Abigail waved cheerily. "Be there soon," she said.

Zoe and Logan slipped out the sliding doors and started down the hill.

"AAAAWWWWWHHHOOOOUUUURGGGHH!!!"

Captain Fuzzbutt trumpeted loudly as he came galloping up to them and squeezed Zoe with his trunk. Logan reached out to pat the mammoth and the Captain bossily nudged his ear under Logan's hand for scratching.

Sunlight bathed the Menagerie, making the green of the grass seem brighter than usual and glinting off the water like spilled diamonds. Suddenly something enormous burst out of the lake, spinning in midair to avoid a tentacle shooting after it. Logan recognized the first creature as Xiang just before the Chinese dragon shrank itself down to the size of a cannonball and plummeted back into the water, neatly avoiding a second tentacle.

"They do that every day," Zoe said. "I think the kraken is beyond thrilled to finally have someone who'll play with her."

"Who's that in the wet suit?" Logan asked. A figure was emerging from the lake hand in hand with Blue.

"Oh, that's Jasmin," Zoe explained. "She came over early this morning so Blue could give her a tour of the underwater castle. It's the first time I've seen him voluntarily get out of bed before nine on a weekend."

"Hey, Logan!" Blue shouted, waving from the shore.

"Hey, Blue!" Logan waved back. "See you guys at lunch!"

Blue and Jasmin headed up to the house as Zoe and Logan continued on.

"So, Jasmin and Blue, huh?" Logan asked.

"Yup, it's official," Zoe said. She tucked her hair behind her ears and smiled at Logan. "Whatever happens, it'll never be as bad as Ruby and Jonathan. Mainly because Jasmin and Blue are both awesome people who could never be as idiotic as my sister or as much of a traitorous backstabber as Jonathan."

"No problems from SNAPA clearing Jasmin?"

"We got the green light last night. She signed all the nondisclosure forms and swore before a caladrius that she'd never expose the Menagerie. And as we told them, this way we have someone to keep an eye on her parents and Jonathan to make sure they don't regress."

The door to the unicorn stable swung open just as Logan and Zoe were walking past.

"Oh." Miss Sameera let out a little yelp. "Hello, Zoe. Hello, Logan."

"Hi, Miss Sameera," Logan said. "How's your first week working out?"

"I love it!" Miss Sameera's brown eyes grew dreamy. "After all these years of searching, I get to spend every day grooming not one but *two* majestic unicorns! Now I'm off to the farmer's market to get Charlemagne and Cleopatra some organic pears."

"That's great, Miss Sameera," Logan said.

"One day, all your dreams may come true, too, Logan." Miss Sameera smiled kindly at him.

Logan kind of thought they already had, but before he could say so, the librarian waved at them and wandered away.

Logan peeked into the stable where the unicorns were hanging their heads out over their stalls. Their manes shone like silk and they looked extremely pleased with themselves.

"It's so nice to finally have someone around who understands our true worth, don't you think?" Charlemagne said to Cleopatra.

"Oh yes," Cleopatra replied. "Although one has to wonder why it took so long to find this serf, when she is so clearly perfectly suited for us."

"Good grief," Zoe sighed quietly.

Logan turned back to Zoe with a grin. "At least she keeps them happy, right?"

Zoe met his smile as they moved on. "And they keep her happy. All we have to do is keep her away from the Aviary and warn her if Pelly's ever coming out for a walk. She actually made that a clause in her contract: absolutely no contact with Pelly unless it's an all-hands-on-deck-the-world-is-coming-to-an-end emergency."

Logan laughed. "That was smart of her. I guess some more of her memories came back."

"Yeah," Zoe said. "I've offered to have Mochi suck out any nightmares of their time together, but she said it wasn't that bad." Zoe sobered as she gazed up at the dragon caves. "I wish we could have done that for Agent Dantes years ago."

"But it's done now, right?" Logan asked. "She shouldn't have any more nightmares about dragons?"

"Right. Between the baku and the kraken ink, everything she's ever known about dragons—and all her memories of her parents' deaths—should be gone. I'm kind of glad she chose that, you know? To have a clean slate and a fresh start," Zoe said.

Agent Dantes—or he guessed he should think of her as Brigid Strong—had been allowed to choose between a SNAPA prison, exile in a distant menagerie, or having her memories wiped. She had chosen a massive dose of kraken ink, which would really give her the amnesia she'd once faked.

"Yeah, I'm glad, too," Logan said. "Now all her memories of her parents are happy ones."

"True." Zoe brightened. "And did you hear the good news about Scratch? SNAPA decided that as an apology for the pain and suffering his family has gone through, they're giving him a monthlong vacation in the Hawaii menagerie."

"That's awesome!" Logan said.

"Of course it annoyed the mermaids to no end. They've been grumbling about it all morning, but the SNAMHP agents told them that if they didn't want to stay here, they'd be happy to discuss a transfer to the Alaska facility. That shut them up fast."

Logan grinned as they came to a stop outside the griffin enclosure. "Well, I'm glad for Scratch."

"Me too. He was so excited, you'd think it was raining sheep," Zoe said. Her eyes went to the dragon caves again and she sighed.

"She is *not* supposed to use him like that," Zoe muttered. "Poor Marco."

Logan followed her gaze to where Keiko was lightly picking her way up the trail to the dragons. Marco was a few yards behind her, laden down with several mops and brooms and two buckets of water that looked very heavy.

"I'm sure Marco doesn't mind," Logan said. "And if he does, he can always stop helping her."

"I suppose. And at least I don't have to do it anymore! Between Keiko getting dragon duty and Miss Sameera taking over the unicorns, I might actually have some free time on my hands. Maybe I'll read a book. Or I hear they have these new-fangled things called 'movies' that sound pretty awesome."

"That is a joke," Logan said, pointing at her. "You are messing with me, but it's not going to work this time. I will, however, take you to a movie next weekend if you want."

"Okay," she said, smiling and looking at her toes. "That would be cool."

Logan wasn't quite sure what to do with his face, where his grin felt much too big.

Captain Fuzzbutt nudged Zoe with his trunk and she patted him affectionately. "The Captain and I should head to Mooncrusher's yurt. See you soon."

"Sure thing," Logan said. He watched Zoe jog away with Fuzzbutt shambling along behind her. He couldn't believe how lucky he was that this was now his world.

Logan was on the run, chased by six agents of a shadowy organization dedicated to wiping out all mythical creatures. He had to find the secret treasure hidden in the cave and activate its magic powers before they—

YAAAAAAAAAAH!

A small furry body collided with his knees.

We've got you now, Tracker!

Another set of paws hit his back, knocking him into a sprawling heap.

Where have you hidden it?

We'll make you confess!

You must give us all your treasure!

Logan was buried in fur and flapping wings and tails smacking him in the face.

Never fear, Logan! I will save youuuuuuuuuuuuuuu!

A wild rumpus ensued on top of him.

Squorp! You're supposed to be on OUR side!

Yeah, we're all bad guys, remember?

Hey! Logan's hands smell like meat!

Six beaks immediately started poking around Logan's hands. He tried rolling up to a sitting position and was knocked over by one of Clink's wings.

Don't even think about moving, Tracker.

Squorp climbed onto his chest and stared beadily down at Logan over his little griffin beak. The other five griffin cubs crowded up behind him, trying to look menacing.

Forget the treasure, Squorp rumbled. **This one has MEAT.**

Yump, the overweight griffin cub with reddish fur, jabbed Logan's side with one of his claws. **Tell us where it is!** he demanded. **Or we will ALL sit on you! At once!**

"All right, all right," Logan relented, laughing. "But let me get it out, okay? I don't need six griffin cubs trying to climb into my backpack at once."

HIS BACKPACK! Clonk and Flurp shouted at the same time. All six of them shot toward the gate where Logan had dropped his backpack on the way into the griffin enclosure. Logan just managed to dive between them and rescue it before it was torn to shreds. He reached inside and pulled out a Tupperware container full of hamburger meat.

COOOOOOWWW!!!!!! Yump cried, flaring his wings.

Mine! Yummy!

Me! Me! Me!

Want! Give!

SO STARVING NEED FOOD NOW!

No, Logan brought it for ME!!! Squorp cried, trying unsuccessfully to fend off his brothers and sisters, whose paws and wings overlapped as they piled on top of him and one another in an attempt to reach the container in Logan's hands.

"Everybody sit!" Logan shouted at the blur of fur and feathers leaping around him. "The first one who sits still gets the first helping!"

The six griffin cubs immediately slammed their butts to the ground and gave him huge, expectant eyes.

That was clever, Nira said from her perch on a boulder. Except that now you'll be in trouble no matter who you decide was first.

"It's okay, I brought enough for all of you," Logan reassured them. Luckily, he'd planned ahead and there were six mini-bowls inside the container. Logan set them each down a foot apart so the griffins could have some space. The cubs attacked the food as if they hadn't been fed in months.

Oh, thank you. Nira's voice floated into Logan's head. That's the first time they've been quiet since five this morning. The white griffin extended her front paws forward in a deep stretch and then arched her back, shaking out her muscles. I'm going for a flight around the lake. You've got them, right?

Nira focused her sharp eyes on Logan. He felt a little thrill that she trusted him enough to leave him cub-sitting. "Of course," he said.

Great. Riff is here if you need him. Nira's gaze flicked to the den, where her mate was sprawled in an exhausted heap, as though he'd collapsed in the middle of a game. She shot Logan a skeptical look. **Although he may not be much use. He only made it through four rounds of chase-the-tail this morning.**

Logan knew Zoe and the Kahns had given Riff a stern talking-to about spending more time with his cubs so that Nira could have a break. He was glad to hear the father griffin was making some effort.

"And thank you again for your help getting back Xiang's pearl," Logan added.

It was no trouble. I quite enjoyed myself. Let me know if there is ever anyone else I need to glare into oblivion.

"Urm, I think we're okay for now," Logan said. It was hard to believe, but it seemed to be true. Whatever Bob had done to the Sterlings appeared to be permanent. As for Agent Dantes, SNAPA had been profusely apologetic about not properly vetting her. The Kahns had been given funds to cover the damage to the Reptile House and enough extra that they were planning a new stable for the unicorns, too.

In fact, nearly a whole week had passed without any creatures escaping, getting kidnapped, or being accused of murder.

This, apparently, was what the Menagerie looked like at peace.

Nira spread her wings and leaped into the air.

That's going to be me soon! Squorp cried, galloping

up and colliding with Logan's legs. **Watch! Watch this!** The golden griffin cub leaped up and hovered a few feet off the ground, flapping his wings madly. **Look at me FLY!!!**

"Hey, Squorp, looking great!" Logan smiled. Squorp thumped back to the ground and wriggled excitedly.

Hey, guys! Let's play Logan is a mountain we have to climb and also a Chinese dragon for us to rescue and also there is a secret tunnel for us to find somewhere in the den!

"Hello, beautiful cubs," Logan's mom sang out from the gate.

"Squorp, I want you to meet my mom," Logan said. The little griffin cub clacked his beak, looking delighted.

Abigail sank to her knees next to them and gravely shook paws with each of the cubs as Logan introduced them.

"Squorp, Clink, Clonk, Yump, Flurp, and Sage."

Logan's mom just like in picture! Squorp pulled a photo from within his fur and feathers, as though he had a pocket hidden somewhere. The picture was of Logan and his parents and he'd given it to the cub as a treasure for him to protect. Which reminded him.

"Clink is the griffin who has been guarding your bracelet for me, Mom," Logan said.

The black cub puffed out her chest proudly.

"Well, thank you, Clink. I'm sure you've been taking very good care of it. May I see it?" Abigail asked.

Treasure is hers? Clink asked, giving Logan a skeptical look.

"Yes, the bracelet is very special to my mom," Logan told her. "She leaves it with me when she travels, but she's back now."

The black cub reluctantly pulled out the silver chain with twelve dangling charms. She hunched her shoulders as she handed it to Abigail.

"We'll find you another, even more special treasure to guard," Logan promised.

Soon! bellowed Clink. **Need treasure soon!**

The cub stalked away muttering. She paused and cocked her head, considering Clonk's pile of fake pirate coins. Clonk came galloping over shouting at her and the cubs began to tussle. Squorp charged over to join the fight.

"Did you hear about Scratch?" Logan asked his mom.

"I did." She glanced around, then leaned in close. "I'm going to let you in on a huge secret. Scratch isn't really going to Hawaii."

Logan cocked his head at her.

"He's going to visit his mom."

"What?" Logan exclaimed. "Isn't she dead?"

"Nope. She's up at the Freezer."

Logan blinked at her, confused.

"It's our Arctic facility, buried under the ice sheet. It's where SNAPA sends all the creatures they've supposedly exterminated." She smiled at him. "SNAPA's whole mission in life is to protect mythical creatures. They would never kill any of them if it could be avoided. But to pacify the worried government types, they have to put on a big show and pretend to sometimes, with scary-looking Exterminators and everything. And then they take the animals up north and hide them in a highly classified facility that only the top tier at SNAPA knows about. Well, and those of us who escort the creatures there. Like me."

"So Scratch and Lacewing will be reunited—that's amazing."

"Yes." Abigail smiled. "I know it will make her century. No mother wants to be away from her kids."

Logan felt tears pricking at his eyes and he blinked rapidly. "I missed you so much, Mom."

"I missed you, too, Logan. Every minute of every day." She pulled him to her side. "I just kept thinking about how tight I'd hug you and how I'd tell you everything when you found me." She fingered the charms on her bracelet, one for each of the creatures she'd tracked. "I'm so glad I get to explain each of these to you now," she said.

"I want to hear everything, all your stories," Logan said.

"And I'm serious about you coming with me on my next trip," she said. "I can't think of anyone I'd rather have at my side. I hear there are rumors of a chimera in the mountains between China and Mongolia." She quirked an eyebrow up at him in challenge.

Logan grinned at her. "So, this is our life now."

"This is our life." His mom beamed back at him. "Griffins, chimeras, unicorns, and an occasional yawkyawk."

Squorp bounded over and nestled into Logan's lap. He purred happily as Logan scratched under his chin.

"I guess I don't need a dog anymore." No pet could ever compare to Squorp.

His mom wrapped an arm around him. "You'll have to come up with something new to ask for at Christmas," she joked. "Maybe you could figure out what hiking gear you'll need at camp next summer."

Logan's eyes widened and his mom nodded, answering his unspoken question.

"Your father and I discussed it, and we think it's a great idea for you to go to Camp Underpaw."

Logan's heart felt like it might burst out of his chest and give his mom, the griffins, and the whole Menagerie a giant hug. His mom was back, the Menagerie was safe, he had real friends, *great* friends, and he'd get to go to Tracker camp next summer. There was nothing else in the whole world he could possibly wish for.

He was finally home.

CAMP UNDERPAW'S GUIDE

TO MYTHICAL CREATURES

A Brief Overview for Trackers in Training

You've made it to Camp Underpaw—your first step on the path to becoming a Tracker!

Now, forget everything you think you know about "mythical" creatures. Being a Tracker is not about riding magical unicorns and cuddling griffin cubs. It is a dangerous career suitable only for the toughest, most committed creature hunters. It takes determination and resourcefulness, guts and brains, and all the skills you'll learn in this intensive, hands-on Tracker camp experience.

And it starts with memorizing this list of the most notable and notorious creatures you're likely to encounter out in the world. Look it over and think carefully . . . is this really the right future for you? Are you ready to face venomous teeth and razor-sharp claws and kraken ink?

If so—welcome to Camp Underpaw!

REMEMBER THESE CREATURES

ALICANTO

Most commonly found in Chile, these birds are easily recognized by their wings, which shimmer and clatter as if they were made of gold and silver. Their primary food source is metal, with a strong preference for gold and silver, but in captivity alicantos are usually fed lesser metals and often survive on a diet of pennies. Search for these birds along waterways and high in the mountains near precious metal mines. You will know you are getting close when you hear a sound like raining coins. Protective earplugs highly recommended.

ANT-LION

A small insect with the body of an ant and the head of a lion. Very aggressive and territorial, but can be mollified with food (other

insects, crumbs, scraps of meat, etc.). Wear thick boots and be careful where you step when tracking these tiny, ferocious biters.

BAKU

A big, gentle, nocturnal creature resembling a tapir. Native to Japan, bakus eat dreams, particularly nightmares. Usually found near humans and can sometimes be summoned after especially vivid dreams.

BASILISK

A deadly, venomous giant lizard; its gaze kills anyone who looks at it. Do not underestimate the threat of these creatures; bring backup and a mirror if you must track one.

The crow of a rooster will put the basilisk to sleep, but only a weasel can kill it.

BONNACON

A giant, vicious creature shaped like a bull with a mane like a horse, horns that curve backward, and fiery dung. Extremely easy to track by its excretions, but approach with caution. Bring nose plugs and a fire extinguisher.

CALADRIUS

A pure-white bird roughly the size of a gull. It is known for being able to discern whether someone is telling the truth or lying.

CHIMERA

A creature that is part lion, part goat, and part snake (and all dangerous); beware its ability to breathe fire.

CHUPACABRA

The chupacabra has the head of a dog, a spiny back, and scaly skin; its red eyes can hypnotize and it leaves a sulfurous odor in its wake. Tends to feed on goats and other livestock, but has been known to bite people as well.

DRAGON (Chinese)

Related to Western dragons, but without wings or fire-breathing; Chinese dragons can change their size and love the water.

DRAGON (Western)

Enormous fire-breathing creatures with scales, talons, and vast wings. Usually they choose the relative safety of captivity and do not require Tracking.

GOLDEN GOOSE

A larger-than-average goose that can lay golden eggs.

GRIFFIN

A lion-eagle hybrid, with the body, paws, and tail of a lion and the wings and head of an eagle; they are traditionally guardians, mistrust horses, and love treasure. If you can identify what treasure a griffin is protecting, they are easier to track.

HALCYON

A small blue bird with white throat feathers that looks something like a kingfisher and can affect the weather.

HELLHOUND

Oversized black dogs with sulfurous breath and glowing red eyes. Try to avoid their slobber as it can sting if it comes in contact with broken skin.

HIPPOCAMP

A water animal with the head and front legs of a horse but the tail of a fish.

JACKALOPE

Only found in Wyoming, a jackalope looks like a rabbit with antlers. Beware its ability to imitate the human voice, as it may lead you on a merry chase.

KAPPA

Water sprites from Japan with scales, faces like monkeys, and turtle shells on their backs. They love cucumbers but will also happily eat children.

KELPIE

A malevolent kind of water horse that lurks by ponds and rivers to lure people into the water for the purpose of drowning and/or eating them. Basically, if you see a horse standing next to a lake, leave it alone.

KITSUNE

Native to Japan, a kitsune's true shape is a fox, but they can also shift into human form, so they are monitored by the SuperNatural Agency for Mostly Human Protection (SNAMHP). They are very difficult to catch because a full-grown kitsune can often read minds, see the future, fly, possess people, and create illusions that mimic reality. A clever Tracker might spot one by its fox-shaped shadow. Dogs are sometimes useful for tracking them as a dog can sniff out a kitsune's true nature.

KRAKEN

Possibly the largest of all mythical creatures, the kraken is shaped like a giant squid and lives deep in the ocean. Their ink can wipe all supernatural memories from your brain, and more than one promising Tracker's career has been derailed by an unfortunate encounter with it. Only specially trained deep-sea Trackers are qualified to search for creatures like this.

MANTICORE

A fierce and deadly creature with a lion's body and claws, a scorpion's tail, and a face like a man with rows of sharp fangs. Extremely dangerous—do not approach!

MAPINGUARI

A giant sloth-like animal found in the dark jungles of South America. They are slow, but willing to eat people, and fearsomely bad smelling—bad enough that they can often be tracked by their terrible scent.

MERMAID

Exactly what you think they are: people with fish tails from the waist down who prefer to live underwater. Classed as Mostly Human and therefore monitored by SNAMHP.

PEGASUS

A winged horse. The primary difficulty in tracking them is that no ordinary saddle will fit around their wings.

PHOENIX

A beautiful scarlet-plumed bird who occasionally dies in a burst of flames and is then reborn from an egg found in the ashes. There is only one in the world, currently located in the Wyoming Menagerie.

PYROSALAMANDER

The mythical cousins of a regular salamander, pyrosalamanders are small, bright red, and eat fire. Handle with caution and be sure to feed them regularly!

QILIN

Sometimes confused with unicorns or called a "Chinese
unicorn," as they are usually found in China or Japan. A qilin
has the slender body of a deer, fish scales along its back, and
one horn pointing backward from its head. They are able to
sense the guilt or innocence of others. Extremely difficult to
track as a qilin passes over grass without flattening it. Take
care when capturing one as it is bad luck to wound a qilin.

ROC

A gigantic bird of prey, usually with white and gold feathers,
capable of carrying an elephant in its massive claws. Found
in the most uninhabited mountainous regions of the world.

SELKIE

Another Mostly Human sea hybrid; selkies take the form
of seals in the water, but can slip off their sealskins and

assume human form while on land. Please try not to bring in ordinary seals who are "acting suspicious," as this happens entirely too often and SNAMPH is not amused by it.

TANIWHA

A long serpentine creature from New Zealand with some of the qualities of a dragon, except that they are usually wingless and prefer to live in the ocean. On land, they can be tracked by the tunnels they leave behind as they dig their way through the earth.

UNICORN

A graceful horselike creature, usually a shimmering white, with a horn in the center of its forehead. Warning: can be rather sensitive and temperamental, so be sure to demonstrate respect when dealing with them.

WENDIGO

These shape-shifters are cannibalistic, ruthless hunters with sharp, jagged teeth and skeletal frames. A rare example of a creature whom Trackers are encouraged to kill in the wild, as they do poorly in captivity and seem to be impossible to rehabilitate or tame. Typically found in cold regions, they turn their victims into wendigos as well and can hunt through a victim's dreams. They can be killed if you melt their hearts of ice.

WEREWOLF

Mostly Human; these are humans who have either been bitten by a werewolf or inherited the gene from their parents. At the full moon, they involuntarily transform into wolves from midnight to dawn; at other times, they may choose which shape to present. Werewolves are the most well-known example, but werecreatures exist in all shapes and sizes, from weremice to werewhales. These creatures fall under the purview of SNAMHP, but occasionally you may have to track a rogue werecreature on their behalf.

YAWKYAWK

Water spirits from Australia who often look like mermaids, but can also shape-shift into crocodiles, swordfish, snakes, dragonflies, or humans. They may have the power to create storms, so try not to make them angry.

YETI

Also known as a Bigfoot, a Sasquatch, or an Abominable Snowman, these huge hairy manlike creatures are covered in fur and generally live in cold climates. Somewhat human, but not Mostly Human, so they are covered by SNAPA instead of SNAMHP.

ZARATAN

A turtle the size of a small island, and yet shockingly difficult to track.

ACKNOWLEDGMENTS

Behind every author is a team of literary experts and a network of friends and family. We are very lucky to have a brilliant team and wonderful network, whom we can't thank enough.

So thank you to our fabulous and patient editor, Erica Sussman, for her guidance, friendship, and never-ending support. Our heartfelt thanks to Stephanie Stein, Tara Weikum, Erin Fitzsimmons, Christina Colangelo, Olivia Russo, Bethany Reis, and the rest of the talented HarperCollins team who not only helps get this series ready for publication, but makes sure readers know about it and can find it wherever they may live.

As always, enormous thanks to our stellar agent, Steven Malk.

For being a true artist and friend, our thanks to Ali Solomon, whose rendering of a baku made us desperately wish for one and fueled our drive to write a character to match.

To all our friends and family, old and new, near and far, thank you for your love and support.

To our fearless parents, Bron and Jim Sutherland, for taking us on many an international journey—from the ancient ruins of Peru to the serene vistas of New Zealand and everywhere in between, inspiring our imaginations, and raising us to follow our dreams, even if they don't lead into banking (sorry, Dad!). Thank you guys also for your more recent hands-on support—we really appreciate all your help in lovingly shepherding your exuberant and energetic grandchildren—you guys are awesome!

To Wyndham: a million, gabillion thank-yous are not enough to cover it! Your enthusiasm, patience, and creativity are boundless and never cease to amaze us. This book literally could not exist without you—two little bears and I want you to know how much we appreciate you!

To Jim and Sue Hoover, a pair of terrific grandparents and super-generous hosts: thank you for everything, including your cheerful willingness to mind Adalyn and crawl around on the floor with her as she explores the world one square foot at a time. To Gwen and Rick Sterns, thank you for being such wonderful, supportive, loving grandparents, for giving the books to everyone, and for your general marvelousness.

To our intrepid husbands, Adam and Steve, who never hesitated to take kid duty after we'd been up all hours of the night writing and discussing plot twists. We love you very much!

Finally, to our incredible children: know that no matter where we are, you are always our hearts and souls.